Leach Library
276 Mammoth Road
Londonderry, NH 03053
Adult Services 432-1132
Children's Services 432-1127

FIT TO BE TIED

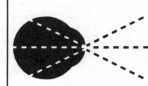

This Large Print Book carries the
Seal of Approval of N.A.V.H.

BUCKLIN FAMILY REUNION SERIES,
BOOK 2

FIT TO BE TIED

DEBBY MAYNE

THORNDIKE PRESS
A part of Gale, a Cengage Company

Farmington Hills, Mich • San Francisco • New York • Waterville, Maine
Meriden, Conn • Mason, Ohio • Chicago

19 Jan 30
B+T
30.99 (29.44)

Copyright © 2018 by Debby Mayne.
Thorndike Press, a part of Gale, a Cengage Company.

Thorndike Press® Large Print Christian Romance.
The text of this Large Print edition is unabridged.
Other aspects of the book may vary from the original edition.
Set in 16 pt. Plantin.

LIBRARY OF CONGRESS CIP DATA ON FILE.
CATALOGUING IN PUBLICATION FOR THIS BOOK
IS AVAILABLE FROM THE LIBRARY OF CONGRESS

ISBN-13: 978-1-4328-5855-1 (hardcover)

Published in 2018 by arrangement with Gilead Publishing

Printed in Mexico
1 2 3 4 5 6 7 22 21 20 19 18

I'd like to dedicate this book to my wonderful agent, Tamela Hancock Murray, who never gives up on me, and to my dear friend Julie Pollitt who inspires me and keeps me sane.

The term *fit to be tied* is an old-school expression that means "upset, angry, or anxious." Southern mamas often use it when they're exasperated by something their young'uns do to annoy them . . . or when they don't know what else to say when they feel like life is whuppin' up on 'em.

1
SALLY WRIGHT

As soon as my Fitbit vibrates, letting me know that Tom Flaherty is calling, I mentally kick myself for forgetting to disengage that feature when I turned off my ringer. Ever since the last Bucklin family get-together, he's called me every single day, bugging me to go out with him again.

When I first met Tom at a children's fashion trade show in Jackson, I thought he was handsome, sweet, and overall pretty wonderful. I even liked going out with him a few times after that. But something snapped during the last reunion — maybe when I realized he wanted to be something he wasn't and never would have the nerve to become — and I lost interest. But how would I have known he hated children, fashion, and children's fashion when that's what he does for a living? I still like him, sort of. But I have no desire to have a romantic relationship with him.

I know I need to talk to him and let him know I'm not interested, but that's hard for me. Even though we're not in a relationship, doing this feels an awful lot like breaking up — something I've never had to do before. I've had dates here and there, but they hardly ever turned into a real relationship. And when one did, it always fizzled out on its own without having a formal breakup.

My wrist vibrates again, and I groan. But when I glance at my Fitbit, I see that it's my identical twin sister, Sara, and I grab my phone.

"Hey, have you checked your email?" The teasing lilt in her voice sounds awfully suspicious.

"No, why? What are you and Justin up to now?"

She laughs. "*We're* not up to anything, but the family is. Mama and Aunt Lady are planning the next family get-together."

"We just had one," I remind her.

"That was four months ago."

I snort. "Seems more like four days ago."

"Yeah, I know."

"Are you going?"

"You're kidding, right?" Sara's voice goes up an octave, so I hold the phone away from my ear. "Wild horses couldn't keep me and

Justin away." She pauses. "Well? Are you going?"

"I'll have to read the email and see if I'm busy that day."

Sara laughs again. "Okay, you do that. In the meantime, I'm going to call Shay and see if she has time to teach me how to make something yummy. I want people fighting over the last bite in my casserole dish."

"I'll probably bring those meatballs I brought last time."

"So you're going?" She lets out a giggle. "You do realize it's during Thanksgiving weekend."

"I know." I pause and wonder if meatballs will go over on Thanksgiving. Then I remember it's the Bucklin family. "*If* I go, that's what I'll make."

"Let me know if you don't so I can bring them. Then I won't have to waste my time learning something new in the kitchen."

The hair on the back of my neck rises. "I have dibs on the meatballs. You have to come up with some other signature dish."

"Don't forget, you stole those from Shay," she reminds me. "So if anyone should have dibs on them, it would be her."

I let out a sigh that I know annoys her, but I don't care. Sara and Justin have gotten on my nerves off and on ever since they

11

eloped a few weeks before the last reunion. Don't get me wrong. I love my sister, and I've gotten past the point of merely tolerating my brother-in-law. In fact, I even like him most of the time. But they say and do things that I'm sure are just to annoy me. I remember when Sara and I used to do that to each other to keep things from getting boring, but the whole dynamic has changed with Justin in the picture. To top it off, they only dated a few weeks, even though Sara reminds me we've known him most of our lives. But still . . .

"Hey, I gotta go," she says. "Justin wants me to go help him pick out a new turkey fryer."

"I thought he already had a turkey fryer."

"He needs a bigger one for the reunion."

I have more questions, like why she would need to get a recipe from Shay if they're frying a turkey and why she has to go with him to pick out a fryer since she knows nothing about anything culinary. But I don't say another word, since I can't wait to get off the phone.

The first thing I do after clicking the Off button is open my laptop and pull up my email. Yep. There it is. A note from Mama, giving me what she calls an *early heads-up* about the reunion so I can be prepared. She puts emphasis on the fact that it's Thanksgiving weekend, so I need to do something extra special.

I close my eyes for a moment to reflect. It seems weird that I've found out about the reunion from Sara, who I used to tease about being flakier than Mama's pie crust. So many things have changed ever since Sara and Justin got married. But now that I think about it, our lives haven't been the same since she and I left our teller jobs and became full-time bow makers.

After Sara and Justin got married, they decided to stay in the condo with me. Now they get out of the condo every chance they get, and I find myself wandering around aimlessly. I always thought it would be fun to be alone, but Sara and I have been attached at the hip since birth, and I find myself missing her more than I ever thought I would.

Our Etsy hair bow business hasn't slowed down, even though Sara isn't as active as she once was. When she first backed off, I increased my workload to accommodate the business, but now I'm starting to burn out. The bloom of success has faded now that I'm alone most of the time. I've even mentioned that we might want to find some other way to earn a living, but she reminds me that this and banking are all we know. Neither of us wants to go back to being a teller.

My frustration comes and goes, and at the moment it's pretty bad. So I start pacing — the same thing I always do when I can't come up with solutions to business problems. My wrist vibrates again, and this time it's an unknown number. Although tempted to ignore it, I pick up my phone and answer it.

"Hey, Sally."

I should have gone with my first instinct. "Hi, Tom."

"Are you going to your family reunion?"

I can hear the hope in his voice. I swallow hard. "How do you know about my family reunion?"

"I have ways." He lets out a low chuckle that I suspect his mama said was cute when he was younger, but it's not the least bit cute now . . . at least it isn't to me. "Actually, your mother emailed me a couple of hours ago and told me about it."

I need to have a talk with Mama.

"So, tell me. Are you planning to attend?"

"I haven't decided yet." Now that he's aware of it, I'll need to come up with an excuse not to invite him. "Why?"

"After your last one, I started working on

some new recipes, and I have a couple new dishes that I think will knock the socks off your family."

"Um . . ." I know I need to tell him — to break it to him that I'm just not feelin' it, but it's hard. "You might want to hold off on that."

"Hold off on what, Sally? What are you talking about?"

"You're not going to my family reunion." The words tumble out of my mouth before I have a chance to stop them, and I cringe. "What I meant to say was —"

"Did I say something to upset you? I thought everything was good between us."

The hurt in his voice is palpable, and I want to crawl under the table. As much as I don't have the least bit of romantic feeling for him, I still think he's sweet, and I would never want to hurt him. I've had coffee with him a couple of times since the last reunion, but I've thrown out some hints that we can never be more than friends. The problem with Tom is he's so desperate to be in a relationship he can't grasp subtle hints and needs to be told. So I suck in a deep breath and as quietly as possible let it out.

"I'm sorry, Tom, but there really isn't anything between us."

"I thought we were friends." He clears his

throat. "I guess I read that wrong."

"We are friends, but that's all."

He sighs. "That's all I thought we were. If I led you to believe . . ." His voice trails off, and he sighs again. "You obviously don't want me around."

Oh man, now he's playing the guilt card. He's done this before, which is why it's been a while since I've tried to explain. But I have no choice now. He needs to be clear.

"No, Tom, that's not true. I do want . . . I mean, I like you . . . as a friend."

"But you don't want me around your family."

That's sort of true, but it sounds so harsh. "I think it might be awkward for us to go together, since I'm . . ." I suck in a breath and blurt, "I have a date."

The instant those words come out, I want to kick myself because I know I can't take them back. What's so crazy about this is that I've never so blatantly lied before.

"Oh, then it makes sense." He sighs again, making me worry that he might hyperventilate. "I don't want to make your new boyfriend *jealous.*"

The way he says that lets me know he's the one who's jealous, but I can't take responsibility for something I can't control. "I'm sorry, Tom."

"Oh, Sally, honey, that's okay. No need to apologize. I understand completely. In fact, I've been worried about letting you down easy. It's nice to know we're on the same page."

"Thanks for understanding." I glance over at my computer, where I see new orders popping into my Etsy queue by the second. "I really need to run now."

"Bye, Sally. Have a nice life."

My heart sinks as I hang up. He makes the end of our conversation seem so final, yet I'm sure I'll see him again next time I go to a children's fashion event. That's where I met him, and that's where we had our first date. Well, not a date exactly, but we had lunch — just the two of us. And that's when I thought we might have been at the beginning of something special. Occasionally, I wish I hadn't taken him up on his lunch offer or gone out with him after the last reunion, but I know the only way of seeing how a relationship can go is by spending time with each other. Unfortunately, he is totally incapable of taking a hint . . . or two or three.

I glance over at the computer as the orders continue rolling in. As frustrated as I am, I can't ignore the business that puts food on the table and keeps the lights on.

So now I scan the orders and come up with a plan of action to make the wisest use of my time. In spite of my argument against orange a few months ago, I realize that Sara was right when she insisted on going heavy on orange ribbon. That is *the* fashion color of the season this year, and our orders reflect it.

I pull out all the orange ribbon we have on hand and realize we're short by several spools. So I use this as an excuse to call my sister again.

"What do you want, Sally?" she asks without a greeting.

"Sorry to bother you, but while you're out, would you mind stopping off at the craft store and picking up more orange ribbon?"

"Yeah, but it might be a while. Justin is still talking to the guy about the turkey fryer."

"That's fine." Out of the corner of my eye, I see more orders coming through — and at least half of them are for orange bows. "You'd better get all the orange ribbon they have."

"Why don't you order some and have it overnighted? Hold on a sec." She covers the receiver, and I can hear muffled voices before she comes back. "Tell you what.

18

Justin said he'll be a while, so I'll take the truck, pick up some ribbon, and bring it to you. But I have to come right back and pick him up."

"That'll be wonderful." The mere thought of spending a little time alone with my sister brings a smile to my lips.

"Oh, by the way, Justin has a few days off, so we thought we'd go down to New Orleans for a second honeymoon."

"When?"

"I'll let you know for sure as soon as he gets a definite answer from his boss. But it'll be soon."

My heart sinks. I'll be alone. Again.

As soon as we hang up, I punch in Mama's number. "Why did you email Tom about the reunion?"

2
SHEILA WRIGHT

I can't blame my daughter for being upset with me, but I honestly don't understand why she doesn't like Tom. He's handsome, smart, and very successful. His mama was a Chi Omega, and his aunt was a Kappa Delta at a southern college, so if they have a daughter who goes to college, she'll be a shoo-in as a legacy in either of two great sororities. In other words, he's everything a mama would want for her daughter.

"I wasn't trying to hurt you, sweetie."

"Maybe not, but you put me in a bad predicament. I had to tell him I have another date."

My heart picks up a beat. Maybe there's hope yet. "You do?"

"Um . . ." She coughs. "Not exactly, but I had to tell him that because I couldn't think of anything else to say when he started talking about what he was planning to bring."

"Oh, Sally, why can't you give this sweet

boy a chance? He's everything I've always wanted for you and your sister, and since Sara . . . well, it's too late for her, but you —"

"That's just it, Mama. He's what *you* want." Her voice softens. "Justin isn't so bad. In fact, he's actually a pretty sweet guy."

"Oh, I know. I like him just fine. It's just that —" This conversation is getting beyond uncomfortable. "I just had something different in mind for the two of you."

"But I have something else in mind."

"I didn't mean —" Actually, I did mean exactly what she thought I meant. "I just want you to find someone to love so you can settle down and be happy."

She laughs out loud. "I don't know how much more settled I can get."

"Sally." I clear my throat. "You know what I mean."

"Just do me a favor, okay? Don't try to force things for me in the romance department. If I meet someone nice, it needs to happen naturally."

"Whatever you say, Sally. But remember, don't choose just any guy. He has to —"

"Please don't do that, Mama."

I close my mouth. Sometimes it's so hard to keep from meddling when it comes to

21

my precious daughters. At first, when Sara married Justin, I was fit to be tied. Fortunately, he turned out to be a good guy, and now I'm worried about Sally. They both tell me I shouldn't worry so much, but I'm a southern mama, and that's what we do.

"Are you okay?" I hear the sympathy in her voice.

"Yes, I'm fine." I decide it's time to change the subject. "Hey, do me a favor and tell Sara we're excited about Justin doing the turkey. I have to admit I'm rather surprised by his cooking abilities."

"I'll tell her." Sally pauses. "Hey, Mama, it's been nice talking to you, but I gotta run."

After we hang up, I sink back in my chair. I can't believe how fast my girls have grown up. It's almost like one day I walk them into their kindergarten class with them clinging to my legs, turn around for five minutes, and when I come back, they're off on their own, running their little bow-making business. I can't help laughing though, because they used to fight me tooth and nail when I stuck those big bows in their hair. Now I realize they were just pullin' my leg. They must have really loved them to start a business making them. What gets my goat is that the bows they're making are big ol' honkin' things that would cover most kids' heads.

I turn around and take a long look at the house I've called home for a few decades. It's a beautiful place that I loved from first glance. It's a three-bedroom house, but we've only used two of them as bedrooms and converted the smallest one into whatever we needed at the time. It's been a playroom, a storage space, and a sewing room. We tried separating the girls when they were little, but they always wound up wanting to be in the same room. At least until they were teenagers.

It's one of those places that, when you walk in, you just know it's right. What I've always liked about it is the flow from the living room, through the dining room, and into the kitchen that is light and bright with rays of sunshine streaming in through the window over the sink. We have a front porch with rocking chairs that we keep saying we'll start using every evening after supper. But so far, we've been way too busy. One of these days we will.

Ever since the girls moved out a few years ago, George and I have been rattling around our house, not knowing what to do with ourselves. He wants to convert the girls' room into an office, but I keep telling him we need to keep it like it is for a while, just in case. I mean, you never know.

Now I'm starting to think he's right, only I'd rather have a sewing room. Maybe one of these days I'll get back to making things — hopefully for some grandchildren.

I hear the sound of a truck coming up the road, so I walk over to the window to see if it's George. It is. My pulse quickens, and that makes me smile. We've been married a while, but just the sight of him makes me happy. However, his truck . . . well, not so much.

Shortly after his cousin went out and bought a tricked-out pickup truck, he decided he needed one too. Fortunately, his company bonus covered it, because I wasn't about to let him get into our emergency fund — not with every appliance in our house living on borrowed time.

"Hey, hon."

I turn around and see my husband's smiling face, looking all proud as punch and pumped up. And suspicious. I narrow my eyes. "What have you gotten yourself into now?"

He mocks hurt feelings as he walks toward me. "I bought you somethin' pretty."

I frown back at the man whose idea of something pretty is a new skillet or something he spotted on the way back to the tool section at the hardware store. "You don't need to be buying me stuff."

He reaches down deep into his pocket and pulls out a box that wouldn't hold any pot, pan, or kitchen appliance. As he opens it, I lean over to see what it is.

"One of my buddies down at the tire store said his wife is sellin' this stuff, so I agreed to take a look at it. I thought this looked like you."

For the first time in years, I'm shocked by his insight. He's right. Lying against the black velvet inside the box is a coral pendant necklace that will go perfectly with half my wardrobe. I open my mouth, but my voice catches in my throat, and nothing comes out.

"Well?" He widens his eyes with a look of concern. "Do you like it?"

"I love it." The truth is, it's so stinkin' pretty that I can't take my eyes off it.

He looks at me from beneath eyebrows that are so bushy I can't see his eyelashes. "Do you really, or are you just tellin' me that so you won't hurt my feelings?"

"Can you put it on me?" Before he has a chance to say anything, I lift my hair off my neck and turn my back to him. Then I stand there and wait . . . and wait . . . until I realize he's not going to do what I asked.

When I turn back around, I see that he's not even in the room anymore, but he's left the box on the edge of the dresser. So I carefully lift the necklace off the velvet and put it on myself. And then I turn and look at my reflection in the mirror. This is about the prettiest thing George has ever given me since he got down on one knee and presented me with the engagement ring I'd shown him in the jewelry store window a week before he proposed.

The sound of cupboard doors opening and slamming shut makes me cringe. George had always been a noisy man, which used to annoy me to no end until I found out he couldn't hear himself. After he got his hearing aids, he asked me if the world had always been this loud.

I decide it's time he sees his gift on me, so I walk toward the kitchen. On the way, I make a mental note that it's time for changing out some of the décor — something I used to do like clockwork when the girls still lived at home. Now I'm embarrassed by the fact that I still have my summer centerpiece collecting dust on the dining room table that hasn't been used in months.

George glances over his shoulder when I enter the kitchen, turns back to whatever he's doing, and then does a double take. A wide grin covers his face. "That thing looks pretty on you." He pauses as his smile fades a bit. "Do you like it?"

I nod and move toward him. "I love it. Thank you."

He shrugs and gives me a shy look. "You deserve it for putting up with me all these years."

My heart does a little flutter, just like it's done ever since I first met him. I close the gap between us as I open my arms and try to give him a hug. But his body stiffens, and he turns his back toward me. Something is definitely wrong with him.

"What's going on, Georgie?"

"I don't know. I have a hard time talkin' about stuff like this."

"Like what?"

"You're awful wrapped up in everything, but . . ." His voice trails off as he looks away.

I let go of George and walk over to the oven, open the door, and see how the casserole is doing. It's starting to bubble, so I turn down the heat. The aroma of Italian seasonings wafts through the air. I've been working mighty hard on making sure this reunion goes well. Thank goodness Georgie isn't a needy man and he understands why I haven't been around as much.

"Smells good, hon."

I turn around and face my husband, who is now shoving half a peanut butter sandwich into his mouth. "You're gonna spoil your supper if you keep eating like that."

"Do you want me to starve to death?" He manages to get the rest of the sandwich into his mouth as he reaches for the glass of milk on the counter.

"What's going on with you, George? You haven't been yourself lately."

He nods toward the necklace. "Are you talkin' about my gift?"

"No, I'm talking about how you've been acting for a few weeks." The family gathering pops into my head. "I want whatever it is to stop before the reunion. They'll know something's up, and they'll assume the worst."

He narrows his gaze. "That's the problem, Sheila."

"What's the problem?"

"Your family. That's all you've been talking about lately — where we're gonna have it, who's gonna show up, who they're gonna bring, what they're cookin' —" He lifts his arms out to his sides and shrugs. "It's like I don't matter anymore."

3

CORALEE BUCKLIN

Mama keeps telling me if I don't grow some boobs soon, I might as well hang up any notion of finding a man, since the only way my chest will get bigger is if I put on some weight. She obviously hasn't seen some of the flat-chested stars who have swarms of men around them. I mean, look at Taylor Swift. She's left such a long trail of broken hearts that she's got decades' worth of song material she doesn't hesitate to use. And there are others, like Cameron Diaz and Gwyneth Paltrow and Nicole Richie and Katie Holmes — way too many to count. It's obvious that having a large chest isn't the only thing that makes a woman. Besides, Daddy's mama, Granny Marge, tells me that the size of a woman's chest isn't nearly as important as the size of her heart.

I pull my sweater down, exposing the small bumps on my chest that don't even need a bra for support, and try to imagine myself being better endowed. If it weren't for Mama, I'd be fine with how I look, but she keeps planting those seeds of doubt in my head.

My phone rings, so I let go of my sweater and pick it up to see who's calling. It's my cousin Shay, who always makes me smile. She and my other cousin, who just happens to be her sister-in-law, Puddin', took over the La Chic Boutique a few months ago, and I'm happy to say she's a whole lot more cheerful than she used to be. And she's never been judgmental like some of my family. I know they love me, but I'm also aware they say things when they think I'm not listenin'.

"Hey, Shay, what's goin' on?"

She clears her throat. "We just got a new line of apparel, and I think it is perfect for your figure type."

I let out a laugh. "You mean my boyish figure?"

"No," she says. "I'm talking about your model-like figure. Seriously, Coralee, you need to stop beating yourself up. Most women I know would chop off their right arm if they could have your body."

"So what kind of clothes are we talking about?" In the back of my mind, I imagine hunting jackets and cargo shorts.

"It's a complete line with dresses, tops, pants, and even some accessories. If you can come in today, you'll have a great selection, but I have a feeling this one will sell out fast."

The excitement in her voice is contagious, and I find my pulse quickening.

I've known Shay all my life, and she's always been low-key, so her aggressive salesmanship surprises me. "I can't afford much right now. I just paid my tuition."

"Oh, don't worry about that, Coralee. You'll get the family discount."

Well, I could use something new, since I haven't bought myself anything in a long time, and being honest with myself, I know it's more because I have a hard time deciding what to buy and what to leave behind than the money.

I need clothes. And according to what I've heard from Mama and some of my cousins, the La Chic Boutique family discounts are pretty good.

"Okay, I'll try to come in later today, but I won't have long. I have an afternoon class that I have to prepare for."

"What time is your class?"

"2:30."

"That gives us plenty of time," she says. "Tell you what. I'll pull a few things that I think will look good on you, and I'll set you up in a room as soon as you get here."

After we hang up, I turn back and take another long look at myself. I'm not exactly ugly, but I'm not one of those women who turns heads. In other words, I'm invisible.

I let out a sigh of resignation and finish getting ready for the day. My sociology book beckons me, so I plop down and try to read the assigned chapter. But Shay's voice rings in my head. Could she be right when she says I have a model-like body? I think about all the famous models and wonder if she's right or just trying to make me feel better about myself. No one else has ever told me that, so I'm not putting too much credence in her words. But still.

Okay, I can't read any more of this sociology stuff. It'll have to wait until I check out the boutique and see what Shay's talking about with this new line.

To my dismay, Puddin' is standing at the counter when I walk in. Don't get me wrong. I don't have anything against my cousin's wife, who will do anything for the family. It's just that sometimes she tries too hard, and it makes me uncomfortable.

"Hey, Coralee. Shay said she called you." Puddin' points toward the fitting rooms. "Why don't you go on in there, and I'll bring you the stuff she pulled for you to try on?"

I walk back to the fitting room area and see that all four of the rooms are vacant. After stepping into the first one, I change my mind and go for the farthest one. It makes me feel claustrophobic, so I dart out of there and just stand in front of them staring at the curtains.

Puddin' grins at me as she walks straight into the second fitting room. "This one is the biggest and has the most hooks." She places the clothes on the hooks and turns to face me. "Come on out when you change so I can see how everything looks on you."

I nod and dutifully walk into the fitting room. This one does feel bigger. As I pull my arms out of my sweater and lift it over my head, that crazy-sick feeling of dread fills my belly. Clothes have never looked good on me. They just hang there like they're waiting for a real woman to come along and put them on.

The first outfit doesn't look like anything I ever would have picked out for myself. It's purple, has a scoop neckline, and there's no waist to it. *It's purple.* I cringe and make a face. But Shay and Puddin' went to the trouble to pull it from the rack, so I put it on and turn around to face myself in the mirror.

My heart nearly stops as I see the transformation. *Are you kidding me?* Just a simple dress makes me look like that? I've never —

"Coralee, are you okay?"

I hear concern in Puddin's voice. "Sure, I'm fine."

"Come on out when you have one of the dresses on. I want to see."

I suck in a deep breath, lift my chin, and push back the curtain. Then, as I walk out into the main part of the shop, I exhale and smile as Puddin's face lights up.

"My, my, my! Don't you look pretty?" She comes around from behind the counter and walks toward me. "Turn around so I can get the overall effect."

I make a slow turn, and when I'm back to facing Puddin', I see Shay coming in the front door. Her eyes widen and light up, and she smiles with her eyes crinkling and eyebrows arching.

"Oh wow." Shay takes a couple of steps closer. "I knew this would look good on you, but I had no idea just how good." She clasps her hands together. "Coralee, if you wear this, every single woman in Pinewood will turn green with envy."

"I wouldn't say that." I sneak a peek at

myself in the three-way mirror off to the side.

"Maybe not," Puddin' says, "but I would. In fact, I'm feelin' sort of jealous right now, and I'm near 'bout old enough to be your mama."

"So how did the other things look?" Shay asks.

Before I have a chance to respond, Puddin' speaks up. "This is the first thing she's tried on." She makes a shooing motion with her hand. "Go change into the next outfit."

"I don't exactly have much time." Truth be told, I'm already feeling overwhelmed by how this dress is making me feel, and I'm not sure I can handle more trying on.

Shay frowns at me as though she can read my mind. "You said your class isn't until two thirty."

"I still have a chapter to read."

She purses her lips and shakes her head. "You have time to try on a couple more things and read your chapter if you just go on ahead and do it."

After a brief stare-down, I finally nod. "Okay."

The next outfit is a pair of slim-fit pants and a tunic with an uneven hemline. I've seen those on the covers of magazines, and I'm not so sure how I feel about them. But once again, I comply.

The pants are super tight — something I've never had to deal with before, since I've always been so skinny. Then I yank the top off the hanger and pull it down over my head. This time, when I turn to look in the mirror, I'm surprised once again.

"You doin' okay in there, Coralee?"

I hear annoyance in Puddin's voice as she gets closer to the fitting room.

"Yeah." I pull back the curtain and step out.

Puddin's eyes widen, and then she turns to Shay. "Look at this girl, will ya?"

Shay nods. "W hen these clothes first came in, you were the first person I thought of. The line is made for women like you, Coralee."

Now I'm confused. I turn back toward the three-way mirror and take in a different angle. "You don't think I look goofy?"

"Goofy?" Shay shakes her head and turns to Puddin', who makes a you've-got-to-be-kidding face at me. "Anything but goofy. Coralee, you look stunning." She pauses. "Runway gorgeous. In fact, next time we have a fashion show, I want you in it. Now go try on the rest of those outfits before you run out of time."

I've tried on a lot of clothes through the

years, but I've never found so many things that fit. In fact, every single piece fits like it was made for me, so I will have to make a decision about what to buy and what to leave behind. The problem is, for the first time in my life, I want it all.

After I put my own clothes back on, I walk out of the fitting room. Puddin' shakes her head. "Such a shame you had to put those old things back on." Her eyes quickly widen, and she lifts her fingertips to her mouth. "I am *so* sorry, Coralee. I didn't mean —"

"Sure she did," Shay said. "She meant every word of it. Your old stuff does absolutely nothing for you. Why don't you put those slim-fit pants and that tunic with the asymmetrical hem back on?"

"But I have class, remember?"

"Yes, and you can wear that outfit to class."

"But —"

Shay holds up a hand. "I know, I know, you don't get why you should waste such a cute outfit on a college class." She grins. "But trust me, it'll be worth it when you see the attention you get."

"I'm not so sure I want —"

Puddin' takes a turn at interrupting me as she gives me one of her mama-bear stares. "Just go put it on."

I'm obviously no match for these women, so I do as they say. When I come back out, Shay darts into the fitting room and comes out with all the things I tried on. "If you have to leave, I can ring these up and call you with a total later."

"I need to know —"

"We'll work it out, Coralee," Puddin' says, tag-teaming her sister-in-law. "You don't have a thing to worry about." Her lips widen into a big ol' honkin' grin. "Just trust us."

I start for the door, but before I get there, Shay calls out to me. "Hold on a sec. I have one more thing for you." Then she comes at me with a long necklace that has multiple chains and some dangly things in the front. I hold still as she puts it on me. She stands back and gives me a clipped nod. "Now you can go."

Since I have so little time left, I drive straight home and quickly read the chapter without worrying about comprehension. At least I've read it, which is more than I can say for most of the people in my class. Then I get back in my car and drive to the campus in Hattiesburg.

As soon as I open the car door and get out, I realize I'm getting double takes from people who have never looked at me or even given me the time of day before. My mouth goes dry and my palms start to sweat as I make my way to the building where my class is.

It feels good to know I look better than I ever have before, so I lift my chin and smile as I glance around. I walk inside and start for the chair in the far back corner, but one of the guys I've helped with his homework motions for me to sit next to him.

What on earth is going on? I know I look better in this outfit than anything I've worn to class before, but this is way beyond an appreciative glance.

4
BRETT HENKE

Parents can be so lame. Mama says I have to go to the family reunion, but I absolutely will not go, even if they ground me for the next year. Last time I went, my cousin Julius dared me to go into the barn with him, saying I was nothin' but a mama's boy and a loser and a dork. I've always been a little shy around people my age, which is why my parents worry about me being immature.

I also think folks forget that I'm almost two years younger than Julius because I'm so much bigger than him. And Mama says he's not any more mature than I am.

So I went to the reunion, and next thing I know, I'm in trouble with the cops because Julius thinks it's fun to light a bunch of firecrackers, all at once. Inside the barn. Who does that? Even I know better than to do something so stupid, and I know I'm not the smartest guy in Pinewood. Not even close.

The last reunion started out boring, which is pretty much what I expect at a family social. So Julius has me hold the matches while he strings all those firecrackers together. Then he tells me to light one of them while he holds it up in front of me. Next thing I know, he's tossing the whole wad of firecrackers toward some bales of hay that have probably been there for years, and within seconds the place explodes. Not long after that, the police are interrogating me.

Fortunately, most people know about Julius, so I don't have to take the whole load of blame from the family, which is a good thing. And now Mama expects me to go back for more torture?

All I can do is keep digging my heels in about this stupid reunion and hoping Mama and Daddy will eventually give up, but that's not likely. Mama should have been a saleslady. No one can say no to her and get away with it.

Maybe I'll just leave town for a while. If they can't find me, they can't make me go to the reunion. But then I remember when my older brother, Trey, tried that stunt, and Mama never let him live that down. My sister, Hallie, will probably get sick the morning of the reunion like she does half the time, so the only one who'll be forced

41

to be there is Jeremy, the baby of the family. I reckon I can just hang out with him.

Julius and I just finished our community service the judge made us do, and actually, that wasn't so bad. We worked with Habitat for Humanity and then spent some time over at the Community Faith Food Bank, where we sorted all the canned goods and helped put together boxes of food for people who can't afford to feed their families. Until doing that, I never realized how hard some people have it. Now I know my family is rich compared to others who need the food bank's services.

But being with Julius isn't good for me. I'm afraid his shenanigans will only get me into more trouble.

Until the last reunion, I have always admired Julius, even though I know he's always up to something. His mama and daddy give him everything he wants, so of course the rest of us cousins are jealous. But maybe Mama is right when she says if you don't have to work for stuff, it doesn't mean as much to you.

Julius was super annoying when we were sorting food at the food bank. He tried to talk me into dumping all the canned food into one bin because he was getting tired of checking the labels. By then, I knew not to listen to him, so I just kept my head down and did as I was told. Julius, on the other hand, did what he felt like doing, so the lady in charge yanked him off sorting duty and told him to clean the restrooms. I guess you can say he went from *sorting* cans to *cleaning* cans. I let out a soft chuckle.

I know that's not funny, but it's the best I can do, considering how this whole situation is so messed up. Mama doesn't seem to understand how hard it'll be for me with Julius and some of my other cousins. And the other people . . . well, I don't really feel like facing them, since they probably hate me after what happened.

I've already gone over to Daddy's cousin Missy's house and apologized. She said she accepted it, but I'm not so sure because she didn't want me to stick around. I mean, who can blame her? If she'd been in the middle of that old barn when it exploded, she could have been killed. Good thing for me and Julius, she was by the back door, so all she had were a few cuts and bruises. And according to Mama, a case of PTSD. Apparently, loud noises still send her into a tizzy.

"Brett, get your fanny in the kitchen right now. I need you to help set the table."

Mama's voice makes my stomach hurt. I know she loves me, but she's always been bossy. And ever since she bought that shop, she's only gotten worse.

"I'll be there in a few minutes," I holler back.

"Get in here right now, Brett Henke," her voice screeches. "And I mean now, young man."

"Coming." I feel my shoulders sag as I slog into the kitchen, where Mama has all the plates, forks, knives, and spoons lined up for me to put in everyone's spot. It would have been just as easy for her to put them out herself, but no, she wants to make me work.

After I lay everything out, I see that there are a couple of extra settings. "What's this for?"

Mama places her hands on her hips, gives me a smug look that scares me, and grins — something that makes the hair on the back of my neck stand on end. I am almost a foot taller than her, but even Daddy listens when she gets like this. "Missy and Foster are joining us for dinner. I thought it was time for you to clear the air with her so it won't be so awkward when we see her at the reunion."

Before I catch myself, I groan. "No."

"Just what do you mean by that, young man?" Mama shakes her head. "You can't

44

say no, because I've already invited them."

"Why'd you have to do that?"

"I've already told you, Brett. You have to clear the air and make sure Missy knows you'll never do anything like that again. She deserves at least that from someone who near 'bout killed her."

Once again, I shudder at the very thought of what could have happened. Mama obviously doesn't realize how traumatic that whole thing was for me. Sometimes I wonder if she thinks I'm as guilty as Julius was.

"So what do you want me to do while she's here?"

Mama shrugs. "It won't hurt for you to do a little grovelin'." She bobs her head. "You can hold her chair, ask if she wants you to get anything for her, and make sure she's comfortable while she's here."

Daddy walks into the kitchen, gives Mama a kiss, and then turns to me. "Did your mama tell you who's comin' to supper?"

Without giving me a chance to speak, Mama nods. "I certainly did, and that's not all I told him. I said he has to do everything in his power to make Missy comfortable."

He casts a look in my direction as he turns to leave the kitchen. "Don't go overboard, son, or no one will be comfortable."

That's what I'm thinkin', but one look at

Mama, and I know I'll have to go way overboard, or she won't be happy. And there's a sign over the mudroom on the way to the garage, reminding all of us that *If Mama ain't happy, ain't nobody happy.*

5
MARYBETH BUCKLIN

I'm totally beside myself with a combination of joy and trepidation about Bucky's whole family coming to our house for the next reunion. I realize Bucky is excited to show off all our new stuff, including our theater room with a dozen rocking chairs that also recline, the billiards room that rarely gets used, the state-of-the-art chef's kitchen that I'll eventually use as soon as I have time to learn how to cook, and a swimming pool in the backyard that's near 'bout the size of a football field. But it's starting to get on my nerves big-time. Sure, I got caught up in the whole charade in the beginning, but the newness has worn off, and I'm not feelin' so good about what too much money has done to us lately.

Bucky walks up behind me and gives me a kiss on the back of the neck, startling me. "What are you doing, Bucky?"

"I've been thinkin'."

"Don't start doin' too much thinkin'. I'm tapped out on all we're doing for the reunion."

He rubs the back of his neck and takes a long look around. "You know how blessed we've been with all that money from striking oil. I think we should have everyone spend the weekend here so they can get a feel for what it's like to be rich."

"No." The word comes out before I have a chance to face him. When I do eventually look at him, he looks like someone slapped him, so I allow the urge to explain to take over. "What I mean is, it's not good to flaunt our money."

He laughs. "Honey, it's too late for that. We've done flaunted our money all over the place."

"You know what I mean, Bucky. Some of the people in your family . . . well, they just don't get it."

He rolls his eyes — something that has always bugged the heck out of me. "That's their problem. Some folks is just too stupid to —"

"Don't say that." That's another thing he does that makes me want to smack him upside the head. "Money isn't as important to some people as it is to you."

"I didn't hear you complainin' none when

48

I brought you home that Mercedes."

True. But if he'd brought me a Buick and straightened out his attitude, I would have been just as happy. "I just don't think we need to have anyone spend the night — at least anyone who lives in town. I'm sure they'd rather go home after it's over and sleep in their own beds where they can be more comfortable."

He gives me a sideways grin. "I bet not a one of 'em has a top-of-the-line Sleep Number bed."

"I think it's ridiculous that we have so many of them." This conversation is going nowhere, so I change the subject. "So, what are you doing this afternoon?"

He shrugs. "I thought I'd go see what's going on at the feed store. One of the guys said he's selling off some pigs, and I just might buy a couple of 'em."

"What are you going to do with a couple of pigs?"

"Eat 'em." He scrunches up his face and gives me a look like he thinks I'm stupid or something. "What else would you do with 'em?"

I shudder at the image of what I originally thought when he said he might buy pigs. The very thought of pigs oinking around in our perfectly manicured backyard that we spent a boatload of money for slams me with old memories that haunt me relentlessly.

When I first met Bucky, he told me he'd take me away from my past filled with squalor, parents who used to scream and holler at each other, saying things that would make me wash my son's mouth out with soap if he ever said them, and wondering if or when the next meal would appear on the table. Mama and Daddy didn't seem to mind living in a house that needed painting, dealing with a toilet that ran nonstop, and having a stove with only one working burner. Daddy used to leave every morning, saying he was going to work, but to this day, I doubt he had a job. Mama chain-smoked, so everything in our house reeked. There was nothing to be proud of where I grew up.

My little sister, Shalimar, and brother, Henry, got involved with drugs when they were teenagers. I'm not sure what kept me straight — maybe it was the fact that I'd started sneaking around and seeing Bucky, who was out of high school when I'd barely started. We ran off to Alabama and got married shortly after I turned eighteen because Mississippi required a parent's consent under twenty-one.

Both my brother and sister have turned their lives around — but it wasn't until they spent time in jail for selling illegal substances. I talked to them about how the love of Jesus could make a difference in their lives. Shalimar listened and immediately started attending church, while Henry needed another stint behind bars for the message to get through his thick skull. One of the men from our little country church started visiting Henry, who didn't have a choice but to listen. The second time he was set free, he straightened up.

Bucky loves Jesus, but he seems to love being rich even more, and that's mostly what the family sees. I see much more than that. Deep down, he's a good man with a big heart who doesn't know how to handle his instant wealth. And when I'm being honest with myself, I admit that I'm often confused too. I mean, it's really weird going from wondering where the money will come from to buy a loaf of bread and a jar of peanut butter to having enough money to buy the most expensive hunk of meat in the grocery store and putting it in the trunk of a car that cost more than my parents' house.

The person who struggles the most with being rich is our son, Julius. That boy pretty much stays in trouble, and he catches all kinds of heck from Bucky and me — behind closed doors. In front of people, it's a different story. In my book, family sticks up for one another. Granted, Bucky's cousins are all family, but I'm talking about immediate family — folks who all live in the same house.

The Bucklins seem to think we let our boy get away with all kinds of stuff, and sometimes we do. But we've tanned his hide and threatened him with everything under the sun, and he still tests us. Half the time I'm too exhausted to deal with him, but when I'm rested, hoo-boy, you'd better watch out. He doesn't know what happened.

Now he's giving us grief about going to the next reunion, which is sort of funny, since it's going to be at our house. And that wasn't my idea. Bucky's grandparents, Grandpa Jay and Granny Marge, thought it would be a good way to make up for what our son did. I'm not sure they're right, but at least if he does something bad, it'll be at our house, and we won't have to worry about the cops showing up like they did when he and Brett blew up the barn.

And that's another subject. I flew off the handle when that happened, and I caught myself blaming Brett. You'd've thought I said that boy was a serial killer if you'd seen

Puddin's reaction. When I even hinted that her boy might have been to blame for the explosion, she came after me, eyes blazing, nostrils flaring, fists tight enough to knock down a wall made of steel. It took her husband and one of her cousins to hold her back. And I can't say I blame her a single solitary bit.

"Marybeth!" Bucky's voice echoes throughout the house. "Where are you?"

"Same place I was last time you saw me," I holler back.

He appears in the doorway, grinning. "I just talked to Grandpa Jay. He says this is the reunion in the rotation that lasts a whole week."

"Whoever came up with that?" I shake my head. "That's downright ridiculous."

"No, it's a good bonding experience." He gives me a serious look. "It'll bring the family closer."

I'm not so sure he believes what he's saying. It seems like he's more interested in showing off than bonding.

"I'm thinkin' it might backfire if we have people here for a week." I shake my head and fold my arms. "One overnight . . . maybe two. But not a whole week."

Bucky comes toward me with open arms. As soon as he touches me, that old familiar electricity sends my senses into orbit. He knows how to get his way.

6
SALLY

Finding orange hair ribbon when it's the hottest color of the season is making me crazy. I'm not telling Sara this, but I should have listened to her when she said we should have bought several cases of it a couple of months ago.

I skim the list of vendors and find one I haven't yet called. After punching their number into my cell phone, I see an email pop up on my laptop, letting me know that I'm in luck. Our main vendor has just located a case of orange ribbon in the back of his warehouse, and it's ours if we still want it. I don't hesitate to claim it, but then I still place my call because one case isn't enough.

"Um . . . yeah, we have a bunch of it — something like six cases," the guy says. "But the Halloween shipping season is over. Why would you want orange?" Before I have a chance to say a word, he speaks. "Tell you what. Since it's clearly not the season for orange, I'll let you have it for half price if you'll take all of it. It's not even worth putting in my catalog."

I mentally high-five myself. "It's a deal." Then his comment about Halloween pops into my head. "It is plain orange, isn't it? I mean, there aren't any pumpkins on it, are there?"

"One case has Halloween designs, but the rest of it's solid orange." He clears his throat. "But you have to take all of it for the half-price deal. It's a final sale too."

My heart sinks. We've already decided to only do business with companies that stand behind their merchandise. I'm not about to make the decision to back off from that without Sara's consent. "Sorry, but I'm afraid that's a deal breaker."

He mumbles something I can't understand before he finally blurts, "Oh, okay. If you don't like it, you can send it back, but you'll have to pay shipping."

"Oh, absolutely." I give him my information before hanging up. I have no idea why that company has so much orange ribbon with it being as popular as it is, but I figure it's the break I've needed lately. It might not be a big thing to most people, but I'll take whatever I can get.

I figure that since we're down to a two-day backlog on making the bows, and it's a much faster process when Sara and I are both doing it together, I can work on our spreadsheet. Even after a couple of years of our business steadily increasing in volume, I still smile when I see the balance sheet. I doubt anyone else would believe how well we're doing.

After a half hour of being deeply immersed in numbers, I decide to leave the work for a few minutes and go get a snack. Sara and Justin are sitting at the kitchen table, hunched over it, looking at a pamphlet.

"I didn't hear y'all come in," I say. "I thought y'all were going to New Orleans."

"We are, but Justin has to go to the shop for a little while this afternoon."

Justin lifts his head. "One of my clients refuses to let anyone else touch his car, and I promised someone at the shop I'd help with his hot rod first."

I try to see what they were so engrossed in, but Sara quickly covers it with a folder. When Justin glances away, I make a face, and she mimics me. I grin as I try to see the pamphlet. "What are y'all looking at?"

Sara shakes her head, but Justin nudges her. "You need to tell her."

"Not now."

He lifts an eyebrow. "If you don't, I will."

Sara rolls her eyes and lets out what Mama calls the *millennial grunt,* which is really a sigh of exasperation on steroids. "Oh, okay, I'll tell her."

I open the fridge and pull out a bottle of water and reach for the bagged salad. "Tell me what?"

"We've been looking at houses." Sara grimaces in what she probably thinks is an apologetic look. "It's not that we don't like being here with you. It's just that —" She cuts herself off as she turns to her husband.

He nods and turns to face me. "We think it's time to be on our own as a married couple."

"Oh, okay, I get it." And I do. It's just that I've never been completely on my own, and I'm not sure what I'll do with myself in this big old condo. And that brings up another point. "How will we deal with your half of the condo ownership?"

Now Sara speaks up. "We'll still use this as our office, if you don't mind, so we won't have to deal with it at all. Justin has been saving his paycheck for a down payment, so I won't need for you to buy me out, at least not now."

"I see." I pull my lips between my teeth to

keep my chin from quivering like it always does right before I cry.

Sara bounds out of her chair and puts her arm around me. "It's not like we're doing anything today or tomorrow or anything. We're just starting to look."

I blink as we make eye contact. "Remember how fast we found this place?"

She nods and looks over at Justin. "She's got a point. Maybe we should put off looking for a few weeks."

"But —" Justin cuts himself off, glances back and forth between Sara and me, and nods. "I reckon you're right. We're not in a big hurry, but we'll need to do something before we have a young'un."

"A young'un?" I narrow my eyes and glance at Sara's belly. "Is that what this is all about?"

Sara shrugs and glances away. "We've been talking about it. I don't want to wait until I'm old, like thirty, before having a family."

"Thirty's not old." I'm thinking I'll be at least thirty before I can start thinking about having kids, and since there's not even a man in my life, it might not even happen then.

"I know, but —" She gives me a helpless look and then glances away. There's something about the look in her eyes that sends off an alarm in my head. "It'll be nice to have them when I'm still young enough to enjoy them."

Sometimes my sister doesn't know when to stop. Justin and I exchange a glance that lets me know he's probably thinking the same thing.

"Tell you what. We'll stay here for a while longer so no one has to worry about anything." Justin smiles at me. "It's just easier for now, but eventually, we really need to find our own place."

I grin right back at him. "At least now I know y'all are looking for a house, and I won't be blindsided when it happens."

"So, have you seen the orders rolling in?" Sara holds up her phone. "I had to turn off notifications because it wouldn't stop."

I nod. "Yeah, and I have to give you credit for something that has totally surprised me."

"What's that?"

"Almost half of our orders are for orange bows."

Sara tilts her head and purses her lips, something she does when she's thinking of a comeback. I brace myself for a tirade.

"We need to get on the stick and find some orange ribbon," she says, her voice cracking.

"Well . . ." I give her a huge grin. "I've already taken care of it. We have one case coming from Notions, Inc., and six cases coming from Value Threads." I lift my chin in pride.

Her eyes widen. "Not Value Threads."

"Why not?"

"Don't you remember? They're the ones whose boxes are all mislabeled, and they never send what we ask for. You even told me we shouldn't ever order from them again because everything we got was messed up."

I close my eyes and let out a deep sigh. Now that she mentions it, I do remember. "Maybe it's not too late to cancel."

Justin stands and pushes his chair under the table. "I need to go help Slick with his new hot rod. See y'all later." He gives Sara a kiss on the cheek. "I'll bring supper home if y'all tell me what you want."

Sara and I both say, "Thai," at the same time.

He laughs. "I should've known. Do y'all want the usual?"

"Yep." Sara turns to me with a questioning look.

I nod. "Red curry chicken."

After Justin leaves, Sara and I stand and stare at each other for about a minute before she finally speaks up. "I hope you know he cares about you."

"He's turned out to be a decent guy." I laugh as I remember my initial reaction to their elopement, since they only dated a couple of weeks. My first thoughts when they got married weren't so good, but over time, I've come to accept some of his strange ways — his ability to sit in a room filled with people and not say a word for hours, the way he gets up and does stuff like fix my car without announcing it, and how he'll go into the kitchen and come out a half hour later to announce that supper will be done in five minutes. It's weird but in a good way.

Sara sighs. "I remember when he used to talk to me in Family and Consumer Science. I loved the fact that he could cook and sew better than any girl in that class."

Most of the time, Sara and I took the same classes in high school, but a few of our electives were different. She chose Family and Consumer Science, what Mama and Daddy said was a fancy way of saying home ec, while I picked Speech and Drama.

I'm about to say it's time to get back to work when my phone rings. It's Shay letting me know they just got a new maternity line in at La Chic Boutique.

I laugh. "Why are you calling me about it?"

A long silence falls between us before she finally speaks. "Um . . . this isn't Sara, is it? I think I pressed the wrong name on my phone."

I glance up and look at my sister's belly. "No, but she's right here. Would you like to speak to her?"

7
SHEILA

I sure wish I knew what's going on between my daughters. They've been acting odd — almost like they don't like each other — lately. Even though I can't quite put my finger on whatever it is, I suspect Sara's husband, Justin, has something to do with it.

There was a time when my girls were totally inseparable, with Sally almost always in the lead. It wasn't that Sara was a follower. I think it was more that she didn't care where they went or what they did when they got there. So she deferred to her sister, who cared about everything, and I mean *everything*.

My own mother used to check and double-check every stinkin' thing she did. Sally obviously inherited Mama's OCD behavior. When she was little, she'd turn off the light, take a few steps, and then look over her shoulder to make sure it was still off. Sara, on the other hand, never cared whether the light was on or off as long as she was comfortable and happy, which was most of the time when she was with Sally.

But over the past couple of days, when I call either of them, I get a polite brush-off. Sara will listen to me for a few minutes, make a brief comment, and then say she has to go. Sally, on the other hand, asks if there's an emergency and then says she can call me back later. That's weird, because in the past, both of them would rattle on and on about their business or some new beauty product, and I was the one who'd have to go.

So I decide it's high time to pay them a surprise visit. Calling first is not an option because I suspect both of them would tell me it isn't a good time.

Armed with their favorite casserole and a basket of muffins, I walk up to their door, shift the handle of the basket to free my hand, and ring their doorbell. My breath catches in my throat as soon as the door opens.

"Hi, Justin. Are the girls here?" I know I shouldn't be so shocked that my daughter's husband is standing in front of me, but it still feels too weird to describe.

He takes the casserole from me as he

opens the door wider. "Come on in, Mrs. Wright. She's in our room, resting. I'll go get her."

Having this boy sharing a room with Sara makes the situation feel even stranger, but I know there's nothing wrong with it, since they're a married couple and all. "Okay."

"Let me put this in the kitchen first." He leads the way, and I follow. "Does it need to be refrigerated?"

I nod. "Yes, that's what I would do."

I'm amazed by how comfortable he is in my daughters' home, until I yank my mind back around to the fact that it's his home too. I follow him into the kitchen and watch in amazement at how deft his moves are. After he shifts a few things around in the refrigerator and slides the casserole onto the shelf, he turns and takes the basket of muffins from me.

"Everything smells good, Mrs. Wright. Thanks for bringing it." He grins and lets out a soft chuckle. "Now I don't have to cook tonight."

I feel my eyebrows shoot up. "You cook?"

"Most of the time. Sally used to do most of it, but she's having to take up some of the slack in the business now, so I figure it's the least I can do." He shrugs and smiles even bigger. "Besides, I like cooking."

Alarm bells ring in my head. "Why is Sally having to take up the slack? What's going on, Justin?"

He starts to step back, but I grab his arm. The expression on his face is a blend of fear and disbelief.

"Is there something you need to tell me?"

Justin closes his eyes for a couple of seconds and then opens them to look me directly in the eyes. "There's something Sara needs to tell you."

"Then go get her. I'll wait right here."

The confident expression he had now changes to one of consternation mixed with fear. After he leaves, I walk over to the table and start to sit, but I quickly realize I'm too anxious to do anything but pace. So that's exactly what I do until I hear footsteps coming toward the kitchen. I stop and turn to face the door.

I blink as I see both of my daughters standing there, hesitating to enter the kitchen. But that's not what surprises me. Sally pretty much looks the same as always, only she has a scowl on her face, while Sara is pale and wearing ratty sweatpants and an oversize shirt that must be Justin's, although he's not that much bigger than her.

"What is going on?" I ask, since neither of them appears ready to talk.

Sally's lips tighten as she turns her attention to Sara. "I told you this would happen."

Sara's chin quivers — one of the traits they both share — indicating that she's about to burst into tears.

"Just tell me."

Even though Sally is clearly annoyed with her twin sister, she puts her arm around her and takes another step closer. "C'mon, Sara. I'm right here."

Sara nods, glances down at the floor momentarily, and then raises her gaze to meet mine. She licks her lips and slowly shakes her head as she sinks deeper into Sally's embrace. "I can't. You do it."

Justin comes up from behind and takes Sara's hand. She appears to pull back, but he doesn't let go. "I'll tell her if you want me to."

"No." The quick response from both girls at the same time lets me know that at least they're still a team.

Finally, Sara sucks in a breath, lets it out, and blurts, "I'm pregnant."

My first reaction is a gripping sensation in my chest and fear for my daughter. But when I take a long look at the three people standing in front of me, Sara sandwiched between Sally and Justin, both of them with arms around her, I realize this might actually be a good thing. Besides, I've always hoped to become a grandmother. It's just that they've been married for such a short time.

Now my chin starts to quiver as I open my arms wide and walk toward her. "Oh, Sara, I am so happy for you. For *both* of you." I look at Sally, whose expression of disbelief almost makes me laugh. "For all of us. How long have you known?"

"I found out when Shay called."

I hear the pain in her voice.

Sara places her hand on Sally's shoulder. "I already told you she heard about it from the lady at the doctor's office."

"I know, but —"

I can't let her continue, or she might say something she'll later regret. I've learned that the hard way, so I speak up. "Don't forget that y'all have been reminding me since you were eighteen that you're adults." I smile at Justin, who appears extremely uncomfortable. Memories of George's shell-shocked expression that lasted until almost a year after the girls were born make me chuckle. "And now that you're married, there's nothing bad about it that I can see."

"Well, that just beats all." Sally breaks away from her sister, walks over to the cupboard, pulls out a glass, and takes it to the refrigerator, where she gets water from the door. "I never saw that coming."

"Saw what coming?" I ask. "The pregnancy or my reaction?"

"Both." Sally leans against the counter, takes a sip, and looks at me for a few seconds. "I thought y'all would wait at least a year or two. Do you realize how this is going to change everything?"

I smile at my bossy daughter. "Yes, sweetie, I do."

"How is that good? Everything was perfect before."

"I hate to burst your bubble, but . . ." I step closer to Sally and pick up her free hand. "Nothing is ever perfect."

"But —"

"Y'all will have to make some adjustments, but over time you'll be just fine." I let go of Sally's hand and walk over to my other daughter and her husband. After a brief hesitation, I take both of their hands and squeeze. "I am very happy that y'all are blessing me with a grandchild. What's the due date?"

"We don't know yet." Sally glances at Justin out of the corner of her eye. "I haven't seen the doctor yet."

"She just took the pregnancy test a few

days ago, after I got worried about her being so sick every morning when she woke up. I thought something was seriously wrong with her."

I smile. "I was sick as a dog when I was pregnant with the two of you." Then something even more alarming pops into my head. "What if you have twins?"

Justin speaks up again. "I've been looking on the Internet, and I'm pretty sure that's not the case, since it's not genetic."

"It's not?" I shake my head. "I always thought it was since Sally and Sara's daddy has a lot of identical twins in his family."

"According to the twin sites and some of the medical experts, genetics only plays a role in fraternal twins, not identical."

I blink as I see my son-in-law in a different light. Before now, in my mind, he was just a goofy kid who liked to work on cars. He's sounding smarter than I ever would have imagined.

He lets go of my hand and wraps both of his arms around Sara, who remains standing there, soldier-straight. "But if we have twins, I'll just have double the love for my kids."

"*Our* kids." Sara's voice squeaks. "Mama, I'm so sorry I didn't tell you. It's just that, well, I thought you'd . . . ." Her voice trails

71

off as she looks at Sally for reinforcement.

Sally takes the bait. "After your reaction to her elopement, she thought you'd disown her."

Sara pulls away from Justin. "I never said that. Mama would never —" She gives her husband a helpless look before glaring at her sister.

"I thought that would get you to talk." Sally emits a half chuckle and then resumes her straight-face demeanor. "Now we're trying to figure out how to get all our work done." She flinches. "And our living arrangements."

At this moment, I'm speechless. My girls have always been on the same page with practically everything in their lives, until now. One of the women in my Mothers of Twins group warned me of this, but I still never imagined how it would play out in our lives.

Justin is the first one to break our momentary silence. "One of the problems we're having now is that we all like this place." He laughs as he rubs his chin in a fashion similar to my husband's. "Who'd've ever thought I'd become a condo man?"

Sally rolls her eyes and shakes her head as she settles her gaze on mine. "So, what do you think about this, Mama? Have you ever seen anything like this?"

"Honey, folks have babies all the time, many of them during their first year of marriage."

8
SALLY

It took me forever to fall asleep last night after Sara and Justin finally went to New Orleans. Justin's boss asked him to wait until he could hire another mechanic. I've been alone before, but this time it feels different — sort of like I'm being pushed out of her life for good.

What's crazy is that even though I barely got six hours of sleep, I'm wide-awake before the sun comes up. Sara and I have both always been good sleepers, according to Mama, but I think that's about to change.

I get up and head toward the kitchen, where I fix myself a cup of coffee. It's so quiet my ears are ringing. Most mornings, Sara sleeps a little later than I do, so I'm used to being alone in the kitchen, but now I know she won't be padding in, rubbing her sleepy eyes, while I'm drinking my coffee.

I pull my phone out of my bathrobe

pocket and see if there are any calls I missed. There are, but none of them are from Sara. The other people can wait.

This is going to be a long day, so I sit at the table and try to figure out what I can do to make it go by easier. Maybe Mama will want to go to lunch. It's still a tad too early to call her, but at least I have hope that there's something I can do to break up the loneliness.

Since it's so early, instead of starting work in my pajamas like I normally do, I decide to take a shower and put on some jeans. Maybe that'll perk me up.

The whole process of showering, getting dressed, putting on a little makeup, and brushing my hair takes a total of twenty minutes. It's still early, but I sit down at my workstation and pull up one of the orders.

Normally, I prefer total quiet when working, but today I pull up my '80s playlist and connect it to the little Bluetooth speaker. Mama used to listen to '80s music when Sara and I were little girls, so I suppose that's when I developed a taste for it. Both Sara and I know all the words to most of the songs on the list.

After completing a couple of orders, I pick up my phone and call Mama. "Hey, Mama, whatcha doing for lunch?"

"I have a club meeting." Her voice sounds breathy, like she's in a hurry. "We're working on the holiday charity event."

"Oh." I sink back in my seat as disappointment floods me. Am I the only person in Pinewood who doesn't have a life?

"Did you need to talk about something in particular? I should be home around 2:00 or so."

"No, I just thought it would be fun to have lunch together."

"Oh, honey, I wish I could join you. Where's Sara?"

"She and Justin went to New Orleans for a few days." I try to sound normal, but even I can hear the disappointment in my voice.

"So you're lonely." Mama pauses. "I'm sorry, Sally, but I always knew one of you would eventually have to deal with this. Maybe you can take advantage of your time alone to work on a plan."

"A plan?" I sigh. "For what?"

"Your life. You can't spend all your time waiting for your sister to come home. I know you're not a social butterfly, but maybe you should consider joining some club."

"I won't know anyone." Sara and I hung around together most of the time, and the few friends we have either moved away or

76

got married.

"That's the whole point, Sally. You'll meet some new friends who have similar interests."

The problem is, I don't have any interests outside of what I'm already doing, and even that's a stretch. But I can't tell Mama that, or she'll try to come up with something for me. "I'll think about it."

"I would invite you to come to my club meeting, but I'm afraid you'd be bored to tears. After we finish the planning for the charity, most of our talk is about our grown kids *and grandkids.* I'm not thrilled about Sara's timing, but at least I have a baby to look forward to."

It's clear that she's giving me a not-so-subtle hint, and it's not something I want to hear. "Okay, have fun at your club meeting. Maybe I'll just go downtown and walk around or something."

"Great idea. Maybe you can stop off and see Shay and Puddin'. They've been bringing in a lot of new lines since they bought the place, so you might find something cute to wear. That always perks me up."

After we hang up, I fill a few more orders before I stand and stretch. It's almost noon, but I'm not hungry, so I decide to take Mama's advice and head downtown to do a little window-shopping. The irony of the situation is that between Sara and me, she's always been more of a shopper. I normally don't see the point unless there's something I need.

It's a nice, cool fall day, so I slip a faux leather jacket over my T-shirt and change from my sneakers to a pair of ballet flats before heading out to my car. All the way into town, I force myself to look at the scenery — something Sara says I don't do enough. She thinks I'm too driven in business and I don't pay enough attention to the other things that make life worth living.

As I pass the library, I notice that most of the leaves have fallen, leaving the trees bare for winter. I don't remember them changing colors, which lets me know that Sara is right. I need to enjoy what Mama always calls *God's amazing decorations.*

There are never enough parking spots on Main Street, so I pull into the first one I see that's a little more than a block away from La Chic Boutique. It feels weird to be doing this alone, since Sara has always been with me in the past, except those times when I went shopping for a gift for her. But I force myself to get out of the car and start walking. It's becoming painfully evident that

I'm not as independent as I thought I was, and it's time to make some major changes.

9

CORALEE

Ever since I started wearing my new outfits, folks have been looking at me different. In some ways, it's kind of nice to not be ignored. But there are times when I wish I could go back to my wallflower self . . . but not enough to actually wear the frumpy rags. The oversize cargo pants and men's tees I used to wear aren't attractive on anyone — especially a woman my age. I know I look good now, so I lift my chin with the newfound confidence these clothes have given me.

I've been called smart all my life, so I'm comfortable when it comes to schoolwork. Hopefully, I'll develop a little more social confidence now that I'm not so embarrassed by how I look.

I've barely gotten out of my car when I hear Kyle calling my name. I turn and see him jogging toward me. "Hey, Kyle."

"Hey, Coralee, wanna go get a burger after

sociology?" He smiles and waits for my answer — something no guy has ever done before.

"I don't know." After the looks I got from the other pair of tight pants, I went back to La Chic and bought them in every color.

"Or we can just walk around campus and maybe stop at the student union for some Starbucks."

The eagerness in his voice gives me a tummy thrill, but I'm not so sure it's because he's the one talking or the fact that someone actually seems to care about being with me. "Coffee will be good."

As we walk toward the building where our class is, I can see guys looking at me in a whole 'nother way — something that would have made me uncomfortable in the past but that actually feels good now that I've gotten sort of used to it. And I can tell that Kyle is fully aware of it too as he reaches for my hand and holds it tight.

This isn't the first time we've had physical contact, but the other two times were when we were alone. So I know he's trying to lay claim to me, which isn't a bad thing, since I really like him.

Once we reach the classroom, there are only a couple of spots available — on opposite sides of the room. The sociology professor doesn't believe in assigned seats.

Kyle whispers, "Want me to see if someone will move?"

"No, that's okay. I need to take notes anyway."

He gives me a reluctant nod before walking across the room and claiming the seat by the wall. I take the one closer to the door.

Almost the instant I sit down, someone taps me on the shoulder. I turn around and find myself face-to-face with one of the football players — the guy who struts around while girls wish he'd look at them.

"Hey, are you and that guy just friends, or are you in a relationship?" He pauses and gives me one of those too-charming-to-trust smiles. "I'd like to hang out with you."

I laugh. "You don't beat around the bush, do you?" Even though I'm getting attention that I never got in the past, I'm still the same inside. I reckon it'll take a while before the confidence kicks in.

He shrugs. "There's no reason to."

"Well . . ." I glance over at Kyle and see the panic-stricken look on his face, and my heart melts. "I am sort of in a relationship with him." That is somewhat the truth, I think.

"If things don't work out between you two, let me know." He settles back in his seat and lowers his eyelids to half-mast. I suspect he'll probably snooze once the professor starts talking, but as long as he doesn't snore, I don't care.

I start to turn back around, and as I do, I glance over at Kyle, who continues to stare. I give him my flirtiest smile and wiggle my fingers in a wave. His lips twitch into an uncertain smile back.

The lecture is more interesting than usual. I take notes as fast as I can, but I'm not too worried because Kyle somehow manages to remember most of what the professor says. At least that's what he tells me. He says the reason he struggles with his grades is that he's never been a good test taker.

I don't know how he does it, but within a second of the class's ending, Kyle is standing beside my desk. "Ready to go get coffee?" His gaze darts to the football player behind me, and then he looks at me as he reaches for my hand.

As we stroll out of the classroom hand in hand, I wonder how things would have worked out with the guy sitting behind me. It would have been fun to see what the big deal is about him, but there's no doubt in my mind it wouldn't last once he got bored.

"You know what I like about you, Coralee?"

I turn to Kyle. "What's that?"

"You're not only beautiful, you're smart and nice. That's an unusual combination."

I tilt my head back and let out a nervous laugh. "Yeah, I'm weird."

"I didn't say that." His brows slam together in a look of consternation. "What I meant was —"

"Don't worry about it. I'm kidding . . . Well, sort of kidding." I ponder my thoughts for a few seconds. "Actually, I am weird, but that's intentional."

"You are?" He gives me a curious look with his nose wrinkling and his eyes all squinty. "It is? What are you talking about?"

I figure I might as well tell him now because if we continue to . . . whatever it is we're doing, he'll find out. "I've always been sort of dorky and not attractive at all."

"You're kidding, right?"

"No, I'm serious as can be." I stop, and since we're still holding hands, he nearly stumbles. "I mean, look at when we got together. You never paid a single solitary bit of attention to me before."

He narrows his eyes and shakes his head. "That's not true. I noticed you before, but you used to seem so closed off — sort of like you didn't want to be bothered."

"I did?"

"Yes, and I don't like to get shot down, so I never said anything."

This puts a whole different light on things. "What made you think things would be different?"

He shrugs. "I don't know, maybe it's just a gut feeling. That day when you came walking in looking like this, you were smiling." He pauses. "And you looked happy and approachable. And then you looked directly at me, and I felt like I'd been struck by a ray of sunshine."

"You did?"

"Absolutely." He reaches out and taps my nose in a playful manner. "And that's exactly what you've been for me."

"Oh wow. I had no idea."

"Now it's my turn." His smile fades. "After I got out of the Air Force, I was offered a couple of jobs that were tempting."

"You were in the Air Force?" This just goes to show how little I know about him, and that makes me feel guilty for only thinking about myself.

"Yep. Four years." He closes his eyes and shakes his head. "Four very long years."

"I take it you didn't like the military."

"Oh, I liked it just fine, when I was in the States. I spent most of my time in Afghanistan."

This puts a whole new light on Kyle. "So why did you decide to go to college instead of taking one of those jobs?"

"The jobs weren't something I wanted to do for the rest of my life, and I figured that I might as well go back to school while I'm still young."

"How old are you?" I ask.

"I'll be twenty-five on my next birthday." He lifts his chin. "So that makes me about a year and a half older than you."

Now I'm embarrassed that I've talked so much about myself and not asked him about his life until now. "What do you want to do with the rest of your life?"

"Well, first I need to finish up here, but . . ." He makes a face. "At the risk of sounding geeky, I'd like to be an electronics engineer."

"Geeky is good." We walk a few steps toward the library before I continue. "Then what?"

"I'd like to find a job. A boring job with a stable company, settle down with a wife I'm madly in love with, and have two-point-three kids."

"Do you go to church?"

"Yeah, I do."

I see his Adam's apple rise and fall as he swallows hard.

"How about you?"

"Yes, in fact, that's probably the most important thing in my life."

He grins at me. "Mine too."

Maybe there's hope for us after all.

10
SALLY

I still can't believe I spent so much money at La Chic yesterday. The second I walked in the door, Puddin' pounced on me and told me she'd start me a room. Sometime while I was trying on my first outfit, Shay appeared with another batch of things she said were perfect for me.

So here I am with a whole pile of this season's fall fashion — three pairs of leggings, a half dozen tunics, a couple of dresses, and accessories to go with all of it — piled on my bed. When I first got home from downtown, I hung everything up, but now I'm thinking I might want to take some of it back. Now I'm trying it all on and looking at myself in the full-length mirror that Sara insisted I hang on my door.

The first outfit that Puddin' said was *so me* is a pair of navy leggings and a V-neck burgundy-print tunic. I never would have put those pieces together, but Puddin' was right. It looks amazing. Okay, I'll keep that one. Next, I try on the other tunic that goes with the navy leggings, and it looks just as good. Another keeper.

After I finish looking at all of it a second time, I'm amazed that I like it even more than when I was in the store. Puddin' clearly has a knack for fashion. Who'd've thought?

Shay isn't so bad either. In fact, I'm starting to see her as the accessories queen. She found scarves, necklaces, and earrings to go with every one of the outfits I bought, and I like all of them. Looks like I won't be bringing any of it back.

I can't help laughing at myself. Neither Sara nor I ever worried too much about what we wore, and between the two of us, I have always been less interested. She'll get a kick out of my purchasing all this stuff.

After getting past the fact that I'm feeling left out, I'm worried about Sara not feeling well during their trip. But I'm sure that having a new baby on the way has created a sense of urgency, since it'll be much more difficult once he or she arrives.

Since Sara called and said she and Justin aren't planning to come back home for another day or two, depending on whether or not they can get tickets to some concert

Justin wants to go to, I know I have to find more ways to occupy my time. I've managed to fill most of the orders that don't require orange ribbon, so I have to do something, and I don't want to sit in front of the TV for hours on end. It's too depressing, and I'm already fit to be tied. I thought I'd gotten used to Sara being married, but obviously not. *How could she have done this to me?*

Now that I have time to think about it, I know it's selfish of me, but we've always talked through things before making a big decision. When the biggest decision of all came up, she pushed me aside and put this boy . . . this man ahead of me. I wonder what she would have done if I'd gone off and gotten married to some guy she barely knew.

Sure, I think Justin is okay, and there's no doubt in my mind that he adores her. It's just that he's the wedge that keeps Sara and me from being as close as we were before he popped into her life. Our lives. I don't know how I'll ever get past that.

There's absolutely nothing I can do about it now, nor would I want to. Truth be told, I've never seen Sara as happy as she is now. Sure, she still has her moody moments, but overall, she seems more confident. More adult. Now that I think about it, she's becoming more of the woman I'd like to be.

Mama's words about joining something and getting involved with people who have similar interests flit through my head. Maybe she's right. But where do I start? The problem is that I don't have a lot of interests, and the only thing I'm good at is making hair bows. That's totally not something I want to do in my spare time.

I open my laptop and do a search on special-interest clubs. Political? No, that's not for me. Coin collecting? I don't see the point. Money's for spending. Cooking? I laugh as I think about how lacking I am in the culinary department. Until we got together with Shay, neither of us knew our way around the kitchen, and we did a lot of carryout. But cooking does interest me now. I peruse the different cooking clubs that have websites, and I see that several of them offer classes. Unfortunately, none of them are in my area.

Maybe the kitchen store downtown offers classes. Mavis Gentry inherited the Chef's Skillet when her parents passed away.

With a new pep in my step, I put my jeans back on and get ready to go downtown again, only this time I'm on a mission. I'm going to find something that I can do without my sister.

Mavis greets me the second I walk into her store. "Hey there, Sara." She narrows her eyes. "Or are you Sally?"

"Sally." I smile.

"What can I help you with?"

I glance around before settling my gaze on hers. "I want to take some cooking classes. Do you offer anything here?"

She shakes her head. "Mama and her sister used to, but unfortunately, her culinary skills didn't get passed down to me. I'm afraid I'm lost when it comes to cooking."

"Maybe you can bring someone in to do them for you."

"Do you volunteer?" A hopeful expression lets me know she's open to ideas.

"No one would want to cook the three things I know how to make if I did it, but I might know someone." Shay is an excellent cook, but I stop before I say her name or volunteer her for anything.

"That would be awesome. I've been trying to figure out a way to pick up business, and that just might be the trick. Back when Mama was still living, she said she sold more during and after her classes than she did the whole rest of the week."

On an even more exciting mission, I back

toward the door. "Let me get to work on this. I know a couple of people who might be interested."

I can think of a few people who might enjoy teaching classes, like Shay, who's a great cook, and also Mama, who claims she's the best casserole maker in all of Pinewood. And then there's Missy with her chili and some of my aunts and cousins who can make all sorts of things, from savory main dishes to irresistible desserts. I have a whole family of people who might be able to teach at Mavis's shop.

Now I head toward La Chic, praying that Shay is in. As soon as I open the door, I see her and Puddin' standing over the counter, looking at the contents of the display case.

"Hey, girl." Puddin' looks me over. "Why aren't you wearin' one of your new outfits?"

"I'm saving them for something special."

"Oh, honey, don't save your cute clothes for something special. Life's too short."

She has a point, but I need to stay on task. "Do y'all remember Mavis Gentry?"

Shay nods. "She's the one who inherited the kitchen store. Why?"

"She's looking to start some cooking classes, and I thought of you —" I don't want to leave Puddin' out. "Er . . . y'all."

Puddin's eyebrows come together. "Do

you think we need to take cooking classes?"

"No, I'm thinking y'all should teach them."

I see a flicker of interest in Shay's eyes, but Puddin' shakes her head. "I don't know, Sally. That'll take a whole lot of preparation, and I don't have much time on my hands, what with the business and the family."

"But I do," Shay says. "I think it sounds like a blast. Tell her I'm interested."

Puddin's chin juts out as she looks at Shay and then at me. "I might be able to teach something as long as it's not too involved and doesn't require a whole lot of planning."

One thing I know about Puddin' is that she can't stand to be outdone or left out of anything. I grin at both of them. "I'll let Mavis know and get back with you."

11
BRETT

Julius is coming over, and Mama says I have to be nice to him. After what he did to me back at Grandpa Jay and Granny Marge's farm, he's the last person I want to see. Somehow I've managed to avoid him until now, but there's no way that would last.

"Do I have to?" I clear my throat to get the whiny sound out of my voice. "Every single time I'm with him I get in trouble."

"It's high time y'all worked through this," Mama says. "I'm not sayin' you have to hang out with him or anything. Just learn to be civil and stand your ground if he tries to lead you astray."

"But —"

"Hey, Puddin'." The sound of Daddy's voice when he walks into the kitchen makes both Mama and me turn around. He grins at me. "So, how'd practice go?"

I shrug. Actually, practice was awesome. Our first-string quarterback got injured at the last game, so the coach is going to let me start the next game. I shrug and pretend I'm not excited. "Okay, I guess."

"That's nice, son." He looks back at Mama. "One of the drivers said his wife needs somethin' fancy to wear to their Fall Ball, and I told him you'd give her a real good deal."

Mama makes her growly sound, trying to make us think she's not happy but really is. "Don't go tellin' everyone I'll give 'em a discount, or you'll put us out of business."

"I know, Puddin', but this is different. She just got out of chemo for breast cancer, and I thought it might cheer her up to have a new dress that she doesn't have to get at the thrift store."

Mama's expression changes, and she nods. "Well, that's different. Tell her to call me, and I'll make sure I spend some extra time with her." She twists her mouth like she always does when she's thinking. "In fact, I might even surprise her with a free necklace to go with the dress."

Daddy grabs her and gives her a big ol' hug and a kiss on the lips, and that embarrasses me. Mama says I'll eventually grow out of that feeling, but I don't think so. About a year ago when I told them to quit doing that, Daddy said if it weren't for the way he's willing to show how he feels about Mama, none of us young'uns would be here. And that embarrassed me even more. Maybe it's because I'm already in high school, but I've never been kissed.

"Digger, go change out of your uniform and help Brett with the leaves." Mama tips her head in my direction. "Just because you're some big-man-on-campus football player doesn't mean you're gettin' out of doin' chores."

Daddy nods. "And just because I'm your mama's super-hunky UPS driver husband doesn't mean I don't have to help you."

Mama giggles, and Daddy winks at her. I turn away before they kiss again.

I'm sure they think they make sense, but I don't see it. Why can't they just say, *Brett, go rake the leaves*? That would be a whole lot simpler. But they always complicate everything — something I've noticed that adults do . . . Well, except Grandpa Jay and Granny Marge.

My daddy's grandparents are the coolest great-grandparents ever. They know when to be adults and when to have fun. Even when Julius and I got in trouble after we blew up the old barn — and they didn't hold back on the tongue-lashing — they were actually nice to us. After they let us

97

know the trouble we caused, they joked around with us and told us they love us in spite of what we did. I'm not so sure Julius appreciates them, though. He later said some ugly things about Grandpa Jay that I'd never repeat. It makes me mad when people make fun of old people. Don't they realize we're all getting older? Maybe not Julius. I don't think he thinks past his own little here and now.

Daddy goes to his room to change out of his brown uniform, while Mama continues to give me orders. You'd think I was in the army or something, and she's my drill sergeant.

I'm actually happy to be in the backyard with a rake. The sound of Mama's voice is starting to get on my nerves. Actually, everything's starting to get on my nerves. I don't know what's going on with me, but ever since I started my junior year, I've been on edge at home and at school.

Sometimes it seems like the world keeps getting crazier — at least it's crazy in Pinewood, Mississippi. I know it's not just me though, because even the teachers say this world isn't the same as it used to be.

I know I sound lame, but there are times when I wish things were simpler, like when Daddy was a teenager. They used to drive around with girls in their cars and go to movies and burger places and stuff. Now everyone just sits and punches buttons on their cell phones — something Mama and Daddy won't let me have yet. Mama says she'll get me one when I'm a senior, but Daddy says I shouldn't have one until I can afford to pay for it. I gripe about it, but deep down, I'm fine without a cell phone. I have a hard enough time typing on the computer keyboard. Whoever decided to jumble the letters all out of order must have been on something strong. Why couldn't they just put the letters in order so folks could find them without having to take classes?

I don't have much of a social life outside of my family and church. Some of the other guys on the football team tell me that my problem is I'm *old school.* Maybe so, but I don't see that they're doing all that well either. Besides, I like hanging out at home when I'm not playing football. A few annoyances aside, most of the time my parents are pretty cool — especially now that Mama has her shop and doesn't harp on me as much as she used to.

My sister and brothers are okay. My older brother, Trey, moves in and out, depending on what's going on in his life. Mama says one of these days she'll change the locks, but I don't think that'll ever happen. I think she just likes to talk tough.

Hallie, my sister, is sort of moody, but she's not terrible. I've figured out how to read her, so I know when to leave her alone and when I can get away with messing with her, which is fun when things get boring.

The coolest kid in the house is my baby brother, Jeremy — the one Daddy slips up and calls their *oops child,* whatever that means. I like him because he keeps Mama and Daddy busy so they're not always watching and waiting for me to make a mistake. He gives them plenty to worry about, like when he yanks the tablecloth off the table or throws his sippy cup across the kitchen when he's mad. I can't help laughing, even though Mama says all I'm doing is encouraging him to be a brat. But then she always turns around and talks all sweet and nice to him, so I think she's as guilty as I am. Maybe even more so.

Me and Jeremy have a special bond. He likes to follow me around the house and do what I do. When I play music, he likes to dance, and that makes me laugh, which only gets him excited, so he breaks out some really crazy dance moves. Hallie rolls her eyes when Jeremy is like this, and that makes us laugh. I can't wait until Jeremy is old enough to hang out. I've got a lot of stuff I want to teach him.

Daddy finally joins me in the backyard. "Good job, son. We need to hurry and get these leaves into a pile so we can go in and clean up before the company gets here."

"Why did Mama have to invite them over?"

"She did it so we can clear the air before the family gets together again." Daddy gives me a sympathetic look. "I know it's hard on account of how he got you in trouble, but you might as well get it over with." He shakes his head. "He's family, and that means you have to love him, even when you can't stand the sight of him."

"I know. It's just that —" I'm not sure how to tell Daddy that when Julius is around I feel inferior.

"Julius is a spoiled brat," Daddy says. "We all know that. He never took responsibility for what y'all did, but you're a better person, and you own up to your mistakes."

"It's not fair." I pull the rake so hard it hurts my shoulder.

"I know, and I feel sorry for Julius."

I give Daddy a curious look. "Why do you feel sorry for Julius? He's the one getting me in trouble."

"You just said it's not fair. What I'm sayin'

is you're the one with the advantage. You have a mama and daddy who know what's goin' on, and we'll see to it that justice is served. When folks make mistakes, they eventually have to pay for them. I think you're good."

The sound of car doors slamming gets our attention. We both stop raking, look at each other, and then walk over to the shed to put our rakes away without saying another word until we get to the back door.

Daddy whispers, "Why don't you go on upstairs and get cleaned up? I'll chat with Julius and his daddy until you're done."

I take advantage of the opportunity to avoid my cousin for a few more minutes, but I know better than to dillydally. After I take a quick shower and throw on a fresh pair of jeans and T-shirt, I ask Jesus to keep me out of trouble, and then I go downstairs.

Julius has a smirk on his face that I want to punch the second I see him. I turn my back and ask Jesus to forgive me for my thoughts, but I can't help thinking them. Mama glances back and forth between us before she walks up to me, puts her hands on her hips, and gives me one of her smiles with a look in her eyes letting me know she means business. "Why don't you go show Julius the project you and your daddy have been workin' on?"

The last thing I want to do is show Julius the tree house Daddy and I have been building for Jeremy. I know he'll make fun of it, and then I'll for sure want to deck him.

We're barely out the back door when Julius leans over. "Hey, we're gonna have some kind of fun at the next family party."

I frown at him. "What are you talking about?"

His eyes spark with mischief. "What we're gonna do will make the barn look like baby stuff."

I can't help letting out a groan. The look on Julius's face lets me know that all that work we did for Habitat didn't do a single bit of good with him.

12
SALLY

I can't remember ever being this excited. In the course of a day and a half, I've managed to line up three cooking classes for Mavis, and she's over-the-moon happy, which delights me to no end. "I don't know if you realize this, Sally, but if this works out, you might have just saved my business. We haven't made a profit in months."

It's a good thing I didn't know that until now, or the pressure might have been too great. The main reason I went to all that trouble was to give myself something to do — something that interests me. In fact, I might even go to Puddin's class on cooking nutritious foods for toddlers just to show support, even though I'm not having any kids any time soon.

Mama calls. "Hey, honey. I've been feeling bad about turning you down for lunch. What are you doing today?"

"I'm caught up with the bows, so now all

I have to do is wait for Sara and Justin to get home."

"Want to go get a bite to eat?"

The pitying tone of her voice sets my teeth on edge. "I'm fine."

"What's that supposed to mean? I didn't ask how you were doing. I just wanted to know if you'd like to go have some lunch with me." Now she sounds annoyed.

"Sure. Since I have to be downtown in a couple of hours, why don't we meet at the Lettuce Leaf?"

"The Lettuce Leaf? I was thinkin' . . . Oh, never mind. When do you want to meet?"

I tell her a time, and then we hang up. Now I have to figure out what to wear. Now that my closet is full of cute things, I find it's harder than ever to decide.

It's a little cooler today, so I pick the brown leggings and the long ecru sweater that makes the perfect backdrop for the coral and brown paisley scarf Shay showed me. Then I slide on my knee-high brown boots. I take a long look at myself in the mirror, and I'm amazed by how grown-up I look. For the first time, I realize how immature my wardrobe was until now — until I took a leap to my zone of discomfort, simply because I was lonely and desperate. Sara could use an update too, but I'll save that for after the baby comes. If she gets her figure back, maybe I can give her some of my things.

The second I walk into the Lettuce Leaf, I spot Mama sitting at a small table by the corner window. She glances at me, blinks, and then her eyebrows shoot up as she smiles. "You look amazing."

I grin as I sit down in the empty chair across from her. "Thank you."

"I think this is the first time in ages I've seen you in anything besides jeans and those long skirts you wear to church." She shakes her head. "You look so pulled together."

"Why, thank you." Now I'm starting to grow uncomfortable under Mama's scrutiny. "It's just a little something I picked up from La Chic."

"Oh . . . yeah, I thought you might find something. They're making quite a splash in town." Mama picks up a menu and opens it. "Any idea what kind of salad you're going to have?"

I almost always get the spinach-pecan-mandarin salad, but I'm in the mood for something different. "I'm thinking maybe the one with quinoa and black beans."

Mama closes her menu. "I have no idea what quinoa is, but I think I'll have that too."

I can't help laughing. Mama has always been game for just about anything, and she used to fuss at Sara and me for staying in a rut. Now I get it. I was in a rut, but after dipping my big toe into the foreign waters of fashion, I think I like it.

"So, why do you have to be downtown?" Mama asks.

As I tell her about the cooking classes I'm lining up, I see her expression change. "So, what do you think?"

She shrugs as she glances down at the table. "I reckon I'm disappointed."

"Disappointed?" I rack my brain trying to figure out what I said that might disappoint her. "Why?"

She lifts her gaze to mine. "Because you didn't ask me to teach a class. You've always said I was the best cook in Pinewood."

"But you're too —" I cut myself off. "Do you want to teach a cooking class?"

She frowns. "I'm not sure I have enough time with the club meetings, committee responsibilities, and church." She pauses. "And there's your father, who thinks I need to spend more time with him."

"That's why I didn't ask you. You're too busy."

Her lips turn downward as she tips her

head to the side. "At least you could have asked."

I make a mental note to go to Mama first next time Mavis wants to start a series of cooking classes. "I'm sorry."

A pensive look washes over her face. "But I might be able to find some time on Tuesdays."

"To teach?"

She nods. "Isn't that what we were talking about?" Before I have a chance to answer, she continues. "How about a class on quick and easy breakfast foods? We can keep it to a couple of nights. That way, I'm not committed for too many weeks. Do you think Mavis is game for a short, two-lesson class?"

That actually sounds good to me. The most difficult meal for me to come up with is breakfast, so I typically fall back on cold cereal, bacon and eggs, or frozen toaster waffles.

"I'll talk to Mavis and make sure she's okay with one more class. Keep in mind that she'll want you to use items she sells in her shop so people will buy what they need when the class is over."

Our salads arrive, so we change the subject to what's on our plates. "What's that grainy-looking stuff?" Mama asks.

"That's the quinoa."

108

She picks up a small amount on her fork, inspects it, smells it, and finally puts it in her mouth. I can't help laughing at her reaction.

"Well?" I'm still smiling. "What do you think?"

She scoops up another bite and holds it up. "It's not bad, but it could use more salt." Then she shoves it into her mouth.

After we finish our lunch, I reach for the check. "This is on me."

"You don't need to pay for mine, sweetie. After all, you're my daughter." She reaches for it, but I yank it away.

"That's precisely why I'm paying. After all these years, don't you think it's my turn?"

Mama frowns and then nods. "Okay, but it's my turn next time."

"You're on."

The sound of sirens rings through the air. Mama looks in the direction of where they're going. "I wonder what that's all about."

I shrug. "Could be anything."

Once we're outside on the sidewalk, Mama looks me over again and sighs. "I can't believe how grown-up and polished you look."

"That's because I *am* a grown-up." I glance at the time on my phone. "I really need to run. Thanks so much for suggesting lunch."

"Tell Sara I said hi and that I love her."

I start walking toward the Chef's Skillet, which is around the corner on the next block. As soon as I make the turn, I see the fire truck with its swirly lights still on, but no siren, parked at the curb in front of the Chef's Skillet. My pulse quickens.

13

MARYBETH

After we get home from Puddin' and Digger's house, Julius hops out of the car and darts into the house. Bucky squints and shakes his head as he stares at the front door of the house of his dreams.

"What do you reckon's gotten into that boy?" he asks.

"How should I know? Maybe it wasn't such a good idea, forcing him to hang out with Brett like that."

"It'll do 'em both good. Julius has to learn how to get along with everyone, even people who aren't up to his —" He shrugs. "You know."

I lean against the car door, fold my arms, and glare at my husband. "No, I don't know. People who aren't up to his what?"

Bucky grimaces. "C'mon, Marybeth. You know what I'm talking about."

"Seriously, Bucky, you sound like a snob."

"I am not a snob." He places one hand on

his hip and rubs the back of his neck with his other hand before he looks back at me. "It's just that some folks in my family are clueless rednecks."

I'm not letting him off on this one, so I intensify my glare. Ever since the oil company started sending us bigger checks than we deserve, I've seen a change in my once-sweet husband whose main goal was to love and protect his family. Now it seems like all he wants to do is to act all hoity-toity and acquire more stuff so he can show it off to his family. It bugs me to no end that he has taken to insulting the people who love him in spite of his snobbishness.

"Why are you lookin' at me like that?" He quickly glances away. "It's makin' me uncomfortable."

"That's exactly how you make me feel when you go braggin' all over the place about buyin' this and buyin' that. Do you realize how many times you did that while we were at Digger and Puddin's house?"

"Are you ashamed of who we are now?" He levels me with a gaze that he always gives me when he thinks he's hit a gotcha moment.

I continue glaring at him as I shake my head. "Sometimes I am."

His shoulders droop. "How can you say

that after I bought you all this?" He spreads his arms wide, gesturing around the property that includes a big ol' honkin' house, more cars than we have drivers, and a beautiful barn that we'll never use.

"I was just as happy before." The memory of our little split-level house in Hattiesburg flashes through my mind. I'd scrimped and saved to buy furniture and decorations to make that house a home, and I was proud of what I was able to do with such a small budget. The place where we live now is decorated in the style preferred by the professional interior designer referred by Bucky's tax guy, who is a little too happy with our windfall.

"You don't seem to mind when I buy you new stuff." His expression has turned into a smirk that I want to yank right off his face. "In fact, if my memory serves me correctly, you were over-the-moon with that new diamond necklace."

"It's pretty, but I would have been just as happy with something not so . . . ." I let my voice trail off as I try to think of a gentle way to say this. Our conversations have become so contentious lately that I know I need to tone it down before we wind up in a full-blown argument.

"Not so what?" He folds his arms and tips

his head to the side as he challenges me with a narrowed gaze.

"Not so showy. I mean, Bucky, when am I going to have a chance to wear that necklace?"

"How should I know where women like to wear stuff like that?" He lifts his arms out to his sides and lets them slap his sides as he blows out a breath of frustration. "Wear it to the reunion."

I can't help but laugh, and it turns into a fit that sends tears streaming down my cheeks. This conversation is going nowhere, and Bucky obviously doesn't get the fact that the only thing people think about our money is that it's annoying and making our boy into the brat he is.

"If you're gonna laugh at my generosity, I'm goin' inside." Bucky turns on the heels of his thousand-dollar boots and takes off in a huff.

As much as I hate to admit it, I'm fully aware that I've contributed to the problem by not making Julius accountable for his actions. Maybe the court-ordered family counseling sessions didn't affect Bucky, but they certainly made me do some serious thinking and reflecting on what we need to improve when it comes to raising our child. So far, I'm afraid we've made quite a mess of things.

Don't get me wrong. In spite of the fact that I was always proud of each little thing I did with our piddly bank account, I'm relieved we're not living paycheck-to-paycheck anymore because the stress was causing friction between Bucky and me. But now I think we've traded one kind of strife for another.

I'll never forget the sick feeling in my stomach when the counselor looked me in the eye and said, "I'm concerned that Julius is suffering from being overprivileged."

Bucky belted out a laugh. "Are you saying we shouldn't give him anything?"

The counselor stifled a smile as she shook her head. "No, I'm not saying that at all. What I'm saying is that he needs to be more accountable."

Bucky stood up and walked out when she said that, but there's no doubt in my mind that she was right. I apologized for his actions, and the counselor told me she understood. "It's not easy hearing this kind of thing, but I'm sure after he has some time to think about it, he'll understand."

"I certainly hope so." I shook hands with her and left the office to find Bucky sitting in the car waiting.

Since we're hosting the next Bucklin family reunion, I came up with a plan to get the boys together beforehand so they could work everything out. Bucky thought it was silly, and he still does for that matter. Julius said he didn't want to go, but he quickly changed his tune when I said I'd take the keys to his car for a week. Bucky started to argue with me, but I shot him a look that let him know I meant business.

Now that we're back from that miserable experience, I have mixed feelings about whether or not my plan has made any difference. On the one hand, both Julius and Brett acted like they'd rather be with anyone but each other. On the other hand, it gave Puddin' and me an opportunity to show a united front — something I don't think we've ever done before.

Ever since we've had money, I feel like Puddin' resents me, yet she still tries to find ways to impress me. I wish she'd quit doing that, but I sort of understand. Throughout the lavish dinner she put together — no doubt a meal that cost her more than her typical weekly grocery bill — she talked about all the changes she and Shay have made to the shop since they bought it.

I have to admit that I get a pang of jealousy when I think about their success that comes from their hard work, while

Bucky and I just fell into some money from land his granddaddy gave us. I'll never be able to take credit for a single solitary thing I own, while she has true bragging rights.

The floodlight comes on, and then Bucky walks back out onto the front porch, puts his hands on his hips like he always does, and looks at me for a few minutes. I take a step toward him.

We stare at each other for several seconds before he eventually speaks up. "Why are you still out here?"

I shrug. "I needed to be alone for a few minutes."

He snorts. "This house is plenty big enough for you to come inside and find a place to be alone."

My cell phone rings in my purse, so I pull it out and see that it's Puddin'. I gesture toward it so Bucky can see what I'm doing before I press the button to answer it.

"Hey, Puddin'. What's up?"

I hear her sucking in a breath before she blows it out. "I'm not sure how to tell you this, Marybeth, but Julius left some pot in Brett's room."

14

SALLY

It's been two days since the fire at the Chef's Skillet, but I've managed to help get Mavis back in business. As soon as I saw the fire truck at her place, I ran down there and found her standing outside, staring blankly at the mess on the other side of the display window.

Fortunately, the fire was contained to the cooking area. She didn't think to check inside the ovens, where she forgot she'd stored a bunch of dish towels that didn't sell. The entire shop had some smoke damage, but the fire department acted quickly, so she managed to salvage almost everything except the stoves.

We've replaced the stoves, scrubbed all exposed surfaces covered in the haze of smoke, and now we're finishing up the painting to get ready for the cooking classes. Her phone has been ringing off the hook from people wondering if she is open yet and asking if she still plans to hold the cooking classes.

She hangs up after the most recent call, rolls her eyes, and groans. "It's getting so annoying having to answer the phone every couple of minutes."

I straighten up from painting the baseboard. "You can look at the bright side. At least we know people will be coming to the classes. I think it's great that they're so excited."

"True." She contorts her mouth — something I've noticed that she does when she's thinking. "Our sales have picked up ever since we announced those classes."

"I'm sure the sale ads haven't hurt." She's running a special that changes daily, thanks to my suggestion to get people motivated to come in. My next recommendation will be to start selling some of the specialty items online. She never paid much attention to some of the business records, so when I pointed out that her mom had arranged to have an exclusive on one of the lines, the idea popped into my head. "And you're still making a profit, even when you mark items down." Until now, I never realized how much profit there was in cookware.

"True." She steps back from the wall she just finished painting. "Ya know, I think this is a boring color. What do you think about changing it up?"

I put down my paintbrush, stand up from my squatting position, and walk over to her. "What color are you thinking?"

"Well . . ." She taps her index finger on her chin. "Last night I was doing some Web surfing, and I saw that certain colors increase people's appetites, while others suppress them."

"Ooh, sounds interesting." I tilt my head and look at her with interest. "What did you learn?"

Her eyes widen as she shakes her head. "I never realized that blue and gray are appetite-suppressing colors."

"Not good for a kitchen store." I look at the wall. "So what color are you thinking?"

"The colors that stimulate the appetite are red, orange, yellow, green, and turquoise." She grimaces. "Too bad, though, because blue is my favorite color."

Another thing I've learned about Mavis is that she's stuck in her own little rut of a comfort zone, kind of like how I've been. "Maybe you'll learn to like one of the other colors."

"I'm not sure."

"Maybe you can paint your office blue and gray but something more appetizing out here so people will buy more stuff."

She glances around and nods. "That might work." A smile spreads across her lips. "And with a blue office, maybe I'll lose my appetite and a few pounds along with it."

I nod. "We don't have much time to change things up if that's what you want to do. I think the two of us can knock it out in a few hours if we get decent paint that only requires one coat."

Her grin widens. "Why don't we get a little crazy and do peach and green?"

"It's your store, so if you want peach and green, that's what we'll do."

"That's what I want." She picks up the can of blue paint and carries it back to the storage room. "I'll paint the office later, but now I need to go back to the paint store. Are you sure you don't mind helping?"

"Not only do I not mind, I want to help." I've actually enjoyed working in the store, since it gets me out of my condo. "While you're getting the paint, I'll go to the Lettuce Leaf and get some salads so we don't starve."

"Perfect."

As she walks out of the store, I see a new pep in her step.

On my way to the Lettuce Leaf, I realize I'm happier than I've been in a while too.

It's obvious to me that I haven't put enough time into cultivating interests outside of the bow business or working on relationships other than the one I've always had with my sister. But why should I have? Until she went and got married, she was always there, and hanging out with her was the path of least resistance, enabling me to stay in my rut.

Even though Mavis is older than me, and we actually have very little in common on the surface, it feels good to have someone else to talk to. Now I'm even more excited about the cooking classes that have sparked interest in way more people than I ever expected. What surprises me the most is how many young moms have signed up to take Puddin's cooking-for-toddlers class.

After we eat our salads, it takes us the rest of the afternoon to paint the wall. Mavis wipes her forehead with her sleeve as she takes a step back.

"Well, what do you think?" she asks.

I look around the room and turn to face her. "I like it. But the most important thing is, do you like it?"

Mavis makes a face and shakes her head. "Not really. These aren't colors I would have chosen."

She actually did choose them, but I choose

not to remind her. I've learned that she gets easily agitated and flustered, and I don't want to trigger something I don't know how to deal with.

"Let's get everything put back in place so you don't have to do anything in the morning." I smile as I gesture toward the pile in the corner. "Just tell me where it goes, and I'll put it there."

As she gives orders, I follow them — only occasionally recommending something different. "I never would have thought to do any of this," she says as we hang a few of the decorations on the back wall. "You seem to have a knack for arranging stuff."

Mama once told me I should be an interior decorator, but I didn't have the desire to go to college for four years and then have to work my way up with a design house, or work in a furniture store. Maybe I should consider it for the future.

"If you ever want a job here, let me know." Mavis gives me a somewhat reserved look before clearing her throat. "I can only afford to hire you part-time, though — at least until I see how much business picks up."

"I don't need a job, but I'll definitely be one of your best customers."

"I'll give you a discount on anything you want, and you can take classes for free."

I shake my head. "I'll take the discount, but I want to pay for the classes."

"Suit yourself." She lifts her hands and lets them fall to her sides. "I need to get my stuff and go home. Raymond expects me there every night when the news comes on." She lets out one of her rare laughs. "He's afraid I might miss something."

"Then you'd better get going." I glance at the time on my phone. "I need to go home too. Justin said he's making lasagna, and I don't want to miss that."

Mavis gives me a curious look but doesn't say anything, probably because she says her husband doesn't even know what a spatula is, let alone how to make a lasagna. She turns off the lights as we leave.

On my way home, my cell phone rings. It's Sara.

"Where are you?" she asks.

"Driving home. Why? Do you need something?"

"Yeah. Can you stop by Freddy's Tire and Lube and ask Justin when he's coming home?"

"But I thought —" I stop myself as my stomach growls. There's no telling how my moody sister will react if I mention that I've been looking forward to Justin's lasagna all afternoon. "Why don't you call him?"

"I've tried, but he's not answering."

"Okay. Want me to pick up something for dinner on the way home?"

"Why would you do that? You knew we were having lasagna."

"How can Justin cook when he's still at work?"

Sara lets out a sigh of exasperation as though I'm annoying her. "He came home for lunch and made it. All I had to do was stick it in the oven and turn it on."

"Oh." I'm relieved that my taste buds won't be disappointed. "Okay, I'll stop off and ask."

Since I've already passed Freddy's, I have to make a U-turn. I pull into the parking lot and look around for Justin's truck, but I don't see it anywhere. Maybe they have a back lot for employee parking.

I get out of the car and walk into the shop. Freddy greets me with a humongous smile. "Hey there, Sara. You sure are glowing. Pregnancy obviously agrees with you."

"I'm not Sara. She called and asked me to stop off and see when Justin's coming home."

Freddy's smile quickly fades as he shakes his head. "He took the afternoon off. Said he had something important that he needed to take care of."

15
SHEILA

I'm sensing a lot of discord between my daughters, and it's keeping me awake at night, gnawing away at my heart. What I don't get is how these two girls who have practically been joined at the hip can be so indifferent toward each other now. It's almost like they don't have a history together.

It hasn't always been this way. I'll never forget the time when Sara fell down and skinned her knee, and Sally cried just as hard as Sara did. In fact, I wondered if some of Sara's nerve endings had spilled over to her twin.

And then there was the time that Sally ran for treasurer of their class back in high school. She lost by a very small number, and Sara marched up to the school office and demanded a revote.

Now when I bring up Sara's name to Sally, she changes the subject. And when I talk to Sara, she manages to turn everything back to what she and Justin are doing. When I asked them about it, they both said the same thing — that they've agreed to talk only about their personal lives and not what the other twin is doing. I respect that, but it sure would be nice to have the scoop from their perspectives. Besides, I'm a mama who worries I'll miss something important.

And Justin is a whole 'nother subject. I used to think he was a nice boy, until he took off with Sara and eloped. Then I went through some serious anger that, at the time, I thought was hatred. Now I realize I was misdirecting my anger toward my daughter for not including her family in what's supposed to be the best day of her life.

Over the past few months, I've come to appreciate Justin and not just because he's always there to fix whatever is broken in the car or house. Granted, I never have to call a handyman anymore, and he repairs my car for the cost of the parts, but there's more to it than that. He's good to Sara, and that beats everything else in my eyes.

Now all I need to do is find a way to get Sally to appreciate her brother-in-law and for Sara to include her sister in more of her life. With a new purpose in life — or *mis-*

sion as my husband, George, likes to call it — I begin to formulate a plan in my mind and set out feeling like my old self. There's nothing I can't do when I set my mind to it. I've always liked a challenge.

I still have a couple of hours before my next church committee meeting, so I head over to the girls' town house, since I figure they'll both be there working. It's nice to see them doing something together.

When Sara answers the door, I have to catch myself to prevent the gasp that wants to escape. Her hair hangs in strings around her very pale, unmade-up face.

"Come on in." She steps aside and closes the door behind me.

"What happened?" I have to overcome an overwhelming urge to pull her into my arms, check her temperature by placing my forehead on hers, and make her something warm and soothing.

"Morning sickness." She sniffles. "I'll never do this again."

"Never do what?"

"Have another baby. It's awful."

In spite of my concern for my daughter, I laugh. "It's just awful for a little while, but once you're holding that sweet baby in your arms, you'll forget all about these mornings."

She shakes her head. "Never."

I can see that she's not in the mood for reasoning, so I figure it's time to change the subject. "Where's Sally?"

"I think she's in the workroom."

Now I'm confused. "You're not sure?"

She shakes her head. "When she came to get me, I told her to go away."

"Oh." Looks like my work is cut out for me. "Can I go on back?"

She holds out her hand toward the back of the condo. "Go right ahead."

I'm disappointed that she's not going with me, but at least it'll give me a chance to gauge how Sally feels about things. When I get to the door of the third bedroom that's been designated their workroom, I see her hunched over a table that looks like someone puked up a slew of orange ribbon.

"Hey, girl." I try my dead-level best to keep my voice light, but even I know I sound fake. So I drop the pretense. "Looks like you're working hard."

She turns and gives me a cursory glance. "Ya think?"

Oh, this is much worse than I realized. I take another couple of steps closer. "Anything I can do to help?"

"Yeah. Make Sara do her share of the

work. I can't finish all these orders by myself."

The sound of shuffling slippers comes up from behind me. "I told you I'd do it after my morning sickness wears off."

Sally jumps up from her chair so fast it topples over. As she turns around to face her twin sister, I see her frustration. "Okay, princess, let's do all this around your schedule . . . when you *feel* like working." She gives Sara a sarcastic face and then closes her eyes and takes a deep breath. A look of contrition comes over her. "Sorry. I should be more sensitive." She winces. "But the work still needs to get done."

Sara sniffles and wipes her eyes with the back of her arm. "I'm trying to be a good wife and a good sister and a good mama and a good . . ." She waves her hand toward the mess of ribbon all over the table. "A good bow maker."

"Look, girls, there are two sides to this. I'm sure that if you . . . if *we* sit down and discuss this like adults, we can come up with some sort of solution."

The room grows quiet for a couple of seconds before both girls pipe up. "Mama, please stay out of this."

I blink. And then I look back and forth between my daughters. Now they're both glaring at me. "But I —" Sally shakes her head, quieting me. "We know you mean well, but you don't need to get involved. This is between Sara and me."

"Yeah." The color has returned to Sara's cheeks. "It only gets worse when other people jump in. Even Justin knows better than to come between us."

They're clearly on the same side now. Looks like my job is done here, even though I'm not quite sure how it happened. The girls are once again showing a united front, and even though I'm what they're united against, in some strange way, I like the fact that they're standing together.

"Um . . ." I glance at my watch and see that I still have a lot more time to kill before my meeting. But I don't want to stick around here, or I might risk reversing the girls' progress, so I back toward the door. "I need to run now. Let me know if y'all need anything."

"Bye." Sara doesn't even look at me as she picks up the chair that Sally toppled and then pulls up another one beside it before sitting down with her back to me.

Sally gives me a cursory half smile but doesn't say a word before joining her sister. They both reach for spools of ribbon and start working.

"I can let myself out." Then, without another word, I leave their condo. As soon as I get to my car, I blow out a sigh of relief. They've argued all their lives, but they also forgive very quickly — sometimes so quickly that I'm not even sure how it happens. There's no denying that my girls are annoyed with me now, but at least they seem okay with each other.

16

SALLY

I think it's sweet that Justin has been saving for an engagement ring for Sara, but she says it's a waste of money. When he brought it home that night I stopped by his shop, she told him to get his money back. I have to keep my mouth shut so I won't say anything that might upset her.

Sara swallows the last bite of her roast beef, stands up, and carries her plate to the sink before turning around to face me. "Where are you going?"

"The first cooking class at the Chef's Skillet."

"I don't know why you want to do that when all you have to do is call Shay. She'll come over and teach you how to cook whatever you want, whenever you want."

"True." I'm not in the mood for sparring with my sister, so I avoid telling her that I need something to call my own now that she has her husband and a baby on the way.

"But it's a fun way to meet new people."

She chews on her bottom lip for a second. "Yeah, you're probably right. Maybe I'll join you."

My heart sinks. It's not that I don't want my sister to go. Well, I guess it is. This is my thing — something I started and want to do without her. But I can't say that, because even to me, it sounds mean.

"Why do you have that look on your face?" She lifts an eyebrow as she stares at me. "Is it okay if I go with you?"

"Of course. Why wouldn't it be?" I can't look her in the eye, so I take my plate to the sink, rinse it, and put it in the dishwasher.

"I don't know why it wouldn't be, but I can tell you don't want me to go with you."

I let out a nervous laugh. "Think we might be a tad too sensitive?"

"C'mon, Sally, I've known you all my life. We've been roommates and womb-mates. I know you as well as I know my own self, and I can tell you don't want me to go."

My shoulders drop as I let out a breath and look directly at my sister. "Okay, so here's the deal. You have Justin and now the baby. I have nothing, so I've gone out and found something that might be fun."

"I get that." Sara contorts her face. "But why do you feel like my being there will take anything away from you? If you love it, that shouldn't change whether I'm there or not."

Of course, I know she's right, but it still seems unfair. I let out another sigh. "Then come along if you really want to go."

"I'm not saying I want to make it a regular thing, but I have to admit it does sound like fun." She leans against the counter, folds her arms, and gives me one of those looks that melt my heart. "May I go with you just this one time if I promise not to keep going?"

I close the gap between us and pull her in for a hug. I think about her baby, so I lean away and touch her abdomen. "My niece or nephew." Tears well in my eyes, and my throat tightens. "I can't believe it."

"I know, right?" She puts her hand above mine and shakes her head.

Now I see a tear falling down her cheek, which totally undoes my composure, and I start sobbing. She chuckles through her tears, which makes me laugh.

She takes me by the hand and pulls me toward the door. "Let's go dry these ugly tears and go learn how to cook some toddler food."

Since Justin has her car at the shop, I drive to the Chef's Skillet. We talk about Mama coming over earlier to check on us, and we agree that tomorrow we need to call and let her know we appreciate her, although she needs to stay out of our squabbles.

"She doesn't understand us," Sara says.

"I know. Oh, did I tell you that I had lunch with her this week?"

"No." Sara pauses. "What did y'all talk about?"

I shrug. "Mostly family stuff."

"Did she tell you that Coralee has a boyfriend?"

"You've got to be kidding. No way."

Sara nods vigorously. "She definitely does. I saw her post on Instagram, so it has to be true."

"Are you sure it was Coralee?" This is so hard for me to believe. I have to admit that like everyone else in the family, I've always assumed Coralee would remain single for the rest of her life.

"Positive. He's a cute guy too."

I sigh. My first thought is that if Coralee has a cute boyfriend, maybe there's hope for me. Then I feel bad. Coralee has always been a very sweet girl, but she's always been rather awkward and gangly — not exactly what most cute guys are looking for. "I hope things work out for her."

We have to drive around for a while to find a parking place. "I wonder what's bringing all this traffic to town at this time of night," I say.

"Probably a sale somewhere." Sara shifts in her seat. "Maybe Shay and Puddin' got some new stuff at La Chic."

"Maybe, but since Puddin's teaching the cooking class, I don't think that's why there are so many cars." I parallel-park in a spot about a block and a half away from the Chef's Skillet.

As soon as we walk inside the cooking store, Sara's eyes bug out. "Whoa. I had no idea so many people would want to learn how to cook."

I look around and see people I know and some I've never seen before, which is mind-boggling because I've lived in Pinewood all my life. Mavis waves us over to where she's standing.

"Look at this, will ya?" She grins as she shakes her head. "I'm not sure what we're gonna do with all these folks. We don't have enough stoves for everyone."

"Didn't you have people call to reserve a spot in the class?"

She shrugs. "I did at first, but it got to be such a hassle I just told everyone who called when to be here."

Mavis obviously has a lot to learn about organization. In the meantime, she has a problem that needs to be solved.

I look around. "Where's Puddin'?"

"Over there in the middle of that crowd." Mavis points to a cluster of a half dozen women in the corner.

Puddin' is short, so I have to get a little closer to see her. All the women standing around her are talking at the same time, so I figure I need to go over and save her.

A look of relief washes over her when I approach the crowd and ask if there's anything I can do to help. She quickly scoots through the crowd and closes the distance between us. "Hey, Sally. There are way too many people here, and we don't have enough cooking stations. What should I do?"

I smile down at her. "You don't have to do anything. I'll take care of it." I look around and see that there are enough people for at least two classes, maybe three. "How do you feel about adding another class?"

"When?"

"Tonight."

She sucks in a breath and puffs her cheeks as she blows it out. "I'll have to ask Digger if he can watch Jeremy an extra hour and a half."

"If he can't —" I stop and think for a few

seconds. "Maybe I can."

Puddin' gives me an odd look before bursting into laughter. "You're kidding, right? What do you know about young'uns?"

"Not much," I admit. "But I'm sure it can't be too hard with just one."

She tries hard not to laugh, but I can see the amusement bubbling beneath the surface. She places her hand on my shoulder. "You're sweet, Sally, but let me call Digger. Can you talk to these people?"

Before I have a chance to respond, she pulls her phone out of her pocket and heads toward the back of the store. I stand in one place as the women close in around me.

I feel completely overwhelmed and frustrated as I try to think of something to say that might calm these women down. As I look out over the group, I finally spot Sara, who winks, smiles, and gives me that special hand signal we used to use to show we had each other's backs. A sense of well-being and a feeling that everything will turn out all right washes over me. Now I'm glad Sara is here.

17

CORALEE

I'm really digging all the attention I'm getting from Kyle. Although there's no doubt in my mind that it's all about the way I look, I'm so long overdue for it that I'll take it, regardless of the reason.

After I got used to the new clothes, I asked Shay for some makeup tips. She showed me how to apply mascara and the benefits of lining my lips before putting on lipstick. I have no idea why I didn't do this sooner. It truly does make me feel better about myself, so I don't feel as uncomfortable when I talk to people.

As I walk across campus to the Danforth Chapel, where we meet before class, I enjoy the slight breeze that lifts my newly styled hair off my shoulders. Maxie, the owner of Maxie's Hair Salon, has taken my transformation to a whole new level. As soon as I walked into her shop yesterday and asked for a new hairstyle, her eyes lit up. "A complete hair makeover? Honey, after I'm done with you, you won't even recognize yourself in the mirror."

And she's right. In fact, I feel as though I'm floating inches off the ground. I spot Kyle before he sees me, and I can tell he doesn't even recognize me as he keeps looking around.

"Kyle, it's me." I'm about ten feet away from him when he finally makes eye contact.

His chin drops. "What did you do to your hair?"

I swing it around so it skims my shoulders as I get closer to Kyle. Maxie put a few highlights in, so I'm hoping the sunlight catches it and makes it sparkle. "I got a new do. Like it?"

He shakes his head. "I don't know why you'd get all that beautiful hair cut off."

"Beautiful hair?" Now I'm confused. "I wanted something more stylish that fits the new me."

"But I liked the old you." The look on his face totally throws me off.

I shift my books to one arm while I plant the other fist on my hip. "The old me was frumpy and dowdy. I figured new hair would make me look even better."

"Oh, I noticed you, all right. I've already told you that. It's just that you never seemed interested."

"I was interested. And it had nothing to do with what I was wearing?"

He scrunches up his face and tilts his head. "I have no idea what you were wearing. Why would that matter?"

I let out what Mama and some of my aunts call the *millennial grunt*. "You're kidding, right?"

His eyebrows come together in a look of concern. "No. I'm not kidding. I don't really care what you wear."

"So, are you saying you didn't mind the fact that I used to wear ratty jeans and sweatshirts that were too big for me?"

He shakes his head. "It didn't . . . doesn't matter to me."

"Do you not like this?" I lift my arms out to my sides and spin around as he watches me.

"Oh, I like this, all right." He lets out a soft chuckle. "*This* looks mighty good."

"So, which do you like better? The old me or the new me?"

"Neither . . . both." He lifts his hands and lets them fall. "You keep going on and on about the way you look. Why are you doing this, Coralee?"

I blow out a breath of frustration. "Don't ever tell me women are complicated."

142

"I never said they were."

"Good." Now that I'm completely confused by his thoughts about how I've changed, I decide this is a topic for a later time. "Let's get to class. I want to make sure we get good seats."

We're in the building and almost to the classroom door when Kyle tugs at my arm. "Wait a minute, Coralee."

I spin around to face him. "What's wrong?"

He clears his throat and licks his lips as he looks around and then meets my gaze. "I don't want you dating anyone else."

A nervous giggle escapes. "What do you mean?"

"I want to be the only — your only . . ." He shifts his weight from one foot to the other. "Can we be exclusive?" He grimaces. "I didn't want to do it this way, but I don't want to take a chance of losing you."

We're almost late for class, so I give him as warm a smile as I can manage. "Can we talk about this after class?"

"I just don't —" He looks at something behind me and then focuses on me. "Okay."

When I turn around to take the last few steps to the classroom door, I see Charlie Zohl, someone I helped tutor last semester, coming toward us.

"Hey there, Coralee. I was wondering if you're not busy, maybe you'd like to do something later."

Before I have a chance to say a word, Kyle steps between Charlie and me. "You've got some nerve, buddy. She's with me."

My heart hammers as I watch these two guys stare each other down. The professor walks over to the door and clears his throat. "Find a seat, folks. I can't wait all afternoon for you to figure out who gets the girl."

Now I'm ready to crawl under one of the desks as I lower my gaze and scurry into the room to the nearest spot. I hear Kyle right behind me, but I don't look up to see if he's found a seat nearby.

It feels strange to have two guys squaring off over me. As the professor continues talking, I try my best to concentrate, but it's impossible. So I finally give up and let my mind wander.

By the end of class, I've calmed down enough to talk to Kyle. He says he wants us to see each other exclusively, and I'm fine with that, but only because I think it would be confusing to date more than one person at a time.

The professor opens the door, signaling he has nothing else to say. So I stand up and smile over at Kyle, who is watching me with puppy-dog eyes. "Well?" he asks. "Have you decided yet?"

145

18
SALLY

Last night started out insane, but thanks to Puddin's husband, who says it's just as much his responsibility to be a daddy as it is hers to be a mama, we broke the group into two classes. And to make up for the inconvenience of having to leave and come back, Mavis gave everyone a huge discount on anything they bought at the store. Granted, she's still making a profit, but everyone feels good about things now, and that's pretty much what this whole plan is all about.

I wasn't a hundred percent sure how good a teacher Puddin' would be, but she's great. Her humor had everyone in stitches, and all the food turned out pretty fabulous. Her mantra of *one for the young'uns, one for me* stuck in our heads as we ate at least as much as we put on the serving dishes that everyone got to take home to their families.

Puddin' is actually a lot more organized

than I ever realized. She came prepared with four different recipes, and while she taught the first class, she had Shay pick up some groceries for the second class. Our cousin Missy is teaching a chili-making class, and since it's getting cold out, we expect quite a group. Mavis is still apologizing about not having a cutoff, and she says the phone has been ringing off the hook, so we're expecting another big turnout.

Today, after I finish making all the bows in the queue, I'm supposed to go back to the Chef's Skillet to help Mavis figure out how to avoid what happened last night. It shouldn't be too hard if she has a class limit and starts sign-ups for a future date once it fills up.

"Last night was fun."

I glance up at the sound of my sister's voice and see her standing in the doorway of our workroom.

"Puddin's funny."

"I know. I guess I never realized that because she and Digger are so much . . ." My voice trails off because I don't want to say what I'm thinking.

She gives me a crooked smile. "Older than us?"

I nod and decide to change the subject. "We have a ton of bows to make today. Are

147

you feeling up to it?"

She clears her throat, walks over to the table, and sits down beside me. "Yeah, I'm doing a lot better this morning. Justin left some crackers on the nightstand before he went to work, so I ate them before I sat all the way up."

"That was sweet of him." I turn my laptop around to face her. "Look at this — more than a dozen orders since midnight. It makes you wonder about folks, doesn't it? I mean, don't you think it's weird that mamas are online shopping when they should be sleeping?"

She shrugs. "Now that I'm pregnant, all I can think about most of the time is this baby. So yeah, it kind of makes sense."

"Huh?" I'm sure she has a connection in there somewhere, but I don't get it.

"People are thinking about their kids late at night and into the wee hours of the morning."

"Oh." I still don't get why they're ordering bows, but I'm not going to argue. First of all, it's profit that keeps us from having to go back to being bank tellers, and second, arguing with my sister while she's pregnant isn't worth the tears later.

We fall into the same comfortable routine we've had until she got married and work for almost an hour before I stand up and stretch. "Want some eggs and toast?"

A grin lights up her face. "That sounds great. I'm starving."

"Come to the kitchen and keep me company. I'll make you some tea so you can relax while I cook the eggs."

A familiar feeling of warmth and contentment washes over me as we spend the next fifteen minutes talking and laughing while I cook and then sit down at the table. With our food on the table, I take her hand in mine for the blessing.

"I'd like to say the prayer," she says.

I lift my head and blink. "You would?"

"Yes. It's been a while, so let me, okay?"

As I lower my head again, I listen to my sister's sweet prayer thanking God for all the blessings of a loving family, a beautiful home, a career she appreciates, and the food we have in front of us. She finishes with "Lord, most of all, thank You for loving us enough to sacrifice Your Son so we can spend eternity with You. Amen."

My heart swells with pride as I open my eyes and see my sister with tears streaming down her face. I squeeze her hand.

She pulls away and wipes her face with her sleeve as she lets out a nervous giggle. "Sorry. These crazy hormones are making

149

me cry at the strangest of times."

I decide not to respond to that, and I change the subject. "So, when will you find out whether you're having a boy or girl?"

"Officially? A few more months." She scoops some eggs onto her fork, shoves them into her mouth, chews, and swallows. "But Justin's aunt did the ring test over my belly, and she says we're havin' a girl."

"The ring test?" I pause as I try to figure out what on earth she's talking about. "What's that?"

She laughs. "She put my wedding ring on a string and then had me lie down on the floor, face up. Then she held the string and let the ring dangle above my belly."

"That's strange. How can putting your ring on a string tell you what you're having?"

"Who knows? She just said that if it goes up and down, it's a boy, and side to side means it's a girl."

"And it went side to side?" I pick up my toast and slather some jelly on it as I try not to laugh. But a giggle escapes.

She makes a funny face. "It went around in circles at first. I thought Justin's aunt would freak out, but it finally stopped before it started moving side to side."

"Seriously?"

"I know, right? I think Justin believes it, but I'm pretty sure I saw her moving her hand."

Now I can't hold back the laughter, since Sara is already chuckling. "At least she has a fifty-fifty chance of being right."

"Well . . ." Sara's laughter subsides. "Justin says she has about a ninety percent success rate, and the only reason it's not better is that a few of the pregnant women wouldn't hold still."

"How many times has she done this?"

"According to Justin, women from all over Lafayette come to her as soon as they find out they're pregnant."

I shake my head as I stand and carry our empty plates to the sink. "I s'pose it's good entertainment."

Before I have a chance to open the dishwasher, Sara walks up behind me, places her hands on my shoulders, and gently pulls me away. "I'll load the dishwasher."

"Are you sure?"

"C'mon, Sally. I'm pregnant, not an invalid."

I clamp my mouth shut to prevent saying something to break her kindness streak. For the past several weeks, I've felt like I've been walking on eggshells around her.

As soon as we get back to the workroom,

her phone rings. I have just pulled out the length of ribbon I'll need for the bow I'm about to make when I hear her gasp.

I glance over at her and see tears streaming down her cheeks, a look of horror on her face. She covers the mouthpiece. "He had an accident."

"Who?"

Her chin quivers as she wipes her nose with the back of her hand. "Justin. He's in the emergency room."

19
BRETT

"Don't you dare go gettin' ideas about wandering off with Julius. I don't care if the reunion *is* at his house. That boy is nothin' but trouble."

"I won't go anywhere with him."

"Dern tootin' you won't. I regret having them over."

"I don't have to go to the reunion."

Mama gives me a look that makes me think she'd actually consider letting me stay home, but then she shakes her head. "That won't do. Not showing up might make folks think you're guilty of something."

I lower my eyes as Mama continues her daily rant. Ever since what happened at Grandpa Jay and Granny Marge's farm, she's watched me with those squinty eyes and that mouth that's all drawn up like she's drinkin' through a straw. And after they came to our house, it only got worse. I don't know why they're blaming me. I didn't invite them.

"Do you hear me, young man?"

"It's not for another two whole weeks." I don't want to push her too much, or she'll never let up, but I need to figure out a way to get some peace. "Besides, I learned my lesson, and I don't plan to wander off anywhere with Julius." It's difficult with her glaring at me like this, but I look directly at her. "If you want me to, I'll just follow you around and never leave your side the whole time we're there."

Her expression changes again, and I can tell I've hit a nerve. One thing Mama hates is for anyone over the age of five to hang onto her, so I decide to drive the point even closer to home. "In fact, I'll even hold your hand so you won't have to worry about me."

She shudders. "Nah, that's okay. As long as I know where you are at all times, I'm good."

Now all I have to do is think of a way to stay away from Julius. "Can I go now?"

Mama's jaw tightens, so I know there's more, but since she doesn't say anything right away, I start backing toward the kitchen door. I'm hoping she'll just let me go without any fuss.

She slams her hand on the countertop, making me jump. Something is seriously

154

going on with her, and I have a feeling I'm about to find out what it is. "Hold your horses there, cowboy."

The look in her eyes scares me. "Did you need something?" My voice comes out in a squeak, so I cough and look down before glancing back up at her. "I really need to go do my homework."

"What you really need to do is tell me what you and Julius were doing in your room."

I shrug. "Just hangin' out."

"I've waited a couple of days, hoping you'd come clean." Mama takes a step toward me with her nostrils flaring. "And since you haven't, I'm starting to think you're as guilty as he is."

Now I'm confused. I'm not lying when I say we were just hanging out, but Mama is clearly in no mood to hear that again. "What did I do?"

She gets even closer, reminding me that even though I'm a few inches taller than her, she's not the least bit intimidated. "Do you have any idea what I found in your room after Julius left?"

"Found in my room?" I start to step back but change my mind. Mama will just get even closer if I do. "Were you snoopin'?"

"Dern tootin' I was snooping. As long as

you live in this house without paying rent, I'll snoop whenever and wherever I please."

This is a house rule, and it's one I know I can't change, so I continue standing there trying to figure out what Mama might have found besides some dirty socks I kicked under my bed or the homework I forgot to put in my backpack.

"Answer me, Brett."

Whoa. She's serious. I just wish I knew what she's serious about.

My insides start to shake and I look her in the eye. "No, Mama, I don't know."

Without a word, she walks across the kitchen, opens her purse, and pulls out her phone. Then she comes back to me and shoves it in my face.

I blink as I see a picture of a plastic bag of something that I've never seen before in my life. "What's that?"

Mama tilts her head and squints as she looks back at me. "You don't know?"

"I have no idea. Looks like a bag of something from the yard and some white sticks."

She turns the phone back around, looks at the picture, and clicks the Off button. "Ya know something crazy? I actually believe you."

A sense of relief washes over me, but I'm

still confused. "What's in that picture?"

"It's something Julius left in your room. After they left, while you were still in the living room talking to your daddy, I spotted it on your dresser when I walked by."

"But what is it?" I sure would like to know what's got her so worked up over that bag of whatever it is.

"It's pot."

"Pot?" I rub the back of my neck.

She nods. "Yes, pot. As in marijuana, an illegal substance that can get you in all kinds of trouble with the law."

I know pot's marijuana, but I'm stunned about it being in my room. Even though I've always seen Julius as someone who does what Mama and Daddy call *pushing the envelope,* this is way crazy, even for him.

"You really had no idea, did you?"

I shake my head, still trying to take it in. I might be fifteen, but Daddy has scared the daylights out of me about hanging out with the wrong crowd and saying that if I was even in the room with someone doing drugs, I'd go to jail. And to think Julius would put it in my room.

"I'm just glad I found it when I did."

That makes me ponder what I would have done if I'd seen it. Since I had no idea what it was, I probably would have brought it to

157

Mama or Daddy and asked.

"Maybe we shouldn't go to this family reunion," Mama says, pulling me from my thoughts. "Julius was clearly trying to get you in trouble, or he wouldn't have left that stuff on your dresser."

I know how much Mama wants to go. I mean, she moans and groans about everyone she'll see, but Daddy and I have figured out she lives for those get-togethers. "We can go. I'll just stay with the grown-ups."

Mama reaches out, places her hand under my chin, and squeezes. Before she goes for the cheeks, I back away.

"You're a sweet boy, but I've already talked to Marybeth about it." Mama makes a strange face. "When I first told her, she was apologetic and said she'd speak to Bucky about what to do. I thought she'd turned over a new leaf. But when she called me back, she was the old Marybeth and said you were probably the one who forgot to put away your stash." Mama shakes her head. "If Marybeth can't see what her son is becoming, there's nowhere for him to go but down."

20

SALLY

Justin has been in the hospital for a day and a half since the car he was working on rolled off the jack and pinned him. He broke a few ribs, but what the doctors are concerned about is brain damage. Sara has been standing vigil in his hospital room ever since it happened.

Mama has never made it any secret that she's upset about their elopement, so when she arrives with flowers for Justin and dinner for Sara, it touches my heart. I'm glad she's finally coming around and understanding that Justin is actually perfect for my sister, even though I don't always admit it.

The three of us sit there staring at the machine that makes all these whirring sounds and an occasional beep, until I feel like jumping out of my own skin. I stand up, place my hands on each of their shoulders, and give them a squeeze.

I'm still holding on to Mama and give my sister an extra-long look. "Since Mama's here, I think I'll go on home and take a nap."

Sara nods and sniffles. "I can't believe this is happening."

I start to say that Justin will be just fine, but I don't know that. So I let go of Mama and put my arms around Sara for a hug as I whisper, "I love you, and I'm here for you no matter what."

When I pull away and look her in the eye, I see tears welling in front of redness. "I don't know what I'll do without him."

That's something I can't respond to, so I don't even try. I give her a sympathetic smile.

Mama walks me to the door. "When can you come back?" she whispers.

"I haven't slept more than a couple of hours since this happened. Why?"

She glances at the clock on the wall. "I have a committee meeting, but I reckon I can let them know my daughter needs me more."

"Yes, I agree. That's probably what you should do." I start to leave but stop and turn back around. "See if you can get Sara to go to sleep. That chair in the corner reclines."

"I'll see what I can do."

All the way home, I pray for Justin, my

sister, and their unborn baby. *Lord, it would be so sad for my sister to lose her husband and just as sad for this child to never know its daddy.* As I continue praying, I think about all the things Sara will have to face, and I make a promise to God that I'll fill any void that might be left.

I've barely walked into the condo when my phone rings. It's Sara, so I answer it. Her voice is muffled with sobs, so I fear the worst.

"I'll be right back," I tell her.

There's another muffled sound — more like shuffling than voices. Mama comes on the phone. "You don't have to come back just yet. Justin's awake, and he's able to talk."

"He's awake?"

"Yes." Mom's voice sounds much lighter than it did earlier, so I let out a sigh of relief. She lowers her voice, and I can tell she's cupping the phone with her hand. "It was really rather strange. Everything got real quiet, and then the monitor suddenly perked up. When I looked at his face, I saw that he'd opened his eyes, so I woke Sara up."

I close my eyes and mouth, *Thank You, Lord.* "Is he able to talk . . . to hold a conversation?"

"Yes, that's one of the things that's so

strange. He's talking to her almost like nothing happened."

"What's the doctor saying?"

"He hasn't been in to see him yet, but the nurses are telling us this is a miracle. They didn't think he'd make it." She lowers her voice even more. "They're still not sure, but the fact that he's awake and talking with Sara gives me some hope."

"We'll have to keep praying." I sigh. "I'm sure he'll have a long road of recovery ahead of him."

"He will. I told Sara that between you and me and anyone else in the family who wants to help, she'll have all the support she needs." She pauses and lets out a soft chuckle. "Maybe more than she wants. You know how our family can be when someone needs help."

"I do."

"And I trust you'll be right there by Sara's side through everything."

"Yes, of course." Exhaustion overwhelms me. "I need to go take a nap. Let Sara know that I'll be back at the hospital in a few hours."

"I'll tell her."

"Mama?"

"Yes, sweetie?"

"I love you."

162

"Well, you know how much I adore you and your sister."

I do know that. Sometimes I think she stays busy with her committees because she's still not sure what to do with twins — even after all these years — and the committee people provide stability and something more predictable in her life. I imagine it's difficult for anyone but another set of twins to understand our relationship.

After we hang up, I set the alarm on my phone, take off my shoes, and plop down on the sofa. I must have fallen asleep immediately, because that's the last I remember before the beeping sound wakes me up. I start to push the Snooze button, but I remember Sara being at the hospital with Justin.

I get a drink of water before calling her. She answers right away.

"How's Justin?"

"He's sleeping now, but we had a nice little conversation when he woke up. Then the doctor came in and told him he needed some rest, so I've been sitting here watching him sleep."

I'm not sure it's a good idea to ask this yet, but I decide I might as well. "What does the doctor say? Will he be okay?"

"He says we'll know more in a couple of

days. He's guarded but hopeful."

"Do you want me to bring you anything?"

"Can you stop off at Sonic on the way here? I'm craving one of their cheeseburgers and a limeade."

I laugh. "Yes, of course. Do you want fries?"

"What do you think?"

The teasing tone in her voice gives me some relief after watching her grieve over fear for her husband's life just a few hours ago.

It takes me a half hour to go to Sonic and get to the hospital. All the way from the parking lot to Justin's room I pray for him, my sister, his doctors, and all the nurses who are taking care of him. I arrive in time to see Sara tenderly stroking his arm.

She glances up and smiles at me, but I catch a tiny tear trickling down her cheek. "I'm starving."

I hold out the bag and walk over to look at Justin. To my surprise, his eyes are open, and he's watching me.

"Well, hello there, brother-in-law. You gave us quite a scare." I have to work hard at keeping my tone light.

The hint of a smile plays on his lips, and then he grimaces. My heart aches for both him and Sara, but I try hard not to show my feelings.

"We need you to get better soon so you can come back to the condo and take care of us." I make a sad face. "As much as I hate to admit it, I miss your cooking."

I see Sara's movement out of the corner of my eye, so I turn toward her. She's holding up a finger like she wants to tell me something.

"Why don't you try to get some rest now so you can go home soon?" I watch Justin close his eyes before I walk over to the tiny table by the recliner where my sister is eating.

"Pull up a seat." She points to a chair in the corner, so I do as I'm told. "They've done some scans of his brain, and they don't think there's any permanent damage. They'll know after the swelling goes down."

"That's a relief."

"I know." Sara takes another small bite of her cheeseburger, chews it, and swallows before leaning back. "Justin and I were talking before this happened, and he said he actually likes living in the condo."

"What are you saying?"

She shrugs. "I don't know if this is the best time to tell you."

"Now that you've brought it up, you don't have a choice." I tilt my head forward and give her one of those looks that mean business.

She rolls her eyes. "Okay, so we were thinking we might stay longer than we originally planned, and now I think we'll have to. I don't want to add any stress when he comes home."

That sounds good, but there is a new little person coming soon, and we don't have room. "How about the baby?"

Sara closes her eyes and moves her lips like she's praying, and then she looks directly at me. "That's the problem we're trying to solve. This place is plenty big enough for the three of us, but once the baby comes . . ."

As we get deeper into this conversation, I realize she's thinking something she's not saying. "Okay, spill it, Sara. What's on your mind?"

"I don't know if this is the best time to tell you . . ." Her voice trails off as she looks toward her husband.

"What? Just say it."

She takes a deep breath, flinches, and blurts, "We were thinking you could move out and let us stay in the condo."

21
MARYBETH

Ever since Puddin' told me about the pot in Brett's room, I've been haunted by awful thoughts about Julius. He's always been somewhat of a rebel. Bucky thinks it's a good thing, and most of the time I do too. But there are times when we need to rein him in.

"Aw, don't break the boy's spirit." Bucky chuckles. "He's just tryin' things. That's normal."

"It's illegal, Bucky. I don't want my son winding up in jail, and at the rate he's going, I'm not so sure —"

He tilts his head forward and gives me one of his hooded looks. "You think a little bag of pot at his age will land him in jail?"

"It might." I lift my chin.

Bucky laughs. "Don't give me that, Marybeth. Even you're not that stupid."

I bristle. "So you think I'm stupid?"

"Nah, you're not stupid. In fact, you mar-

167

ried me, so I reckon you're pretty smart." He gives me what he seems to think is an attractive look, but it makes me cringe. "Wanna do something tomorrow night, just the two of us?"

"Don't change the subject."

He rolls his eyes and lets out a long-suffering sigh. "Okay, so what if Puddin' is right and the pot belongs to Julius? We don't need other people stickin' their noses all up in our business."

"But it is their business. Why would he leave the bag of it in Brett's room?" I would have taken Julius straight over there and had him apologize, but Bucky said no — that would just be an admission of guilt.

"Look, Marybeth. You and I both know it's normal for boys his age to try stuff like that."

"It might be normal, but it's still not right. We never did anything like that."

Bucky gives me a slight head bob. "That's what kids do these days."

"I simply don't buy that, Bucky. Like I said, it's illegal." My heart hurts at the very thought of my son using illegal substances. "Just because —"

He holds up a finger to shush me. "You heard me, Marybeth. I can deal with him. We don't need to get the rest of my family involved."

"In case you haven't figured it out yet, Julius has already gotten the rest of your family involved by leaving the stuff on Brett's dresser."

"How do we know it was Julius?" Bucky tilts his head in the other direction as though he's trying to see things from a different angle. "Maybe it's Brett's weed, and he's lyin' to his folks."

I disagree with Bucky, but he's so prideful when it comes to his family that I know he'll argue until the cows come home, and I'll never get my way. But I have to make at least one more effort, and I use a little psychology to try to sway him.

"Between the two of them, Julius has always been the leader, so maybe —" I shrug when I see Bucky's expression changing and closing me out. He'll never listen to me.

It really bugs me that Bucky still thinks he did something to get all this stuff. He went from being the very sweet, unassuming man I fell in love with almost twenty years ago to having a head as big as our mansion and snobbery pouring out of his mouth with almost every single word. When something goes wrong, it's always someone else's fault. Those thoughts keep rattling around in my head, and I'm struggling to find a way to get back the man I fell in love with and not some spoiled-rotten rich guy who always has to have his way.

I know people see me in the same way, but all I'm trying to do is present a united front. It's hard, though, when I know people in his family probably blame me. At least that's how it would be with my family, who refuses to let me bring Bucky around anymore. Mama says he's gotten too big for his britches. Daddy says he needs a session behind the woodshed to beat some sense into his brain from the other end. Daddy has warned me that if we don't get a grip on Julius's behavior now, we'll be spending all our oil money bailing him out of jail.

As much as I love my son, I'm afraid he's turning out to be one of those rich kids who don't seem to have a conscience. No matter how much we give him, he wants more. Bucky actually went out and bought him a brand-new car that he wrecked the second week he had it. And then Bucky went out and bought him another one with the insurance money.

When I kicked up a fuss about it, Bucky gave me a look of disbelief. "I thought you were getting sick and tired of totin' him around."

"I am . . . I was, but you keep rewarding him for bad behavior."

I look back on that conversation and realize I need to be more forceful, or we'll lose our son. As it is, I can't even talk to him without worrying he'll try to pull something over on me.

Bucky keeps saying how bright Julius is. "He's a whole lot smarter than me and you." He chuckles as though our son has never done anything wrong.

He might be right about Julius being bright, but I prefer for our son to use his smarts for something that will make the world a better place, not to pull fast ones on his parents and everyone else around him. I would say that to Bucky, but he'll keep having comebacks until I'm left with nothing to say, or I run out of energy.

With Bucky's family reunion coming up soon, I need to get my thoughts ironed out. It's not like I have a choice about going, since it will be here at our house. I sure do wish I hadn't let my mother-in-law talk me into hosting it. One of the issues is that our house is not only grand and lavishly decorated, it's big enough to hold the entire Bucklin family and all their plus-ones.

I actually like a lot of his kinfolk, and I think they used to like me. But that doesn't seem to be the case anymore. I've picked up a few hints that they all think I'm the snobby one, and it rubbed off on Bucky. The truth of the matter is that he feels like he has something to prove to his family. He used to be the jokester among the cousins, so no one ever took him seriously. As much as he hates to admit it, that bugged him to no end. Now he thinks they look up to him, but even I can tell that's not the case. They look at him and shake their heads when he turns his back — something I suspect they do to me too.

At this point, it's probably too late to change Bucky's and my image, but I feel like I need to do something for Julius. I'd hate for him to grow up being the "bad cousin" — the one no one else wants to hang out with, or worse, the one they don't claim to be related to.

For the first time in our marriage, I decide to go behind Bucky's back and appeal to the two people who seem to have their heads screwed on straight and might actually listen to me — Shay and Puddin'. Yeah, I know Puddin' is still ticked off about what she found in Brett's room, but I think that if I grovel enough, I might get her attention.

After Julius goes to school and Bucky takes off for wherever he goes every day, I pick up my phone and punch in the number of La Chic. I'm relieved when Shay answers.

"I need to start looking for holiday clothes. Do y'all have anything in my size?"

She lets out a good-natured laugh. "Marybeth, you are the perfect size, so you shouldn't have a bit of trouble finding the perfect outfits. Can you come in today?"

"Yes, in fact, today is the only day I can come."

"Want me to pull some things before you get here?"

I think for a few seconds. "Thanks, but no. I'd like to just wander around and look. Will Puddin' be there?"

"She should be here after she gets Jeremy to school. He threw something into the toilet this morning, so she had to wait for the plumber."

I laugh. I remember those days when Julius's mischief was more focused on Bucky and me. I wish our problems with him were still that simple.

"I'll see you in a little while." After I hang up, I rock back on my heels and try to think of how to approach the topic I want to address. I find a notepad and jot a few thoughts before slipping it into my purse and heading out the door.

I hate the fact that Bucky insists on buying me a brand-spankin'-new luxury car every single solitary year when the new models come out. I'd be just fine with something more understated and keeping it for several years.

He gives me some "spendin' money" every month that I don't have to account for. It's way more than I need, so I've been socking some of it away in an account that's only in my name. Even though the oil company seems to think there's a lifetime supply of oil, I know anything can happen, and I don't want to be caught penniless. I reckon my pauper roots run deep.

I see Puddin's car parked at the curb in front of the shop. My hands sweat as I park behind it, but I can't let my case of nerves stop me from doing what I need to do.

As awkward as it feels, I apologize to God for not going to church as much as I should, and then I pray for guidance. Maybe it's just me, but when I open my eyes, I feel a little bit better. With a slightly shaky hand, I open the car door and get out, hesitating long enough to catch my breath that's also wobbly.

As I walk up to the front door, I look up at Puddin', who's standing by the door, and see her eyes pop open wide. She narrows her eyes, juts her chin, and glares at me. I don't blame her for not wanting to see me, but I can't let that get to me.

My nerves are so rattled that the bell on the door seems to jingle louder than normal. Shay walks around from behind the counter to greet me while Puddin' darts to the back room.

"Can I talk to you?" I ask, my voice barely audible, even to me. "Both of you?"

Before Shay has a chance to answer, Puddin' hollers from the back room, "Tell her I don't want to talk to her."

Shay gives me an apologetic look. "Sorry."

I try to stop my hands from shaking, but it's impossible. I still have to plow forward. "I'm the one who should be sorry. Puddin', please let's talk." I look directly at Shay, whose smile has faded. "I really need help from both of you. My family is in trouble, and I'm fit to be tied."

22
SALLY

I'm blown away by how resilient Justin is. Not only has he come off the life support machines, he's sitting up in bed asking for some of the meatballs Shay taught me how to make before the last family reunion.

"I'll bring you some next time I visit." I turn to Sara, who hasn't left her vigil next to Justin since he arrived. "Why don't you go home and get some rest?"

"I don't —"

Justin interrupts her. "I agree with Sally. You need to go home, take a long hot bath, and get some sleep."

I look at my brother-in-law and smile. He keeps getting better the longer I know him.

"Sally will stay here and make sure I behave," Justin continues.

Sara tilts her head and glances back and forth between Justin and me. I can tell she wants to get away for a little while, but she's not sure she should do it.

I put my arm around her and walk her to the door, picking up her purse on the way. Before I have a chance to give that one last shove, she turns around to face me. "Thank you so much, Sally. I don't know what I'd do without you."

"Go on, get out of here."

She sniffles and nods. As she turns to leave, I glance over my shoulder and see Justin watching us with interest.

Once she's gone, I pull a chair up next to Justin's bed. "So, how're you feeling?"

"Miserable. I'm still not sure what happened."

"A car fell on you, and you hit your head pretty hard."

"Yeah, I know that." He reaches up and touches the bandages on his head. "Funny thing is I don't even remember going to work that day."

"There'll probably be a lot of things you don't remember, but that might not be a bad thing."

He chuckles. "Maybe, but I do know one thing. I love Sara with all my heart, and I'll do anything to keep her happy."

"Getting better will make her happier than anything else you can do right now."

He smiles and then grimaces. "I'm workin' on it."

I tip my head forward and look at him for a few seconds, wondering if I should bring up the fact that she's carrying his baby. Yeah, I think it's okay. "Do you remember that she's pregnant?"

"That's what I've been trying to remember. I knew there was something."

I laugh. "At least you remembered there was something."

He scrunches up his face. "It's so hard, though. I don't want Sara to have to go through it alone."

I pat his arm. "That's why you have to do whatever it takes to get better."

"Oh, trust me, I will."

A very professional woman holding a clipboard walks into the room. I'm not sure who she is, but she clearly means business.

She brushes past me as she smiles at Justin. "Mr. Peterson, I understand you are one very lucky man."

"Lucky?" He grins at me before scrunching up his face and looking back at her. "No, I'm blessed."

Ms. Professional crinkles her forehead as she gives him a curious look. "Call it whatever you want. It's amazing you're able to talk to me now."

"The Lord clearly has plans for me."

"I don't know about that, but I do need

to take down some information before we admit you to therapy."

"Do I need to leave?" I ask.

Before Ms. Professional has a chance to say anything, Justin speaks up. "No, don't leave. I want you to stay right here. I don't have to take my clothes off, do I?"

"No." The woman glances at me with a big frown. "Are you related to the patient?"

"Yes. I'm his sister-in-law."

She looks back and forth between us. "Oh."

I can tell she's not sure what to say to me, so she goes back to her business of asking Justin a bunch of questions — some of them repeating what she's already asked. I'm starting to get the feeling that she's hanging around longer than she needs to. I shift my weight from one foot to the other, until I've listened to about all I can handle.

"I'm sorry, but this has been going on a long time. My brother-in-law has been through a lot, and he needs his rest."

"But the therapy —"

I gently touch her elbow and turn her toward the door. "Why don't you come back tomorrow and finish up? I'm sure he'll still be here."

To my relief, she doesn't resist. As soon as she's out the door, I close it and go back to where I was sitting.

Justin lets out a soft chuckle. "That woman really got under your skin, didn't she?"

I glance over at Justin. "Oh yeah."

He starts to smile and then grimaces. "She was rather overbearing."

"So you'll start therapy soon, which is probably a good thing."

"Yeah, the nurse said I'll have to learn to walk and talk again, but since I'm lying here talking just fine, we can concentrate on the walking." He clears his throat. "Now that I remember what's coming soon, I just want to make sure I'm home in time to greet our new baby."

Since he's in such a talkative mood, I decide to bring up the topic of looking for a place to live. "You're obviously not in the position of moving."

He gives a slight nod and grimaces. "I s'pose you can say that."

"And since the baby will need a nursery, either we can give up our workroom or I can move out."

"I'd never ask you to move out of your home."

"But I thought you and Sara wanted me to find another —"

He shakes his head. "No, not really. I think

she was just putting the thought out there."

"It's still probably a good idea for me to start house-hunting."

"You were kind enough to let me barge in when Sara and I eloped. Asking you to leave would be mean."

"That's something I need to worry about."

He shifts a little in the bed and lets out a groan. "I've never had such a bad headache in my life."

"Why don't you try to get some sleep?" I need to ponder what I'm going to do, since there isn't much time before the baby comes. "I'll just relax in the recliner until Sara comes back."

Without another word, Justin closes his eyes. Once I hear a soft snore coming from his bed, I allow myself to drift off to sleep.

The sound of my sister's voice as she enters the hospital room jolts me awake. "I found the perfect place for you, Sally. It's in the next building over, and it has all new appliances. It even has a built-in vanity by the master bathroom."

I rub my eyes and pull the chair into an upright position. "You what?"

"A condo just came open. Remember that woman no one knows because she's hardly ever home?"

"The one who drives the Jaguar?"

"Yeah. I saw her when I pulled in, and she asked if I knew anyone who's looking for a condo — either to rent or to buy."

23
SHEILA

"You're doing what?"

Sally has stopped by on her way home from the hospital to tell me she's looking at another condo in the same complex where she lives with Sara and Justin. "It's an identical floor plan, so at least I know I'll like the layout."

"But it's so expensive. Why would you move out?"

"The baby."

"Don't you have a three-bedroom place? You can use the extra room for the nursery."

"I've told you before that we need a work-room."

"Why can't you just use your dining room like you did in the apartment? That's what I'd do if I were you."

Her sigh of exasperation goes all through me. I know she doesn't understand why I'm so frugal, but she's never had to be. Even after she and Sara started complaining

183

about having to share a room, George and I decided to stay put in the small house we purchased when we first got married. Now I'm glad we did, because the house is paid for, and we have almost no debt.

"Mama, I'm not like you." She gives me an apologetic smile. "Our business has grown, so we need plenty of storage space and room to work."

"You can always move back here. I haven't touched your room." I look at her, hoping to see a sign that she might at least consider it.

She shakes her head. "Sorry, Mama, but you know I'm not going to come back. It would be too hard."

"But the cost——"

"We make enough money for each of us to have our own place."

"You can save that money for a rainy day." I know my argument is futile, but I have to make at least one more effort to reinforce what I think is the right thing for them to do.

"That rainy day is here. Sara and Justin need their own place, and this is the most logical thing for me to do, since it'll be too difficult for her to move while he's recovering from his accident."

It's obvious that she's not going to heed

my advice, so I finally let out a sigh and shrug. "Do whatever you feel you need to do. So, when are you planning to make this move?"

"I haven't even seen the condo yet. Sara told me she met the lady who lives there, and she's wanting to either rent it or sell it as soon as possible."

"Why don't you rent it and see if this is what you really want? If so, then you can buy it later." I remember one of my friends from high school getting on a lease-purchase plan where some of her rent applied to the down payment. That's the only way she and her husband could afford to buy a house.

A thoughtful look comes over her. "That might be a good plan. I'll ask her when she shows me her place."

"When are you planning to see it?"

Sally glances at the time on her cell phone. "I'm supposed to be there in an hour."

"Want me to go with you?"

She shakes her head. "I appreciate the offer, Mama, but I really need to make this decision on my own."

"But I have experience."

Her face widens into a smile. "So do I."

She's right. In fact, she has as much experience buying a home as I do — maybe even more, since I deferred to George and didn't pay much attention to what I was signing. "True."

She gives me a kiss on the cheek. "I think I'll go home and freshen up before I go look at the place."

After she leaves, I fix myself a cup of tea and carry it into the living room. George won't be back until early evening, so I have the house to myself until then. What's so strange is that for the first time in my entire adult life, I'm not sure what to do with all the time on my hands. All the committees can run themselves, there are no meetings today, and there's nothing much to do at the moment.

It's tempting to call some of the people on my church committee to see if anyone wants to come over, but I don't. Last time we got together socially, some of them started gossiping, and that annoyed me. I don't think they're mean people, but I do think they've justified their self-righteous behavior by asking for prayer before telling everything they know — and I suspect some things they've made up — about their subjects. As soon as someone starts a sentence with "We need to pray for her because . . ." I know there's some juicy gossip to follow.

And I have no doubt that some of their

tongues wag about me when I'm not there. Last time I walked into a committee meeting, I saw the looks on their faces as they instantly stopped talking.

It breaks my heart that so many of the things the Bible speaks out against are making their way into the church. Sure, they're compassionate and donate their time and money to those who need help. But that still shouldn't give them something new to gossip about.

What bugs me even more is that I've been guilty of doing it more than once. I never felt good afterward, so I prayed that the Lord would forgive me and deliver me from the desire to spread rumors — even if they are true. Sometimes the temptation is still there, but if I remove myself from the group, I can generally find something else to do with my time and my thoughts.

But right now I'm feeling out of sorts and kind of lonely. Even though this isn't the first time my daughters have told me they're not coming home when I've asked them to, I think it has finally sunk in that my girls are grown and probably won't ever move back into the room that I've assured them they can have any time they want it.

George has been after me to convert their old room into a craft or sewing room. He's already converted the garage into what he wants. We used to park our cars in there, but one day I came home from the part-time job I used to have, hit the garage door opener, and nothing happened. When I went into the house, he hollered for me to come look at what he'd done to the garage.

He'd taken the day off from work to create his man cave with a big-screen TV, his old ratty recliner that I removed from the living room, some carpet remnants he'd picked up from the home renovation store, and a curb-recycled foosball table. I thought the garage looked hideous, but he was so proud of his space that I just smiled and accepted the fact that my car would be exposed to the elements in our driveway from now on.

The garage is still in the same condition, only now he rarely goes out there anymore. It's a little too hot in the summer, even though he brought in a portable air conditioner, and a little too cool in the winter because the space heater can't even begin to take the chill out of the air. Every now and then I mention that it might be nice to convert it back into a garage, but he just shakes his head. I think he sees that as a place he can go if he wants to, even though his favorite spot is still his newer chair in front of the high-definition TV in our very comfortable, climate-controlled living room.

When the phone rings, I expect it to be one of the twins, but it's not. It's George. "Hey, honey, I have a surprise for you."

"A surprise?"

"Yeah. I would wait until I get home to tell you, but it's gonna be a while, and I can't wait."

"What is it?"

"Are you sitting down? If you're not, you'd better take a seat now."

I lower myself into the closest chair. "Okay, I'm sitting."

"I've booked us for a cruise right after the family reunion."

"A cruise?" We've talked about it many times, but I'm not ready yet. I have so much to do — starting with losing at least twenty pounds and putting together a decent cruise wardrobe — and that's not enough time. "But —"

"I know, I know. You have other things that are more pressing, but we keep talking about it, and if we don't do it now, we may never get around to it."

"What about the girls?" I pause for a second but not long enough for him to answer. "Justin is still in the hospital."

"Sheila, you really need to stop doing this.

Ever since the girls were born, you've centered your entire life on them. Now it's time for us . . . for you and me to bring back the spark we once had."

24
SALLY

Sara will be so jealous. We thought our place was nice, but wait until she sees the one I'm fixin' to buy. It's the same floor plan, but it has all bamboo flooring throughout, except in the bathrooms and kitchen, where the current owner, Jeanine, has put in travertine. Stunning gray, taupe, and white subway tile backsplashes offset the light, sparkly quartz countertops in the kitchen and bathrooms. Every room in the house has extra detail, like chair railing, wainscoting, tray ceilings, and ambient lighting with dimmer switches. The only place I've seen with this many upgrades is on HGTV.

The bathrooms are breathtaking. The master bath has a garden tub with jets and super cool faucets and a shower with a rain head.

I think I've died and gone to heaven, and then I walk into the kitchen that features state-of-the-art appliances, including a range with a double oven, a microwave in a drawer, and a dishwasher that you can't hear running, even when you're standing next to it.

The whole place is ultrasleek and contemporary, but her traditional furniture tones it down a bit and gives it a homey look. I absolutely love everything about it.

Once I've seen the whole place and picked my chin up off the floor, she stops, turns to me, and smiles. "Well, what do you think?"

There's no way I can act coy about my feelings. "I love it!"

"I thought you might." She hesitates. "But there's just one problem. This is my second home, and I don't need the furniture. I'd really like to include most of what's in here so I don't have to find a place to put it."

I swallow hard. "That might not be a problem if I can afford it."

"I'm sure we can work something out. Did your sister tell you I'm motivated to do something quickly?"

"She said you were willing to sell or rent the condo out."

Jeanine nods. "Of course, I prefer to sell it, but if that doesn't happen quickly, I'll consider renting it out."

Now it's time to ask the hard question. "How much do you want?"

"Well . . ." She looks off into the distance before turning back to me. "I did put quite a bit of money into the place, and it's in perfect condition."

I brace myself for a price I'll never be able to afford. When we went looking at flooring and some of the other things Jeanine put into this place, we were stunned by how expensive it all was.

"But since there isn't a Realtor involved, and I want it to happen quickly, I can give you a good deal."

I swallow hard. "What kind of good deal?"

She quotes me a price that's a little out of my comfort zone, but if I'm careful, it might be doable. Based on her expression, I think she interprets my hesitation as reluctance to go through with the deal.

"I'm pretty motivated, so make me an offer."

This is a huge decision that I'll need to make all by myself. When we purchased our current condo from Shay, we knew who we were dealing with, and I was in it with my sister. But I don't know Jeanine other than waving to her in the parking lot, and I'll be doing everything without another person to offer support.

"Can I give you an answer in a couple of days?"

She smiles. "Sure, I understand. This is a big decision. Your sister says y'all have a business together, and she'd love for you to live close so she and the baby can see you whenever they want."

"Sara said that?"

Jeanine nods. "Yes, and she told me you've always been extremely close." She sighs. "I've always thought it would be nice to have a sister, but instead, I have brothers who picked on me unmercifully."

After I leave Jeanine, I go home to think about what to do. I'm so used to talking things through with Sara that I feel overwhelmed. Granted, she has always leaned on me too, and most of the time I'm the one who has made the final decision, but she normally questions everything.

I check our orders and fill the ones that have been in the queue the longest. Normally, I would be frustrated with Sara for not helping, but she has her hands full and enough to worry about at the moment.

Mama calls me, and as soon as I click the On button, she starts talking. "I'm worried about your sister."

"Why? What happened?"

"Nothing happened. It's just that she looks so gaunt."

"She's not getting much sleep." I'm concerned about her too, but I don't want to alarm Mama. "I'll relieve her as much as possible, but I know she wants to be there in case Justin needs her."

"I'm sure she does, but she still has herself and the baby to consider."

After we hang up, I lower my head and pray for my sister and everything she has to deal with. It seems as though everything is happening all at once, and to top it off, our orders for the holidays are picking up. Based on experience, I know we'll be slammed within a month.

A humongous rush order comes in that typically takes both Sara and me an entire afternoon to fill. I take a deep breath, pull out all the ribbon I'll need, and get started on it, knowing it'll take me at least a full day to finish it. I probably should have taken down the option for rush orders, but we don't get many of them, so I didn't think it was necessary.

Sara and I have learned that organization is the key to filling these orders, so I line everything up in the order things need to get done by. Then I print out the page with everything on the list and tape it to the side of the small case that sits on the edge of the worktable.

As I work, I try to think about the girl or

girls who'll be wearing these bows. Since there are so many in each style, I suspect it's for resale, or perhaps it could be gifts.

I'm glad I listened to Sara when she said we needed to order extra clips early in the season to make sure we don't run out. Last year the types of clips we prefer were on backorder, so we had to use some that weren't quite as good.

I get as caught up as I can, take a shower, and go back to the hospital. There's no one at the nursing station, so I just keep walking all the way to the end of the hall. Hopefully, I'll be able to talk Sara into going home for some food and rest.

When I get to Justin's room, I stop. His bed is empty, and there are no signs of his ever having been there. A strange, sick feeling washes over me.

25
CORALEE

Being in a relationship is odd for me. I'm not used to having a guy always there, paying a lot of attention to the details of my life, and having to check in on a regular basis. That part gets annoying. Plus, I'm seeing some things about him that I'm not crazy about.

Sure, there are things I like about being with Kyle. He's a sweet guy who makes me feel special. A lot of people are drawn to him because he's cute, smart, funny, considerate, and comfortable to be around. But we're so different. In spite of what he says about how alone he was before we got together, he seems very comfortable in social situations. But the only way I can recharge and regroup is to be alone . . . like I've been most of my life.

I used to think I was alone because no one wanted to be with me. Now I realize it's more because that's what I chose.

There are times when I need more space than I get now. Granted, in the past, I had way too much space and time on my hands. But now I find myself on sensory overload.

The strangest thing about this whole relationship thing is my grades are improving. I have less time, but I study more because that's the one thing Kyle and I have in common. And there's something else I never knew about myself until now. I'm competitive.

Yeah, that's probably the biggest surprise of all. After we get our grades back from exams, papers, projects, or whatever, I get a strange rush of excitement when I score even one point higher than Kyle. He doesn't seem to care though, because he says he's a lot more secure than I'll ever be. That smugness bothers me too.

I've tried to talk to him about my need for more time alone, but the hurt look on his face completely undoes my resolve to communicate my needs. I hate inflicting pain on someone else, so I always back down.

"My mom and dad are coming down for a visit soon." We just left sociology, and he's making small talk while we walk toward the exit. "I can't wait for them to meet you."

I gulp. Kyle is from Maryland, and I know very little about people who aren't from the

South. I fake a smile. "I'm looking forward to meeting them too."

He puts his arm around me and squeezes my shoulder as a playful grin pops onto his face. "No, you're not."

I pull away a little bit. "What makes you say that?"

"Look, Coralee, I've been studying you for a long time. I can read you like a book."

I sigh as my shoulders droop. "Okay, so you're right. What's the big deal?"

"Why don't you want to meet them?"

The tenderness in his voice touches the core of my heart in more of a sad sort of way than anything.

"I think you'll love them."

Now I know I can't hide my insecurity. "I'm sure I will, but I'm not so sure they'll like me."

He scrunches up his face. "What on earth are you talking about? My parents will love you."

My lack of sophistication has always rendered me nervous around people who seem worldlier, but I don't want to come right out and say this. "Do they know about me?"

"Do they know about you?" He tips his head back and laughs. "Of course they do. In fact, when they call, you're pretty much all I talk about. My mom can't get over the fact that I'm more interested in a girl than I am *Minecraft*."

"Are they okay with that?"

He shrugs. "I've never asked them, but I think so. One thing I do know is that Mom is happy I'm getting out and doing real things instead of sitting in my room with my eyes glued to the computer screen. She says you're making me be social again."

"I don't make you —"

"You know what I mean. Since we're together so much, and you like to go places, that's what I have to do to be with you."

I narrow my eyes as I think about this statement. "Am I the only reason you . . . go places?"

He chuckles. "Pretty much, yeah."

"You seem a lot more social than I am."

He grins. "Maybe that's an act. Have you ever thought about that?"

"But I don't —"

Before I can finish my statement about not wanting him to do anything he doesn't want to do or to feel like he has to act, he gently places his fingertips over my lips. "Hey, I'm not complaining. I've never been so happy, and that's a big deal."

"You haven't?"

He shakes his head. "And another thing

you're doing for me is showing that there are other things in life besides geeky stuff. In fact, I'm seriously thinking about changing my major to psychology."

"You are?"

He nods. "I've always wanted to work with troubled kids." He looks off in the distance before meeting my gaze again. "The only problem is I'll need my master's degree to become a licensed counselor."

"But I thought you wanted to be an engineer."

"That was actually my second choice, but I never told anyone what I really wanted to do because I didn't think I had it in me to stay in school long enough to get my master's."

Oh wow. I'm stunned. I've known from the beginning that he's better around people than I am, but I thought his heart was set on becoming an engineer.

"To put it into your words, cat got your tongue?" He tweaks my nose and then pulls me in a different direction. "C'mon, let's go get you some of that pumpkin coffee you like so much. My folks sent me a Starbucks gift card."

"You don't have to spend your gift card on me."

"Don't be silly. You're the reason I got it.

My mom told me to share it with you." He smiles. "I think she feels like she owes you something for getting me out and about."

"Well, in that case . . ." I point toward the coffee shop. "Let's go get some pumpkin spice coffee."

As we sip our coffee, he tells me that the reason he's majoring in electronics engineering is that it comes easy to him after spending time in the military in that field. "But it's not my passion."

"Why do you want to work with troubled kids?"

He purses his lips and sighs. "It's sort of a long story."

"I have time to listen if you want to tell me."

As he talks about one of his friends he'd met in elementary school having to deal with issues his parents inflicted on him, I hear the pain in his voice. "Stan was just a kid, and he couldn't deal with all the craziness in his life with his dad being a drug dealer and his mother taking off for days at a time. My mom and dad sort of adopted him, and he stayed with us a lot until high school. Then he got caught up in the middle of one of his dad's drug deals, and he wound up in juvie. My parents tried to get him out and begged the court to let him stay with us, but the judge turned them down."

"Wow." I lean back in my chair and stare at the logo on my cup. "That's awful."

"I know."

"Have you heard from Stan lately?"

He clears his throat and gives me the saddest look I've ever seen. "He died in prison a couple of years ago." He sniffles. "It's bad enough that happened to my buddy, but there's more . . ." He pauses before adding, "That could have been me."

26
SALLY

I can't remember ever being so upset — and scared — in my entire life as I was yesterday when Justin's bed was empty. As bothered as I still am about their elopement, I would never want my sister to become a young widow. If it weren't for the nursing assistant who saw the color drain from my face, I might have passed out right then and there.

"Mr. Peterson is doing great. They moved him to the rehab unit." She smiled and gestured for me to follow her. "C'mon, I'll take you there."

Now I'm standing next to my sister, watching Justin walk with the help of two physical therapy assistants. Sara is leaning on me, so I put an arm around her waist so we can hold each other up.

It's difficult enough for me watching Justin struggle to walk, but I can only imagine how hard it is on Sara. She sniffles as she never takes her eyes off her husband.

"He's doing great." I clear my throat, willing myself to believe what I'm saying. "I'm sure he'll be back to his old self in no time."

"That's what his doctor says."

"Then trust him." I think about it for a few seconds. "But more important, we need to trust the Lord to do His will."

"I know." She gives me the same puppy-dog look we both have always given our parents. "But it's hard, ya know?"

"Yes, I do know." Out of the corner of my eye, I see movement, so I look back at Justin, who has just taken a few steps on his own. "Look."

Her hand immediately goes to her mouth as tears stream down her cheeks. If I ever had any doubt about my sister's love for her husband, I wouldn't now. It's amazing how some of the best lessons are learned through tragedy.

I let out a sigh and smile at the same time. "Yeah, he's going to be just fine."

"Looks like he's making some progress."

The sound of Mama's voice behind us gets both of our attention. We turn to see her standing a couple of feet from us.

She nods toward Justin. "To be honest, I'm amazed by how well he's doing, but I shouldn't be. A good man will do whatever it takes for his family, and I suspect that has a lot to do with all the work he's putting into getting better."

Sara pulls away from me and puts her arm around Mama. "Do you really think so?"

"Yes, sweetie, I do." Mama's eyes glisten with tears. "I'm so sorry I reacted the way I did when you first married him. He's actually a pretty wonderful man and . . ." She sniffles and swallows hard. "And the ideal husband for you."

I'm touched by the fact that Mama has finally accepted Justin and that Sara loves him so much. "I agree," I say.

"Then why don't we all pray right now?" Mama looks back and forth between us with an expectant look on her face. We huddle closer with our arms around each other. Mama doesn't hesitate to begin the prayer, thanking God for her many blessings, asking for the Lord to heal Justin, and adding that she's thankful to have him in our family. Then I say a few words, followed by Sara, who gets choked up. Mama ends with her "Amen," followed by Sara's and mine.

When we turn back toward Justin, we see him standing between the therapy bars but not holding on to them. A grin widens his face, and he gives us a thumbs-up.

Sara blows him a kiss, and his face lights up even more. I have to admit they're the sweetest couple I've ever seen. And I'm happy that Mama is there to witness this show of affection between them.

Mama touches my arm and mouths that she'd like to talk to me, so I turn to Sara. "We'll be back in a few minutes."

She nods. As Mama and I walk away, I glance over my shoulder and see Sara moving toward Justin.

We round the corner, and Mama stops. "I spoke to the doctor on my way to the therapy center."

My heart thuds, and my voice catches. I clear my throat. "And?"

"He says Justin should make a full recovery." Mama's voice quivers. "Justin almost died shortly after he got here. The doctor says he's never seen anyone more motivated in all the years he's been practicing medicine."

"That's good. I still can't believe we almost lost him."

"I know." Mama shivers as her chin quivers, and I can tell she's struggling to find the right words. "I feel really bad that I didn't give him a chance before now, but I promise to do better now that there's no doubt they're perfect for each other."

"Sometimes it takes a near disaster to realize that."

207

Mama gives me a half smile. "What are you planning to do now?"

"Right this minute?"

She shakes her head. "No, I'm talking about the living arrangements."

"I'm not sure. The condo I looked at is perfect for me, but the price is a little steep, and the rent is even higher than the mortgage payment will be."

Mama gives me a sympathetic look. "I'm sure you can stay right where you are. Eventually, something else will come along."

"I know." But the condo is even more perfect than the one we're currently living in, so I plan to try to figure out a way to finagle it. Maybe Shay will have some ideas. However, I don't need to worry Mama about it, so I change the subject. "What are you planning to bring to the reunion?"

"The usual. How about you?"

"Meatballs and whatever else I learn how to cook at the next Chef's Skillet class."

"Oh, did I tell you that I'm going to be teaching a dessert class? Mavis called and said you told her I make the best pies."

I actually never told Mavis that, but I don't want to burst Mama's happy bubble. "When?"

"She wanted me to start before Thanksgiving, but I'm too busy between now and then with committee meetings. I told her we'd do a short two-week session on Christmas cookies and cakes, and if those go well, I'll do one on Valentine's treats." She glances at the clock behind the nursing station. "I need to run. Your daddy is expecting supper in an hour, so I have to hustle to get it on the table."

"Mama, you spoil him rotten."

She giggles. "I know, and I love doing it."

I've always thought our parents had the best marriage ever. Sure, they disagree on a lot of issues, but overall, they're always doing little things to make each other happy. My hope is that one of these days I'll meet someone I can have that kind of relationship with. I wasn't sure it existed for anyone else, until I realized that Sara found that with Justin.

Sara wants to stick around for a little while and have dinner with Justin, but she says she'll be home soon. "He's exhausted, so I think I need to leave him alone so he can get some rest."

I start to tell her she looks like she could use some rest too, but I clamp my mouth shut to prevent hurt feelings. She's been mighty sensitive lately.

All the way to the condo, I think about how different everything is now that Sara's married. I should have known this would happen sooner or later, since we have both talked about wanting families. For some reason, I assumed that time would come in the distant future.

As soon as I make the last turn toward our condo, I see the woman who has the place up for sale walking around like she's looking for someone. She glances up as I approach, and when she realizes it's me, she starts waving madly.

27
BRETT

I'm pretty sure Mama believes me when I tell her I had nothing to do with the pot Julius left on my dresser. But she still gives me strange looks when I go into my room at night. Sometimes she even follows me in there and looks around, like she might find something.

I've tried talking to Daddy about how much I dread going to the reunion. Seeing Julius and knowing he's probably up to something to get me in trouble will make me nervous the whole time I'm there.

Daddy says he'll talk to Mama and try to get me out of it, but I know better. He doesn't want to be there any more than I do, but she always makes him go. What I don't get is that she complains about it, but she still acts like it'll be the end of the world if we're not there.

My sister, Hallie, is threatening to run away from home if Mama makes her go. To my surprise, Mama smiles and says, "That's fine. I'll help you pack your bags." I know she doesn't mean it, and so does Hallie. Maybe that's what you call child psychology, even though Hallie is practically a grown-up.

Every single day leading up to it is a day closer to when I'll have to face Julius and whatever he's planning, and I have no doubt he's not kidding when he says he's planning something even worse than last time. Daddy once said that if Julius put as much energy into something productive as he does being a spoiled brat, he'd make the world a better place. I agree.

He's a smart guy who uses his brains wrong while he gets everything he wants — from the latest video game to the coolest cars. And he complains like he has to live in a Third World country, which annoys me to no end. The latest video game I have is one my older brother, Trey, left behind the last time he moved out. It has to be at least three years old. As for cars, Daddy says I can have whatever wheels I can afford when I'm old enough to get my driver's license, which means I won't be driving my own car for quite a while.

The doorbell rings, and since no one else in the house seems to care, I answer it. As soon as I fling the door open, I see my cousin Wendy standing there with a smirk on her face. I groan. "What do you want?"

She fakes surprise. "Is that how you talk to a cousin you haven't seen in months?"

I hear footsteps coming up from behind me, and when I turn around, I see Mama scowling at me before she looks at Wendy and smiles. "Come on in, Wendy. Whatcha got there?"

Wendy holds out a stack of casserole dishes. "Mama told me to bring these to you. She said you'd probably need them for the reunion."

Mama looks at the dishes but doesn't take them. Instead, she gestures for Wendy to follow her. "Come on back to the kitchen. I just made some muffins, and you can have one hot out of the oven."

I've been smelling the muffins for the past half hour. I don't want to be around Wendy any longer than I have to, but the sweet cinnamon and apple aroma is more than I can handle, so I'm right behind them.

"Brett, be a sweetie and get some glasses out for milk." Mama gives Wendy her biggest smile. "Or would you rather have orange juice?"

"Milk is fine." Wendy looks at me with the same smirk she always has. "So, Brett, are you still seeing that girl you were with at the movies last month?"

I want to run and hide as Mama slowly turns around and gives me one of those looks. "You were with a girl? What girl is that, and why didn't you tell me?"

"He didn't tell you?" Wendy flashes a smile in my direction before turning back to Mama. "They were so lovey-dovey I was sure you'd know all about her."

"Lovey-dovey?" Mama's eyebrows go up to her hairline as she twists her mouth to the side. "No, I don't know about her yet, but I will soon." She tips her head forward with her Mama-means-business expression. "Won't I, Brett?"

"Yes, ma'am." As soon as Mama turns back to the basket of muffins, I make a face at Wendy, who is working hard not to laugh out loud.

"Wendy, do you want one or two?"

"One is fine. I've been puttin' on some weight lately, so I have to be careful."

"I understand." Mama puts one muffin on a plate and looks at me. "How about you, Brett?"

"I've changed my mind. I'm not hungry." I back toward the door. "I think I'll go finish my homework."

As I turn and run toward my room, I hear

Mama and Wendy laughing about something — probably me. If I could have a do-over, I would have ignored the doorbell.

Wendy is a few years older than me, but I used to think she was the prettiest girl in the family. In fact, if she weren't my cousin, I might have had a crush on her. Now I can't stand to even be in the same room with her. She still looks the same, but these days she acts all high and mighty, since she's in college now. If that's how college girls act, I don't want any part of them.

I look at myself in the mirror Mama put over my dresser, even though I told her I didn't want it there. What I see is a scared boy, when what I want to be is a confident man. Trey still hasn't figured out who he is, so I don't have high hopes for myself any time soon.

I pick up my books and carry them over to the beanbag chair I've had since I was in middle school. Before I open my math book, I look at the history project that's due next week, and then I lean back and close my eyes. I hate history, but then I hate math too. In fact, there's nothing about school that I like anymore. It used to be fun, but all I ever feel when I go there now is humiliation. I went out for football because Daddy said that would be good for me socially. I'm not so sure about that, though. Julius gets a lot of attention from the girls, and he doesn't play on any teams. That girl Wendy saw me with is new at school, and as soon as she found out I was a football player, she got friendly with me. But someone must have said something on Monday, because now she won't give me the time of day.

When I hear Mama's voice saying my name, I open my eyes and try to focus in the near darkness. She flips the light on and looks at me for a few seconds. "May I come in?"

"Sure."

She walks over and sits on the edge of my bed, folds her hands in front of her, and leans her elbows on her knees. "I think it's time for you and me to have a mother-son chat."

I shrug. "I don't feel like talking."

"Oh, but I do. Whatever is going on with you needs to stop. First, you blow up a barn. Then we find pot in your room —"

"I told you that wasn't mine."

Mama shrugs. "And Julius told his mama and daddy it wasn't his either. Who should I believe?"

"You don't believe me?"

"Why should I?" Mama pauses. "At first I believed you, but now I know you're not

216

bein' truthful with me and your daddy. You've clearly been holding back secrets, like about that girl Wendy saw you with." She tips her head forward and does her look again before letting her eyelids droop a little. "Want to tell me about her?"

28
SALLY

Ever since Sara and I started talking about the incredible opportunity I have to move to my own place that just happens to be in the same neighborhood, I've seen a sense of relief in her eyes. In all fairness, she's the one who should move out, but I know that she's not up to moving. There are still some things we need to work out.

First of all, Jeanine has come way down in her price, and she's offering to throw in most of the furniture for nothing extra. And to top it off, she actually told me I can stay there for a couple of months for free if I want to try it out before signing a contract. When I asked why she's doing this, she said she found out how much money she'd be able to save on the real estate commission, and then there's the matter of waiting for it to sell.

"At least you know you like the neighbor-hood," she admitted. "The one time I rented it out with an option to buy, the couple decided condo living wasn't for them."

"You know I like it. Let me think about it for a couple of days, and I'll get back with you."

When Sara's expression changed, I knew I had to accept the offer, so I called and accepted the offer right away. Now Sara and I are sitting in the living room we share and talking about when and how to make the move.

"Aren't you the slightest bit suspicious of her wanting to do this so quickly?" She gives me one of her half smiles that almost seems apologetic. "And the fact that she's willing to cut the price so quickly and for so much . . ." She shrugs. "I don't know, maybe it's me, but it seems mighty fishy, since she barely knows you."

I have thought about that, but the offer is so good I'm afraid not to jump on it. "What do you think she might be up to?"

Again, Sara shrugs. "Who knows? Maybe she has a body buried somewhere, and she wants out before —"

"Ew, gross. Don't even go there."

"Just sayin'." Sara stands and staggers for a couple of steps before she gets her footing. She's barely showing a tiny bump, but she says she's off balance with the extra weight. "Want some ice cream?"

"I'm not hungry. Besides, isn't it too cold out for ice cream?"

"It's not cold in here." She holds out her bare arms. "Ever since I found out I was pregnant, I've been hot when everyone else is freezing."

I laugh and point toward the kitchen. "Go get your ice cream."

As soon as she leaves me alone in the living room, I pick up my phone and punch in Jeanine's number. "I want you to know how much I appreciate your offer, but I am concerned about a couple of things."

She clears her throat. "Like what?" I can tell she's nervous.

I voice my concerns, like why she's so eager to drop the price and why she's letting me stay in the place for free before we close on it. She whimpers for a couple of seconds and then bursts into a sob — a very stunning, loud sob. It's clear that there's something else going on here.

It takes me a couple of minutes to calm her down. Finally, she tells me a long story about how she's fallen onto hard times, and she doesn't know what else to do.

Sara finally walks back in with a heaping bowl of ice cream. She gives me a questioning look, so I mouth that I'll tell her when I hang up.

Finally, I press the Off button and put the phone on the coffee table. "You were right." My shoulders sag from the weight of disappointment. "There is more to the condo than I realized."

"Like what?" She scoops a spoonful of ice cream and shoves it into her mouth while she waits for me to explain.

"She's eight months late on her mortgage payment, and she got the notice that the bank is foreclosing next month."

"I'm surprised they let her go so long without kicking her out."

"I know. I asked her how she was able to stay so long, and she said she told them she'd have the money any day now." I shrug. "I suppose they got tired of hearing that and decided to move forward with the foreclosure."

Sara swallows and gives me a look of confusion. "Then how did she think she could sell it to you if she won't even own it after next month?"

"She obviously wasn't thinking clearly. That's not even the half of it. She hasn't paid her power bill, water bill, or association fee in a couple of months, so whoever buys the place will have to cover all that."

"Oh wow." Sara stares at her ice cream for a few seconds before meeting my gaze. "What are you gonna do now?"

"I really like her place, but until I know how much I'll have to pay, I can't go through with our plan. I told her to make an appointment with an officer at the bank, and I'd go with her to figure out something."

"I'm really sorry, Sally. I know how much you want that place."

"Yeah, it's a bummer, but maybe something can be worked out." I'm not holding my breath, but I don't need to let her know I doubt I'll be able to go through with it.

"Don't get your hopes up. Besides, it's not like you don't have a place to stay."

"I know, but I was hoping —"

"It might still work out, so don't lose hope."

I smile at my sweet sister, who has completely turned the tables on me. I've always been the voice of reason, and when that becomes too difficult to handle, I find a silver lining. Now she's doing it for me.

"Speaking of hope . . ." Sara pauses as her smile widens. "Justin is now able to walk a few feet completely without a walker. The head of the physical therapy department said that as soon as he can make it across the room and finish his speech therapy in the hospital, he can come home."

"Are you equipped to deal with everything?" I ask. There's no doubt in my mind he's doing much better, but I'm still realistic and know it won't be easy for either of them. "I mean, you are pregnant, and you shouldn't be lifting heavy things."

"He'll have some home health care until he doesn't need it anymore."

I bite my tongue to keep from saying what I'm thinking — that this condo will get mighty crowded for a while, unless I'm able to move out soon. Based on her expression, I suspect she's thinking the very same thing. But neither of us wants to actually come out and say it.

After she finishes her ice cream, she leaves for the hospital. I walk around the condo and try to figure out where we'll be able to work if I'm not able to move out. I finally have come up with a plan when my phone rings. It's Jeanine.

"I have an appointment for us to meet with someone at the bank tomorrow morning at 10:00. Can you be there?"

That's typically when I'm in full swing making hair bows, but I'll get up early and try to knock out as many as possible. "Sure, I'll be there."

"I've been warned that your credit will

have to be impeccable for them to even consider making another loan on it."

I don't bring up the fact that not only do I have great credit, I have enough money for a hefty down payment. I can actually pay cash if they'll allow me to pay her rock-bottom price, but I don't want to deplete my savings. She gives me the address of the bank in Hattiesburg, and I jot it down. The remainder of the day, I work on a spread-sheet with my income and expenses, and then I pull up my previous years' tax infor-mation. This is one time I'm thankful for such a thorough accountant who annoyed me to no end about dotting all the i's and crossing all the t's. Now I get it.

I lie in bed staring at the ceiling as all kinds of scenarios creep into my head. It's strange to want something this badly but feel helpless about being able to get it. In the past, I felt as though I had more control, but now I realize that was just naive.

I'm not sure when Sara got in last night, but I wake up to the sound of her clanking around in the kitchen. When I walk in there to get coffee, I'm taken aback by her energy.

"You're not supposed to have more than one cup of coffee per day," I remind her.

"I haven't even had that." She practically bounces over to the refrigerator, where she pulls out a carton of eggs. "Justin not only walked across the therapy room, he walked me to the nursing station when it was time for me to leave."

"Sounds promising, but what does that mean?"

"He's doing great with his speech therapy, so they're thinking he should be home by the first of next month." Her shoulders rise as she takes a deep breath. "And they're letting him out to go to the family reunion with me."

"That's great news!" I pour myself a cup of coffee and sit down at the table while she finishes filling me in on Justin's progress. Then I tell her about my appointment at the bank.

"I sure hope this works out for you. I know how much you want your own place, and it'll be wonderful to have you so close."

I nod. "Yeah, but I still don't want to get my hopes up too high."

She scrambles the eggs, dishes them out onto two plates, and carries them over to the table. I say the blessing before we dig in.

As soon as we clean the kitchen, she heads toward the workroom. "Let's see how many bows we can make before you have to leave."

With the two of us working, we knock out

more than half of the orders that have come in before I have to go. "Why don't you take a nap, and we can finish up when I get back?"

She nods. "Let me do one more order, and then I'll take a break. I'll say an extra prayer for you."

I put on a nice pair of slacks, a silk shirt, and a blazer for my bank appointment. I rarely get this nervous, but my palms are sweating and my breathing is shaky. As soon as I find a parking spot in the bank lot, I lower my head and pray for the Lord's will to be done.

Jeanine and the mortgage officer are waiting for me when I walk in. It's hard to read them, but it appears that they've already had a nice conversation.

"I'm Nate Hawthorne," the banker says as he extends his hand. "I've heard nothing but good things about you."

I turn to Jeanine. "Thank you."

She shakes her head. "Not from me. Apparently, you and Nate have some friends in common."

"Oh." I can't help frowning at the thought of this man who holds my future in his hands knowing more about me than I want him to know.

"I've heard that you have quite a success-

226

ful business," he states. "I'm friends with your cousin Shay, and she can't say enough nice things about you and what a good business mind you have."

I let out a sigh of relief because Shay would never say anything to hurt me. "She's one of my favorite cousins," I admit.

He holds my gaze, making my stomach do one of those roller-coaster flippy things. Nate's close-cropped hair, piercing blue-green eyes, and wide smile with the slightly imperfect teeth nearly undo my attempt at a professional demeanor. He doesn't look a bit like any banker I've ever met.

Finally, he gestures for us to follow him. "Come on, ladies. Let's go on back to my office where we can talk in private."

As soon as we sit down, Nate picks up a stack of papers and then looks at Jeanine. "You are fortunate that we've been too busy to do anything before now." He states a number that she owes the bank, and I'm surprised by how low it is. Then he turns to me. "Based on the circumstances, I'm trying to get the underwriter to do something different to expedite this sale. We don't want more properties on the books — especially condos. We already have more than normal."

I narrow my eyes. "So you're saying we might not be able to do this?"

"No, that's not what I'm saying." He leans toward me and holds my gaze for a couple of seconds. "If you can come up with what the bank is owed and cover the lien from the condo association and utilities, I think I can make a good case for you to purchase it."

I start to say something, but Jeanine interrupts. "Wait a minute. What am I going to get out of this? I put one-third down on the place, and I've been paying for years."

Nate puts down the papers, folds his hands over his desk, and gives her a long look. "What you'll get is better credit for not having a foreclosure on your record."

She scowls. "Then I'm not letting the furniture go with it."

This whole scene is getting more uncomfortable by the minute, and I'm trying to figure out where to look. Then I come up with an idea. "I can buy your furniture."

She tilts her head and gives me a look as though I've suddenly become her worst enemy. "I'm not letting it go cheap."

Then I name a number, and her chin drops. She starts to say something, but only a squeak comes out.

Nate grins. "That's quite generous, Ms. Wright. Do you feel that the furniture is worth that much?"

Deep down, I know I've offered more than double what she would have gotten anywhere else, but if I can get the condo for what she owes, I'm still ahead. In fact, I can plunk down more than half of the balance from the cash I have saved without batting an eye or having to sell any of my investments. "I'm willing to pay that if she accepts."

Nate and I both look at her and wait. When she doesn't say anything, he clears his throat. "Well, what do you think, Jeanine?"

She swallows hard as she widens her eyes. "I'll have to consider it." She fidgets for a moment. "I don't like the idea of losing money, but it looks like you're playing hardball, and I don't have a choice."

He frowns at her before he turns and focuses on me. "Are you sure this is something you want to do?"

I nod. "Positive."

Nate picks the papers back up and stacks them. "If you ladies don't mind waiting out in the lobby, I have a few phone calls to make before we have you sign the paperwork to get the process started."

As soon as we're alone, Jeanine turns to me with a suspicious glare. "Why are you offering to buy my stuff?"

I try to give her a reassuring look. "Because I think the condo is worth more than what the bank is willing to sell it for, and I want you to at least walk away with something."

She shakes her head and looks down at the floor before raising her gaze back to mine. "You wouldn't happen to be interested in a two-year-old Jaguar, would you?"

29
MARYBETH

It's a little more than two weeks until Bucky's family comes for the reunion, but I still haven't gotten through to Julius about what I'm sure he left in Brett's room. He hasn't broken down and admitted anything yet, but I think that's only because Bucky is giving him the benefit of the doubt.

"You need to have a long talk with him." I look Bucky in the eye without blinking, something that never fails to get to him. Even after all the things he said about kids trying things, he says he believes our son.

He glances down at the floor as he shakes his head. "If Julius says he didn't do it, then I believe him."

"Brett says he doesn't know where it came from."

"He's the one who's probably lying."

"Maybe so, but I'm not convinced." The fact remains, I don't trust my own son because he has such a habit of lying to me that I rarely believe anything he tells me anymore.

Bucky finally looks directly at me as he lifts his hands in surrender. "Okay, okay, I'll talk to him."

"What are you going to say?"

He blows out a sigh of exasperation. "I don't know. Prob'ly something like *your mama doesn't believe you.*"

"That's not good. You need to ask him what they did in Brett's room, what they talked about, and if he saw anything on Brett's dresser when he first got there."

Bucky squints as he shakes his head. "Why don't you talk to him? I can't remember all that."

"Okay, I think I will. It's just that you said he was better with you."

"He is." Bucky lifts his chin and glances away again. "But you're the one with the bone to pick. I'm fine with what he says — that he had nothing to do with that weed on Brett's dresser."

As he turns to leave, I run after him. "Where are you going, Bucky?"

"To a place where there are no nagging wives."

I know what that means. He's going to Bud's Bar and Pool Hall in Hattiesburg. "I don't want you drinking and driving."

"I'll just have a few beers." He pulls his jacket together in front and makes a production of zipping it. "I'll be home for supper."

As he leaves, I slink back against the wall behind me. Bucky was never a drinker before, but when one of his friends he met when the oil company was putting in the oil rigs invited him out for a beer, he said it would be a nice goodwill gesture. And now he goes a couple of times a week. Last time he went, Bud called and told me to come pick up my husband because he'd had too much to drink to drive home.

It all seems to come back to the money — something I'm constantly reminded of. I realize that money itself isn't the root of all evil, but loving it too much sure can bring out the worst.

I was perfectly fine with the split-level house we have in Hattiesburg. It has four bedrooms, two baths, and a two-car garage — what I still think is plenty of room for our small family. But no, Bucky just had to spend some of that oil money that started burning a hole in his pocket the minute we got our first check. Every once in a while, I drive by the old house and long for the good old days.

The sweet little family road-trip vacations we used to take are now first-class flights to

Europe or weeklong cruises in luxury cabins on some swanky cruise ship. Sure, I enjoyed seeing the Eiffel Tower in Paris and the Parthenon in Greece the first time, but I don't want to keep going back. It dilutes some of the joy and wonder. Bucky, on the other hand, gets a kick out of saying, "Last time we went to Paris . . ." It doesn't matter what he says after that, since he's going for touting the fact that we keep going back.

Before we came into so much money, I could always find something to do. Now I find myself getting bored. With everything.

Bucky talked me into joining the Pinewood Junior League. I have to admit I was excited about it at first. Now that I look back on the three years I went to meetings, baked cookies for the Junior League bake sale, participated in their annual ball, and *did lunch* with some of the ladies close to my age, I know I don't fit in. They speak a language I'll never understand, no matter how much money we have or how much I try to be like them.

Don't get me wrong. Most of them are very sweet women who are often misunderstood by those who have never been part of their group. If they come across as snobby, it's more the result of being uncomfortable around people they don't know well than being uppity. Granted, there are some who are too big for their britches, but they're the minority — and unfortunately the ones who are the most vocal and visible in town.

It makes me sad that my old friends from *before money* have forgotten about me. Bucky says not to fret about it because they're not worth worrying over and they'll feel awkward in our world. I disagree, but I do know things will never be the same for me here in Pinewood. I've actually talked to Bucky about selling everything and moving to a place where we don't know anyone so we can start over. He laughs and says everything will get better if I learn to accept who I am now.

The only problem with that is I don't know who I am. Deep down, I think I'm still the bargain-hunting, thrift-store-shopping woman who doesn't mind diving to the bottom of a pile of clothes to find that one wonderful piece that will make me happy for years. I miss bragging about the deals I've snagged off the Walmart clearance racks.

I'm relieved when Bucky comes home from Bud's an hour later. "The place was dead. No one good was there."

I give him one of the looks he hates and leave him standing there. Our communication is at an all-time low because there's nothing left to talk about. I search the shelves for a book to read.

Bucky appears in the doorway and stares at me until I look up at him. "When ya goin' shopping for some new stuff to spruce this place up?"

I sigh. "I don't think we need anything new."

"But you love a good shopping trip. What's wrong with you, Marybeth?"

Now that folks are coming to our house for the next reunion, Bucky wants me to go out and get some brand-new pieces of furniture and shiny knickknacks. He's been working on me for weeks. Granted, I don't particularly care for the stuff we have in the living room, but the thought of putting that much energy and money into something that'll probably get ruined when one of Bucky's uncles gets carried away with one of his hunting stories and splashes sweet tea all over the place makes my stomach hurt.

"Everyone's seen all this stuff before. We don't want their tongues waggin' about how we've fallen onto hard times."

I don't really care what they think anymore, but I can't tell Bucky that. So I shake my head and counter. "A few colorful pillows, a new burnt-orange throw, and a couple of extra lamps will make it seem like a whole new place."

Bucky squints. "Are you sure?"

"Positive." I cross the room and pick my jacket up off the back of the sofa that I hate sitting in but can't bear to replace. That thing cost more than our entire living room set in our last house.

"Want me to go with you?"

"No." The word comes out a little too fast, so I hope he's not suspicious.

"Okay, that's fine. I'll leave the décor up to you." He snickers. "If I had my way, one of these rooms would have a whole wall of wild turkey, deer heads, and whatever else I can shoot."

You can take the redneck out of the woods . . .

30
SALLY

We still don't know the final decision on the condo yet, but Nate has called a couple of times to update me. I've stopped by to bring him some papers from our accountant, and every time I see him, I get that same belly-flopping feeling.

"You keep talking about that guy at the bank." Sally giggles. "All I hear is *Nate this* and *Nate that.*"

"He's very nice."

"Oh, I'm sure." She shoots me a teasing grin.

I glance away. "At any rate, I'm learning quite a bit about the mortgage business. I never really thought about what would happen if you didn't pay the mortgage."

"Speaking of which," Sara begins, "we'll need to buy out your half of this place."

I shake my head. "Don't worry about it."

"I'm not worried about it, but we want to do it. Justin has been saving, so we should

238

have enough to cover it."

"Only if it doesn't put a hardship on you."

She sighs. "As long as you and I have our business, I think we'll be fine. Since Justin can't go back to his job at the automotive shop yet, we might even put him to work doing some of the stuff you and I don't like to do."

I laugh. "It'll be fun to watch your manly guy making hair bows for little girls. He really was pretty good that one time."

Sara laughs. "I know, right? Just don't laugh too hard, or he might dig his heels in."

As annoying as Sara can be sometimes, I love the fact that she never tries to take advantage of me. And Justin seems to have the same values.

My cell phone rings, and Sara shoots me a look. When I glance at my phone and see Nate's name on the screen, my heart kicks up the pace. Sara laughs.

When I say, "Hi, Nate," she mouths it right back to mock me. I turn away. "What's up?"

"Um . . . would you mind coming in . . . um, to sign some papers?"

I glance over my shoulder and see that Sara is staring at me with a smirk on her face. "What time?"

"How about 11:30? After you sign, maybe we can go to lunch."

Now my heart is totally pounding out of control, so I clear my throat. "I think I can make it there at 11:30."

"Good. See you then."

After I click the Off button, I do my best to take on a nonchalant expression before looking at my sister. But she knows me too well and can read me like a book.

She lifts an eyebrow. "Where do you have to be at eleven thirty?"

"The bank. I have to sign some papers."

"And then what?"

I finally blow out a breath I just now realize I'm holding. "We're going to lunch."

She rolls her eyes. "Finally."

I shoot her a curious look. "Huh?"

"He's been calling you and acting like a lovesick puppy, and you're behaving in a way I've never seen you act before. It's about time the two of you had a date so we can get this romance rolling."

"It's not a romance." I quickly look away.

"Tell me that after you get back from lunch." She points to the bow I have a death grip on. "Do you want me to finish making that so you can get ready for your . . ." She smiles and giggles. "Your *business* appointment?"

"I'll finish it." I turn back toward the worktable and redo the bow with fresh ribbon. Once I'm finished, I push my chair back and stand. "I'll be back right after lunch to help finish the orders."

She gives me a knowing grin. "Don't rush. I've got everything covered here."

After I freshen up my makeup and change into something more appropriate for a bank meeting than the yoga pants and oversize T-shirt I've had on all morning, I leave for my appointment. To my surprise, Nate is standing by the door of his office.

"Hey, you're right on time." He gestures for me to follow. "Let's go get this paperwork signed so we can grab some lunch. Unfortunately, I only have an hour."

"We can do it some other time."

"That's what I'm hoping." He looks me in the eye as understanding flows between us. "We'll have lunch today and dinner on another day. How's that sound?"

"Sounds like —" Why can't I come up with something witty? My cheeks grow hot, and I fidget with the strap on my handbag. When I realize what I'm doing, I sigh. "Sounds good."

We sit down, and he passes a paper across the desk. "Just put your initials where you see the yellow highlights and sign on the line on the last page."

I flip through the pages and see my signature on the last line. "I've already signed this."

"So you did. Oops. My bad." He smiles as he takes the paper. "Ready for lunch?"

I nod. My appetite left the second he looked into my eyes. I've heard of people losing their appetite when they fall in love, but I barely know this guy. Is it possible? Nah, not this soon. Mama always said there's no such thing as love at first sight because it takes time to grow and develop into more than a physical attraction. But I sure do like how it feels to be with him.

As we walk through the lobby, it seems like everyone is watching us, but I don't care. He holds the door and leads me to his pickup truck — something I didn't expect. He opens my door and lets me in before running around to the driver's side.

He slides in behind the wheel and puts on his seat belt before turning to me with a smile. "You look baffled."

"I do?"

He nods. "Did I say something wrong?"

"No." I grin at him. "I'm a little surprised you drive a truck, but I like it."

He laughs. "Most people who know me from way back are shocked when they find out I work at a bank." He pauses as he starts the engine and backs out of the parking spot. "And people who meet me at the bank seem to expect me to drive something different."

I shrug. "Most of the men in my family drive pickup trucks, so I think it's great."

He pulls up to the stop sign at the edge of the parking lot and faces me. "I like you, Sally. There's something different — something unpretentious about you."

"What's there to pretend? If I try to be someone I'm not, anyone who gets to know me will eventually find out. I don't want anyone to think I'm a poser."

"That's what I'm talking about." He points to the Gold Post, my favorite po'boy shop in the area. "Do you mind eating fast food for lunch if I promise to take you somewhere nice when we go out on a real date?"

"Only if I can get the roast beef po'boy and fries smothered in gravy."

"You're definitely my kind of girl. That's what I like too."

A few minutes later, as we sit across the table from each other, chatting about everything under the sun while munching on our sandwiches with gravy dripping on our plates, I feel like there might be something beyond physical attraction. We click. Mama would say that's silly, but Nate and I have so much in common I feel like we've known each other for years.

The only bad thing is that we have to keep an eye on the time that is whizzing by at lightning speed. When he says we need to head on back, I feel a strange blend of sadness and anticipation welling in the pit of my belly.

We continue our conversation until he pulls into the bank parking lot. "I'll walk you to your car, but I need to get in there for my first afternoon appointment." As soon as I unlock my car door, he opens it and holds it for me as I get in. "I'll call you tonight."

All the way back home, I think about our conversation and how we've already established so many things we have in common. I love the fact that he's multifaceted and not just some stuffy banker who doesn't have interest in anything but counting money and selling mortgages.

As soon as I walk into the condo, I spot Sara pulling on her jacket. "I'm going to the hospital for a little while."

"Tell Justin I said hi." I shrug out of my own jacket and put it on a hook on the closet door before going to the kitchen for a glass of water.

"Sally!"

I spin around and see Sara's eyes widen as she stares at me in what appears to be disbelief. "What?"

"You're floating, and that can only mean one thing." Her expression softens as she chuckles. "You're totally smitten."

31
SHEILA

"I don't know how many times I have to tell you, I'll go on this cruise, but not until after the reunion." I'm getting more and more frustrated with George, who insists we take advantage of a last-minute special weeklong cruise. I appreciate the fact that he's thinking about romance, but there are times when other things are more important.

"That's when we're going — right after the reunion."

"But I'll need some time to get ready for it." I purse my lips and give him a look I know he hates. "If we go on this one, I won't be able to go to the reunion."

"C'mon, Sheila." He reaches for my hand, but I pull back. "It's the best deal out there. You can skip the reunion this one time, can't you?"

"Nope. I promised your mama I'd be there, and she's the last person I'd want to disappoint."

He winces, letting me know I hit him right in his weak spot. "Yeah, you're right. Mama's been good to us, and if you told her we'd go, we have to go."

"Besides, I'd much rather wait until it's a tad warmer so I can enjoy all the amenities on the ship." Then a thought hits me. "Will you be able to get your money back?"

George hesitates and then nods. "I haven't actually paid for it yet."

"Then you didn't actually book it?"

He shakes his head. "They told me they have a lot of empty cabins, so I figured there would be one available."

I start to laugh but catch myself. My husband clearly has a lot to learn about things like this.

George sighs and gives me the hint of a smile. "I appreciate the fact that you're worried about disappointing Mama. She's always adored you."

What I'm really worried about is missing some of the most important events in my children's lives. Justin gets to go home the day before the reunion, and I want to help out any way I can until he's back to normal. Sally is holding her breath, waiting to find out if the bank is going to let her buy that condo she's been so excited about. And

Sara has hinted that we might be getting another son-in-law soon. She says she's never seen Sally so smitten. That disturbs me though, because it's some guy I've never met and she's only known a short time. I want her to settle down, but I don't want her jumping into something that might break her heart.

"Sheila, honey?"

I turn around at the sound of my husband's voice. "What?"

"Let's pray together, like we used to."

I start to give him an excuse, like I have to start supper or call one of the girls, but the look on his face touches me to my core. George used to groan when I wanted to pray with him, so I lift my chin and nod. "Okay."

As we join hands and lower our heads, I feel a sense of peace . . . of togetherness washing over us. And it's not just George and me. There's no doubt in my mind that the Lord is right there with us, loving us and forgiving us for putting Him in the backseat.

I listen to my husband offer thanks to the Lord and awkwardly ask for forgiveness for not being the kind of husband I deserve. Tears spring to my eyes as he continues on about what a blessing I've been in his life. I don't doubt that he believes every single solitary word he's saying, but I know I don't deserve such kind and loving words.

As difficult as it is, I listen to him going on and on about how wonderful I am and what a wretch he is. He pauses, so I take the opportunity to say a few words about how blessed I am to have George because he's a loving husband and father, a good provider, and someone who has always come home at night — unlike the husbands of several of my friends.

We finally say, "Amen," and open our eyes to face each other. A smile tweaks the corners of his lips, so I smile back. Next thing I know, we're holding on to each other and sobbing. The emotions happen so fast they catch us both by surprise. This has been a long time coming.

It's like a tidal wave that grabs hold of us as we sniffle and laugh at the same time. I'm not sure exactly what has happened, but it's completely different from anything I've ever experienced, and it gives me a combination of relief, curiosity, and excitement about what the future holds.

When we finally let go of each other, George shakes his head and rubs the back of his neck. "What just happened?"

"I don't know." I take his hand in mine

and squeeze it. "But whatever it was, I'm sure it was long overdue."

"Something came over me, and I couldn't do anything about it." He blinks as he lets go of my hand. "I reckon God is happy we're both on the same page."

Spent from emotion, I jump back. "Hey, I have an idea."

"What's that?" As he watches me and waits for my answer, I look deeply into his eyes that now twinkle with the fun that attracted me to him many years ago.

"Why don't we have pancakes for supper tonight? We haven't done that in a long time."

"With blueberry syrup?"

The hopeful look on his face touches my heart. "Sure. And we have some pecans in the freezer."

"What are we waiting for?" He takes me by the hand and tugs me toward the kitchen.

Something I learned early in our marriage was that he likes to help in the kitchen, but he's clueless and tends to get underfoot if I don't assign him a specific task. So I pour twice as many pecans as we'll need into a bowl, place it on the counter in a spot that isn't in my way, and give him instructions on how to break the nuts into small pieces.

As he pops a nut into his mouth before

chopping the next one, I smile. Everything remains the same on the surface, but deep down, past the facade, we both know everything has changed. In fact, we are now more like we were when we first got married than all the years in between. At first, after the girls moved out, I wasn't sure how George and I would get along, and being totally honest, we didn't. It's been a little more than a couple of years now, and we're just starting to reignite that spark.

"Is that enough?" He lifts the clear bowl for me to see.

"How many do you have left?"

He picks up a handful, puts them in his mouth, and then shows me the empty bowl. I laugh.

Fifteen minutes later, we're sitting at the table with a huge stack of pancakes between us. His eyes twinkle as he points to them. "That's mine. Where's yours?"

Throughout our delicious pancake dinner, we talk about the cruise. He tilts his head to one side and gives me the look that has always melted me from the inside out. "I think a winter cruise would be romantic."

"If we go in the late spring, I'll be able to enjoy the sun," I argue.

"But —"

I hold up my hand. "This is our first

cruise, George. I really want to prepare for it so we can get the most out of it." Then I make the pouty face that I know he can't resist. "Please."

He inhales deeply as he closes his eyes, and then he looks me in the eye. "Okay, Sheila, if that's what you really want, I'm fine with going in the spring."

"That means we can give each other new cruise stuff for Christmas."

"Like what?"

I stand and pick up the plates to carry them to the sink. "We'll both need whole new wardrobes, and of course I'll want to lose a few pounds first so I can fit into the cute vacation clothes they're getting in at La Chic."

He makes a face. "So that's why you want to wait until spring?"

I laugh and nod. "One of the many reasons."

"And that's one of the reasons I'll never understand women." He rolls up his sleeves and loads the dishwasher with plates, glasses, and flatware while I start scrubbing the pans.

"It's good that you don't fully understand us. We like to keep you guessing." I nod toward the living room. "I'll finish cleaning up. Why don't you go get comfortable, and

252

I'll join you in a few minutes?"

It takes me all of five minutes to get the pans washed, dried, and put away. When I step into the living room, George is reclining in his La-Z-Boy chair with the TV remote in his hand, his chin dropped to his chest, and a soft snore wafting through the room. I smile as I gently take the remote, put it on the table beside him, and cover him with a soft throw that I keep in the living room. This isn't the first, and I'm sure it won't be the last, time he'll sleep half the night in his chair. I don't have the heart to wake him, even though he'll probably complain about it in the morning.

I'm on my way back to our room to put on my nightgown when the landline rings. I rush back to the bedroom to answer it and see on the caller ID that it's Sally.

"I hope I didn't wake anyone up."

"No, I haven't gone to bed yet, and your father can't hear high-pitched sounds anymore, so you're good." I glance at the clock and see that it's only 8:07. "What's up?"

"How do you know when you're in love?" Before I have a chance to get past the surprise of her question and answer her, she continues. "I mean, how do I know that it's love and not just some silly infatuation just because he's cute and sweet and loves the Lord?"

32
SALLY

I had hoped Mama would surprise me when I told her about Nate and express joy that I'd found someone wonderful and maybe even ask to meet him. But no, she said it's too early to have the feelings I have and that I need to wait for a while.

I'm not sure if Sara understands what I see in Nate, but then again, she's only met him once. I had to pick up the disclosure statement from the bank, so I brought her with me, hoping she could get to know him — at least a little bit. Unfortunately, he was busy with clients, so he didn't have a chance to chat.

"He seems a bit stuffy," Sara says. "I agree with Mama. You need to give it some time before you say you're in love."

I pull my head back and lift my eyebrow as I wag a finger in front of her face. She hates that. "Wait just a minute there, sis. It's not like you dated Justin for years and years before you eloped."

She bobs her head right back at me. "But don't forget, I've known him most of my life."

I want to tell her she never really knew him until they got married, but I'm not in the mood for an argument. What I really want to do is play some happy music and dance because I have a date with Nate tomorrow night.

My silence must have worried her because she closes the distance between us and puts her hand on my shoulder. "I'm sorry, Sally. I know what it's like to be crazy about someone and have other people try to ruin it for you."

"No one can ruin what I'm feeling. You might be right, since I've never dated a guy more than a few times. This might not be love, but I definitely feel something I've never felt before."

She grins. "Or maybe it is love. Who am I to say it's not?"

That's my Sara. I give her a big grin. "Okay, so what should I wear?"

She taps her index finger on her chin. "Where are y'all going?"

"He says we can go anywhere I want."

Sara's face lights up. "Why don't you pick the Purple Parrot?"

I shrug. "I'm more in the mood for Mack's."

"Seriously?" She rolls her eyes. "You just don't want to dress up, do you?"

"I'll dress a little nicer." An idea pops into my head. "Speaking of dressing for a date, do you want to help me pick out something to wear?"

"You have enough new clothes in your closet to start your own boutique. Why do you need help?" Before I have a chance to respond, she's on her way to my room and heads straight for the closet.

"How about this?" She pulls out the ecru sweater and holds it up.

I shake my head. "I've already worn that twice."

A look of amusement washes over her as she makes a couple more attempts. Finally, she replaces the last outfit, turns to me, and holds out her arms. "Why don't we go get you a completely new outfit so there's no chance of Nate ever seeing you in the same thing twice?"

I smile and gesture toward the door. Fifteen minutes later, we're walking into La Chic. Shay glances up from the counter, and when she sees that it's us, a humongous smile spreads across her face. As she comes around to greet us and give us one of the

257

hugs that I've come to count on, she says, "It's great to see you ladies. Did you come to shop, or are you just stopping by to say hey?"

"Both, actually." I turn to Sara, who nods before I look back at Shay. Before I can open my mouth, Sara speaks up.

"She has a big date, so we need to get her something nice." Sara gives me a smirk. "Something *date-worthy*." Her emphasis on date-worthy makes me cringe.

"You should have something date-worthy," Shay says.

Before I have a chance to say a word, Sara speaks up again. "Something no one has seen her in yet."

Shay does her best to hide her amusement, but I know she's laughing deep down. I cut a glance of annoyance toward my sister, but she pretends to ignore me.

"We got a few new things in over the past several days." Shay leads us to a corner that features a mannequin wearing the cutest jeggings, tunic, and infinity scarf. "We have shoes and boots to go with most of the outfits too. Why don't the two of you peruse the racks? I'll start you a fitting room with whatever you pick out."

Sara has her eye on what the mannequin is wearing. "Hey, Sally, how about this?"

I nod. "Yeah, I like it."

Shay comes up from behind. "We also have some ankle boots that are perfect for that outfit." She looks at the tag on the tunic the mannequin is wearing. "This one's your size, so let me take it off her. Find a couple more you like and go on back to the second fitting room."

I'm amazed by how happy a new outfit makes me feel. Ever since Shay and Puddin' bought this place, it's like everyone in Pinewood cares about what they wear. You'd think that with this one small shop dressing everyone in town, people would all be wearing the same outfits, but that's not the case. They only get a few pieces in each style, and they change everything out several times per season.

When I walk out of the fitting room, Puddin' has joined Shay and my sister. Everyone's eyes open wide, and they smile, letting me know they approve. Sara gives me a thumbs-up. "That's what I'm talkin' about."

Puddin' walks toward me and turns me around as she looks me over. "Have you ever thought about being a model? This outfit looks amazing on you."

I let out a nervous giggle. I love how I feel in these clothes, but I'm not used to people fussing over me like this. It's one thing to get attention because I'm an identical twin, but to be noticed individually is a new experience for me. The only other time I've felt this way was my last visit to La Chic, which is one of the reasons I get warm and fuzzy feelings when I come in here.

"No surprise, they all look great on you." Puddin' follows me back to the fitting room. "Which one are you getting for your hot date?"

"Hot date?" I let out a nervous laugh. "We're just going out to dinner."

"Oh, sweetie, this is just the beginning. If he still likes you after dinner, he'll ask you out for another date, and then another."

Shay joins us. "And if *she* likes *him* after dinner, *she* just might ask *him* out for the second date."

Puddin' shakes her head. "True, but I'm still having a hard time wrapping my mind around that concept. I reckon I'm sort of old-fashioned."

"Yes, you most certainly are," Shay agrees. "And that's one of the things we love most about you."

Puddin' casts a pretend look of annoyance to her sister-in-law before turning back to me. "So which one's it gonna be?"

I look everything over and try to pick one that stands out the most. The problem is that I like every single thing I tried on. "I don't know."

"Then get all of 'em." The sound of Sara's voice gets our attention.

"I don't exactly need a new wardrobe." I pause and look her over. "You're the one —" I cut myself off before I trigger another hormonal crying jag.

"Well . . ." When she gives me one of her sarcastic expressions and head bobs, I let out a sigh of relief. "After this baby is born, I plan to talk you out of some of the things in your closet, and then I'm going to come in here and fill in what I still need."

Puddin' reminds me of the family discount. "If you're worried about the cost, that'll make a huge difference."

Sara and I exchange a glance. Most of the members of our family have no idea how much money we're making, and we're fine with that.

The one person who does know is Shay. She smiles and winks but doesn't say anything.

"In that case, I suppose I can get a few more items." I look over at what I just tried on and zero in on a couple of my favorites.

Sara steps up. "I can't wait until after the baby comes so I can get some cute clothes."

"You don't have to wait till then to get

261

some cute clothes. We just ordered some darlin' maternity coordinates. They're nothin' like the lacy tents I used to wear when I was preggers."

"I hate that word." Shay shudders.

Puddin' laughs. "I know you do, which is why I like to say it. Your reaction is funny."

I glance at Shay, who rolls her eyes and grins. "The abuse I take —" She and Puddin' exchange a look that is more sisterly than sister-in-lawly.

Sara shrugs. "Since I work at home, I don't need a bunch of new maternity stuff. I can just wear sweatpants and Justin's T-shirts."

"No, honey. You need some cute clothes so you don't feel like a whale." Puddin' points to Sara's belly. "Girls these days like to show off the bump."

Puddin' has never been known for filtering what's on her mind, so I'm surprised she doesn't insult Sara for looking like she just stepped out of a Dumpster. Instead, she gestures toward the cash register. "If you're interested in any of the jewelry in the case, everything on the right-hand side is seventy-five percent off."

Now, that's a serious discount. I walk over and look at all the necklaces, earrings, and bracelets and see that it's going to be just as difficult to narrow down my selection with accessories as it was with the clothes.

Sara is right there beside me. She nudges me and whispers, "Why don't you get half of the clearance side, and I'll get the other half? We can share."

I nod before looking back at Puddin'. "We'll take all of it. Just split the cost in half, and Sara will pay the other half."

Puddin' looks shocked, and Shay laughs. "This guy you're dating must be pretty special. Anyone I know?"

"Nate Hawthorne from the bank in Hattiesburg." I pause.

Shay's smile quickly fades. "Nate Hawthorne?" She clears her throat. "I didn't realize you were dating him. You and I need to talk."

33
CORALEE

Ever since Kyle told me about how he slipped into a phase of doing drugs with his friend, I've looked at him differently. Granted, he doesn't do them now, and hasn't in a very long time, but still . . .

"It's been years." His voice sounds desperate. "I wish I hadn't told you."

"No, I'm glad you did." In a way, I regret his telling me, but deep down I know it's best for stuff like that to come out now rather than later.

He scrunches up his face. "Do you still like me?"

I let out a nervous laugh. "Of course I do."

"I wasn't sure."

"Do you ever have the desire to take anything now?" I pause and study his face for any signs I might have missed. "I mean, are you tempted when you're with people who do that stuff?"

He laughs. "First of all, I try to stay away

from those situations, but no, I'm not tempted." His expression becomes more solemn. "When you watch a friend go through some seriously bad stuff because of drugs, it makes you stop and think." He closes his eyes and then looks directly at me. "That could have been me."

"Well, it wasn't, so let's change the subject." I know deep down that even if we talk about unicorns and butterflies and strawberry parfaits, I'll be thinking about what he just told me.

"So, what are your plans for Thanksgiving?" he asks.

I shrug. "My family is having their reunion during Thanksgiving weekend, so I'll go there."

"That sounds like a blast."

"It is. Sometimes. We always have a ton of food, and it's fun to see some of my cousins that I only see at these things." I chuckle. "And then one crazy thing always happens, like at the last one when a couple of my teenage cousins blew up the old barn."

Kyle's eyebrows shoot up. "Sounds dangerous. I hope no one was hurt."

"Someone was hurt but not bad. I think it hurt the guys who did it more, since they had to go to court." I look around and then back at Kyle. "How about you? Are you going home to your parents' house?"

"I normally go back home, but my parents are going on a cruise this year." He sighs. "I'll probably sleep in and try to find a restaurant that has a decent buffet."

Now I'm feeling guilty. "Would you like to join me and go to my family reunion?"

"I wouldn't want to impose." The hopeful look on his face contradicts his words.

"Trust me, you won't be imposing. You'll get a lot of stares, and some of my more aggressive aunts and cousins are likely to grill you with questions, but if you think you can put up with that, you're welcome to come."

He laughs. "Sounds like my family." He takes my hand in his, kisses the back of it, and looks me squarely in the eye. "I would love to go to your reunion with you."

I was sort of hoping he'd say no, but I'm going to try to make the most of his acceptance. "A bunch of 'em will be camping out at my dad's cousin's mansion, but I don't think I'll do that."

"Why are they doing that?"

I shrug. "Who knows? I'm thinking it's so they can show off how big their house is. They have enough rooms for everyone, and I'm talking about a lot of people."

"Is your family rich?" He clears his throat and grimaces. "That came out wrong. What

I meant to say was —"

I laugh. "Some people in my family are rich, but it's not like they had to do anything for it. After my grandparents started giving out land, some of them let the oil companies drill."

"And they obviously struck oil." Kyle shakes his head. "Some people are just lucky." Then he tilts his head, scrunches his forehead, and gives me a half smile. "Did your parents get some of that land?"

"They did, but Daddy says he doesn't want the ugly oil rigs on his property, even though they're in plain sight from my aunts and uncles who have them."

"That's interesting. So what is your dad doing with the land?"

I shrug. "He's talking about farming, but he and Mama still live in town, so I'm not sure what they'll wind up doing."

"Will you get some of that land?"

His question annoys me, pretty much like everything he says and does lately. "Why do you want to know?"

"Just curious."

"I have no idea, and quite frankly I don't care." My feelings for Kyle have already started fading, and this conversation is adding fuel. In fact, all I want to do right now is get away from him so I can think. "I need to go home now."

"Want to do something later?"

I shake my head. "Not tonight."

He gives me a look of concern. "Are you mad at me?"

"Not really. I'm just tired." I don't want to tell him I'm tired of him. Tired of this conversation. Tired of being unsure of what I want. Maybe leaving that out is lying by omission, but I don't have the energy to explain anything. Besides, I have way more thinking to do now.

"Okay, then. I guess I'll see you tomorrow?"

"Sure."

After I'm by myself, I let out a deep sigh. This is one of those times I wish I had a sister. I'm the youngest one in the family, and the spacing between all of us is such that I'm pretty sure I wasn't planned. My three older brothers are married and busy with their own lives, and as much as I like their wives, I wouldn't even think about turning to one of them for advice.

Instead of going straight home when I get to Pinewood, I decide to drive around town. As I turn onto Main Street, I see Puddin' standing at the window of La Chic. Maybe she or Shay will have time to chat. They're both pretty cool.

There are a couple of empty parking spots on the side street, so I don't have to walk far. Puddin' is still by the window, so she grins when she spots me coming up the street.

"Hey there, Coralee." She looks me up and down. "Don't you look cute? I've always thought you'd be darlin' if you only dressed a little better, and look at you. You're cuter'n I ever even imagined."

Shay laughs as she approaches. "I think you're embarrassing the poor girl. Come on in, Coralee. What can we do for you? Are you looking for another outfit?"

"No, I'm looking for something else." I clear my throat and lick my lips. "Actually, I need some advice."

"That's something we have in abundance." Puddin' nudges Shay in the side. "Right, Shay?"

"We do, but I'm not sure it's always good." Shay turns to face me and gives me her full attention. "What's going on?"

34
SALLY

I'm stunned. If anyone but Shay had told me what she did about Nate, I wouldn't have believed it. But the fact that Shay has always been such a reliable source of information makes me think there's a serious problem here.

Apparently, Nate has quite a history in the romance department, and it's not good. He's been engaged three times, and in each case, he's either broken it off at the last minute or simply not shown up for the wedding.

When Shay told me that, I tried to laugh it off and pretend I was just trying to have a good time and never expected more from the relationship than that. But deep down, I'm hurt because I've been thinking there might be something special between us. No other guy has had me thinking about him all my waking hours. The guys I've gone out with before wound up being friends for a while until they met other girls. Now I get the whole relationship thing.

When I see something interesting or hear something funny, I can't wait to tell him. I should have known it's too good to be true. It really hurts to think that what we have isn't as special as I thought.

"Maybe it'll be different with you," Sara says.

I lean my head toward her and give her a look she hates. "You're kidding, right? Mama always said a leopard doesn't change its spots."

"No, I'm not kidding. Maybe those other girls weren't as sweet or as pretty as you."

"You and I both know guys don't fall in love with a girl just because she's sweet and pretty."

Sara smiles at me like our mother used to when I was a teenager. "But those other girls probably weren't as committed to their faith as you are."

"I don't even know how committed to his faith he is."

"That's a pretty important conversation y'all need to have before you get serious."

"Did you talk about it with Justin before y'all eloped?"

"Of course we did, silly." Sara shakes her head. "I wasn't about to let myself fall in love with a guy and commit to being with him for the rest of my life unless he felt the same way about the Lord that I do."

"Oh." That's something I didn't know, but I believe her.

"Maybe if you talk about it . . ." Sara's voice trails off. "But you might not want to bring up his failed engagements. You don't want to betray Shay's confidence."

"She didn't tell me in confidence, but I can ask her if she minds my discussing it with him."

"Then what are you waiting for? If Shay says it's all right, you and I both know that's exactly what you should do."

I ponder that for a moment before nodding. "I'll do it, but I have to figure out how to bring it up."

"Why don't you just say something like 'Have you ever been in a serious relationship before?' That gives him a chance to tell you what happened without backing him into a corner."

I smile at my sister. "Ya know, Sara, you're smarter than I ever realized."

"People always think you're the smart one, but that's just because I don't talk as much as you do."

I plant my fist on my hip and give her one of those eye-popping looks. "Seriously?"

She laughs. "I think we're both smart, but you have more to say."

We both laugh. "Okay, it's settled. I'll talk to him."

"Tonight?" She lifts her eyebrows as she waits for my answer.

"Yes, tonight."

She places her hand on my shoulder and puts her face inches from mine. "Don't chicken out."

"Okay, okay. I'll talk to him as soon as we finish eating."

"Why don't you just get the question out of the way early in the date?"

"Why?"

Sara shakes her head. "Because I know you, and you'll have a miserable time until it's all out in the open."

"Yeah, you're right."

She points toward my room. "Now go start getting ready. I don't want to have to entertain him while you put on your lipstick."

I take a shower and get dressed in the outfit I've picked out for tonight. Then I apply some makeup and stand back and take a long look at myself in the full-length mirror. Overall, I'm happy with my reflection, but the one thing I can't cover up is the fact that I couldn't sleep last night.

Concealer took care of the dark circles, but the bags and redness are still there.

When I walk out to the living room, I'm surprised to see Nate sitting there talking to my sister. She glances up and smiles. "Why don't I get y'all something to drink before you leave for Mack's? How about some ginger ale?"

I blink at her and then turn to Nate. He nods. "Yeah, ginger ale sounds good." Then he looks back at me. "There's something we need to talk about first."

As soon as Sara leaves us alone, Nate takes my hand. "Shay called me this afternoon and said she told you about my past." He purses his lips and shakes his head. "I'm glad she did that because I want to start fresh with you."

I gulp. This is totally unexpected, and I have no idea what to say.

He takes a deep breath, closes his eyes for a few seconds, and then looks directly at me. "I've liked a lot of girls in the past, but I'm not so sure I ever really understood what love was all about."

"But you got engaged, right?" I pause and look him in the eye. "You must have thought you loved them."

He shrugs. "Maybe, but I think it was more that after dating them for a while, I thought that was the next step I was supposed to take."

Now that he's explaining, I have to ask what's on my mind. "I can understand once, but three times?"

"I know that seems like a lot, but there's a reason for all of them."

I lean back and fold my arms. "So tell me about it. I'm all ears."

Sara comes out of the kitchen with two glasses of ginger ale on ice. "Here ya go. I'll be in my room if you need me."

After she leaves, Nate picks up his glass, takes a sip, and puts it down. "The first time I got engaged, it was to the girl I started dating our junior year in high school. Her daddy always liked me, and he assumed we'd get married one of these days. We'd just gotten back from having dinner with her folks, when she said she wanted to talk about our future. I was so young then I didn't know what to say when she asked if I was serious about her."

"You obviously told her you were."

He nods. "I did but only because I was afraid she'd start crying — something she did quite a bit when she didn't get her way. As soon as I said I was serious, she squealed and ran inside to tell her parents we were about to get engaged. Her parents came out

275

and congratulated us, and next thing I knew, I was caught up in a whirlwind of insanity."

I can see how that might happen. "Was it hard to break up with her?"

He grimaces. "I didn't exactly break up with her. I went to the church for the wedding, but as soon as I saw everyone sitting there waiting, I turned around and drove to Biloxi."

"That's terrible. I can only imagine how upset she was."

"Yeah, she was upset, but I don't think she was as mad as her daddy. I actually feared for my life — at least until she finally met someone else in college."

"How old were you?"

"That was another problem. I was only twenty." He shrugs. "I had no idea what I was going to do with my life, other than the fact that her daddy wanted me to work for him in the tractor business."

"Okay, that's one situation. How about the other two?"

"The second one was completely different, and so was the third."

"Okay, so tell me about them, one at a time." I lift my eyebrows to encourage him to continue.

"The second one was pretty aggressive.

She always called herself assertive, but in all honesty, she took it a step too far. We were sitting around a table with a bunch of her friends, when she stood up and turned to me with this big old smile on her face. I wasn't sure what was going on, until she told me it was time for us to cement our relationship and get engaged."

"That's awkward," I admit. "Did you have any idea she might do something like that?"

"No. She totally blindsided me."

We sit in silence as I process everything. I actually detect some similarities between the first two engagements. "How about the third one?"

He sighs. "She was super sweet, and I truly thought I was in love. Everything was going just fine, until I proposed —"

"So it was actually your idea this time?"

"Yes. But within days of my proposal, she started getting snarky and embarrassing me in front of my friends and family. She put me down constantly, until I couldn't take it anymore."

"Who broke things off?" I ask.

"I did. I told her she wasn't the girl I thought she was. She didn't sound too surprised, because she came right back at me and said that was the problem. She wasn't a girl, but I was still a boy, and she wanted a real man."

"Wow. Her fangs really did come out, didn't they?"

"They sure did." He takes my hand in his and grows silent as he stares at the floor. Then he looks directly back at me. "Thanks for being such a good listener. I suspect you have some questions, so go ahead and ask."

"The first one makes sense because you were so young. But the second one . . . why didn't you tell the one who proposed to you that you needed to talk to her alone before answering her in front of her friends?"

"I know now that's what I should have done." He shrugs. "I was so caught off guard I wasn't thinking straight."

"And the third one . . . How long did y'all date before you got engaged?"

"About six months."

I think about how my sister dated Justin for just a couple of weeks, and they seem perfectly suited for each other. But she's right. They've known each other for years, and they had that talk about faith.

He clears his throat as he looks down. "I know that's not long, but I thought I knew her well enough, and she seemed perfect in a lot of ways."

"Did you love her?"

"I thought I did, but now I realize it was

278

something else." He raises his gaze to mine. "More fascination than anything. She always did things to surprise me, like blindfold me and drive me to a park where she had a picnic set up."

"I can see how you might get caught up in the excitement."

"So . . ." He forces a smile. "I met Shay through her brother who delivers packages to the bank. Digger and I became fishing buddies, and one day when he dropped off some stuff around noon, we decided to go for lunch. Shay stopped by, and then she and I became friends."

"Were you and Shay . . ." I'm not sure how to ask, so I start over. I know he's quite a bit younger than Shay, but that doesn't matter to some people. "Did you ever —"

"If you're trying to ask if Shay and I were ever romantically involved, the answer is no. I like her a lot, but we're more friends than anything. She helped me through the difficult time after Amy and I split up."

"Does Shay know all the details of your three engagements?"

He shakes his head. "Only what I told her. She knows I've been engaged three times, though, which is why she said she told you."

I'm much more confident now, but I'm not sure what to say next. He picks up his ginger ale and stands.

He reaches for my hand. "Now that you know about my sordid past, do you still want to go out with me?"

35

BRETT

I don't care what Mama and Daddy say, I'm not spending the whole weekend at Julius's house. Being there for the food is one thing, but overnight? That can only spell trouble. And I can't believe Mama doesn't get that. The thought that she might be testing me has crossed my mind.

Daddy has always been pretty clueless about what us kids are going through, even though he spends time with us. He's more our fun person, but Mama's always there for everything else. She always has a lot of things to say about everything, and one of the things she has said over and over is, "Don't put yourself in front of trouble, or it will take you down."

She's right. So why would she put me in the position of having to deal with Julius for the whole weekend?

For some reason I don't understand, Mama's worried about our relationship with

Daddy's family. Sure, Grandpa Jay and Granny Marge are cool, but there aren't many people my age, and I get bored around the rest of them. It's like all they do is talk about jobs and houses and who has what.

"Hey, Brett, can you give me a hand with something?" Daddy's standing in the door-way grinning at me, looking like he's got something up his sleeve.

"What?"

He turns and motions for me to follow him. "Come on. You'll see."

I put down the book I've been hiding behind and slide into my sneakers. I've started for the door before I decide to tie my shoelaces because Mama will fuss at me if she sees me walking around with the laces flopping around. If it were up to me, I'd take the laces out because it's such a hassle to tie and untie them every single time I put them on and take them off. But I don't want her accusing me of being lazy.

The back door slams, letting me know Daddy went out to the backyard. So I head in that direction. When I get there, I see him standing beside a big wooden box without a top, a bunch of metal poles, and some wheels.

"Well?" He holds out his hand. "What do you think?"

I walk around the pile of stuff and try to figure out what he's doing with all this junk. "What is it?"

"It's a boxcar. At least it will be when we finish with it. I thought you and I could build it together." He's rubbing his hands together, looking, as Mama calls it, *pleased as punch.*

"Why?"

His expression changes from happy to confused. "It's a father-son project. I thought you'd enjoy it."

I walk around the box again and pick up a couple of the pieces to look at them more closely. "Doesn't look like much of anything to me."

"Not yet, it doesn't." He picks up a rod and holds it above his head. "I'm thinking this thing'll make a good roll bar."

Sounds dangerous if it needs a roll bar, but I don't want to totally diss Daddy, since he's trying so hard. "So where do we start?"

"Well . . ." He picks up the wooden box and turns it over like he's inspecting it. "Some of the guys at work gave me some tips. One of 'em said he'd even give me some plans and drawings he used when his kids were teenagers."

I don't know how to tell Daddy this, but guys my age aren't into boxcars. They're pretty old-school, but that's something else I don't want to say. He's been having issues with losing his hair lately, and I don't want to make it worse. When Mama teased him about male-patterned baldness, he started spending more time in front of the mirror, inspecting his hairline.

"What are we supposed to do with it after we finish building it?" I sure can't imagine myself ever riding one of these things.

"Oh, that's another thing." His face widens into a big ol' honkin' grin. "I've entered you in the Annual Pinewood Boxcar Race that's comin' up on December first."

This is *so* not good. I'm already considered somewhat of a dork at school, even though I'm on the football team, and this is the very thing that'll seal my reputation for good.

His grin widens. "Come see the other stuff I got. I figured if you're gonna race a boxcar, you need a cool-looking helmet to go with it."

I follow him to the garage, where he pulls a black helmet with fluorescent lime-colored flame decals on the side out of a bag, followed by cans of paint with matching lids. "They won't be able to miss you when you come down the hill in this."

I let out a low groan. Sounds like my biggest nightmare.

"I figure if you wear black pants and a black jacket, you'll be someone to reckon with." He chuckles like we're in on some sort of joke. "We can call you *The Intimidator.*"

I don't want to be called *The Intimidator.* I don't want to wear black pants and a black jacket. I don't want to wear a tacky helmet and drive a boxcar. I look at him and open my mouth, but the hopeful look on his face stops me from saying what's on my mind.

Daddy expects me to help build this thing, and I've never been all that good at stuff like this. So maybe there's hope we won't have it ready in time for the race.

"Ready to get started?" He looks so happy, and I can tell he can't wait to start working on it.

I shrug. "Sure. I guess."

"Worried you won't do a good job?" He gives me a playful punch in the shoulder. "Is that it?"

Actually, I'm worried either way — that I'll do a great job and have to drive this thing or do a terrible job . . . and have to drive this thing. "Maybe."

"C'mon, son. I've done this before, so you have nothing to worry about. We'll have this thing running like a fine-tuned race car in

285

no time."

I shudder with dread. The very thought of crawling into that box in public makes me want to run away from home.

"I bet Bucky's never built one of these things before."

Bucky is Julius's daddy, and this is one time I envy Julius. "Prob'ly not."

"Knowing him, he'll try anyway." Daddy laughs. "That should be a hoot. It'll probably fall apart before it leaves the starting line." He picks up his toolbox and gives me a satisfied look. "But I doubt he'll bother because Julius has his own real car. Where's the fun in that, right?"

Oh, I can think of where the fun in having my own car would be. I'd be able to cruise around town, check out some of the girls who don't give me the time of day now, and maybe even get a date with one of them.

"Speaking of Bucky and Julius, they're stopping by in a few minutes." Daddy gives me a long grin. "I figure it's my turn to brag about something."

Please tell me it isn't so. "Why do they want to come over?"

Daddy's smile turns sheepish. "Because I asked them to, and I might have told them I have something that'll blow their minds."

I'm pretty sure this pile of wood and metal

won't blow their minds, but I'll let Daddy find out for himself. I don't want to be the one to disappoint him. If things go like I think they might, they'll let him know how lame his idea is, and he'll give up on the boxcar dream before they leave. Granted, I'll have to be there for him when he beats himself up and wonders what he'd been thinking. But that's a whole lot better than being the one to upset him. I let out a sigh of relief.

Almost as if it were planned, Mama sticks her head out the back door and hollers, "Digger, you and Brett have company."

Daddy waves his hand over his head. "Send 'em on out. I want to show them something."

As Bucky and Julius walk toward us, a sense of dread floods me. I brace myself for the humiliation from Julius's smirks and comments.

Bucky makes a face and points to the pile. "What on earth is that?"

Daddy folds his arms over his chest, raises his head, and gives them a great big ol' smile. "That's about to be a boxcar that me and Brett are gonna make. Together." Daddy looks at me. "Right, son?"

"A what?" Bucky walks around the pile while I cringe. I can't bring myself to look at Julius, who must be sneering by now.

"A boxcar. I've entered Brett in the Annual Pinewood Boxcar Race."

I want to run inside the house and hide, but I can't bring myself to hurt Daddy's feelings. He's been by my side through everything, no matter how bad it was, although he's never really understood. But at least he's been there.

Bucky snickers. "I wouldn't even know where to begin."

"One of the guys from work has some plans," Daddy says. "I think it'll be fun."

"It's stupid." Bucky shakes his head. He looks over at Julius and gives him a look that makes me feel terrible for Daddy. But I just stand there and keep my mouth shut.

Before Daddy can defend himself, Julius steps toward the pile, bends over, and picks up one of the wheels. "I think it's cool." He turns to his dad. "Dad, I want to build one of those things and be in that race."

36

SALLY

Dinner at Mack's was fun, but I had a hard time getting past knowing how many times Nate has been engaged. Now I'm second-guessing myself and wondering about my judgment of men.

Shortly after high school, I liked a guy and thought there might be a future for us, but my interest waned when I realized he wasn't as manly as my dad. I've tried to find something to like about different men, but none of them measured up. And there's Tom. I had the biggest crush on him until he started getting on my nerves because he kept trying to be the man he thought I wanted, when all I really wanted was to find out who he was. It got to where I couldn't stand to be around him or even see his number on my caller ID.

After pouring my coffee, I walk into the workroom. Sara looks up and shakes her head.

"You look miserable." She pauses. "Was your date really awful?"

"No, it was actually quite fun."

"But — ?"

"I can't get past the fact that he's been engaged so many times."

She makes a sympathetic face. "Yeah, I can see that being a problem."

I shake my head and glance down before looking back up at her. "But it's something I need to work through."

"Remember that no one is perfect. Everyone has something messy in their past." Sara points to the shiny silver ribbon. "We just got slammed with holiday orders, so let's see how much metallic ribbon we'll need to order."

I appreciate the fact that Sara is willing to change the subject, even though I know she's dying to hear more about last night. We fill most of the orders before she finally stands up, stretches, and walks toward the door. "I'll go make us some lunch. Do you want soup and a sandwich or leftover pizza?"

Until she got pregnant, we ate a lot of salads, but those don't satisfy her anymore. Both Justin and I have put on a few pounds right along with her.

"Either is fine." I grin up at her. "Surprise me."

"Okeydokey. Give me a few minutes and I'll have lunch on the table."

After she leaves the workroom, I study the orders that have come in since we started. We're busy year-round, but if this year is anything like it's been since we started, the orders will grow exponentially until about a week before Christmas. Then our sales will drop like a bomb. The first time that happened, we freaked out, but orders started right back up the day after Christmas.

I jot down some of the things that I think we need and bring the list into the kitchen, where my sister has been working hard to fill the table with food. "Pizza, sandwiches, *and* soup?" I sit down at my normal place. "Girl, we're all gonna be fat if you keep this up."

"I can't help it." She lifts a slice of pizza off the serving plate and puts it beside the sandwich. "I'm always hungry. This baby is taking a lot out of me."

As we eat, we chat about the orders, and she agrees with me on what we need. "So, when are you planning to go see Justin?"

She lifts her soupspoon and sighs. "Around two. I wanted to go earlier, but they told me he doesn't work as hard when

I'm there too much."

"I wonder why that is."

She shrugs. "Apparently, I'm a distraction. I sure will be glad when he's able to come home."

"It won't be too long." I know she's worried sick about her husband, and to be honest, I'm concerned too. They've been married less than a year, and now she might be looking at a lifetime of caring for an injured husband as well as a small child. He's doing quite a bit better, but we're still not sure if he'll ever be back to his old strong self.

"Have you heard anything about your new condo?" She shoves the pizza crust into her mouth and chews. She never used to eat the crust, but now she doesn't leave even a crumb on her plate.

"Nate says Jeanine's starting to dig her heels in."

She gives me a questioning look. "Again?"

"Afraid so. She's acting awfully skittish."

"I wonder why." Sara frowns. "It seems like she'd be happy to get rid of the place, since she can't afford it."

"Apparently, this is pretty common behavior for someone who is about to be foreclosed on. He probably shouldn't have told me this, but she had an offer before me that would have brought her a little extra cash, and she turned it down."

"That doesn't make sense."

"I think she's acting on emotion. At any rate, I'm concerned it might fall through."

"When will you know for sure?" Sara asks.

"At the closing. Nate says he's seen deals fall through all the way up to the point when it's time to sign the papers."

"Wow." Sara takes another bite and shakes her head as she chews. "That's nerve-racking."

"Tell me about it." I stand and carry my plate to the sink. "Want me to go to the rehab place with you? I'll wait in the lobby after I say hi to Justin."

"You don't mind doing that?"

"Of course not. I want you to know I'll be here for you, no matter what." As soon as those words leave my mouth, I regret saying them, knowing Sara is an emotional wreck. I look up at her and see the tears glistening in her eyes.

She wipes her face with the back of her hand. "Sorry about that. I can't control the tears."

"I understand. Now go splash some cold water on your face, and let's go see Justin."

Sara spends a little extra time with her face, since she says she doesn't want him to see her all blotchy and red-eyed. I understand. She only gets to see him for a couple of hours a day now, and she wants to present the best front possible. However, I know she's a basket case with her emotions compounded by her pregnancy.

All the way to the rehab facility, she chatters nonstop about how well Justin is doing. The doctors and physical therapists are surprised by how much progress he's made over the past five weeks. I mostly listen, with an occasional comment thrown in to let her know I'm not tuning her out.

When we pull into the parking lot, she reaches over and places her hand on my forearm. "I want you to know how much I appreciate what you're doing." Once again, she tears up.

"I'm happy to do it. Let's get in there before you start an all-out crying jag."

The receptionist grins when she sees us walk in. "Hey, ladies. Go on back."

Something about the way the receptionist smiles makes me suspicious, but I don't say anything because I don't want to get Sara worked up. As soon as we round the corner toward Justin's room, we both stop in our tracks.

Justin is standing outside his room without a walker, wearing his favorite outfit of jeans and a logo T-shirt from the shop where he works. A grin covers his entire face as Sara runs toward him.

She stops about a foot in front of him and gives him a tentative look. He opens his arms wide and pulls her close for a hug. Now it's my turn to cry, and I can't help the heavy flow of tears streaming down my cheeks.

"Surprised?" He holds her back and laughs.

"When —" She gulps. "How — ?" She scrunches up her face and tilts her head. "I just saw you yesterday, and you weren't —"

"I've been walking for several days now, but I wanted to wait until I could make it all the way down the hall and back before showing you."

"So, what does this mean?"

He winks at me and then hugs her again. "It means I'll for sure be out of here in time to go to the family reunion with you."

I say a few more words before excusing myself. "I'll be in the lobby answering hair bow queries on my phone."

She nods and waves before turning back to Justin. Looking at them now makes me wonder why I ever thought they weren't a good match. They're clearly perfect for each other.

There are more than a dozen questions

about our hair bows, so I sit down and thumb-type responses into my cell phone. My phone rings, and I see that it's from Shay.

"Hey there. How'd your date go last night?"

"It was good. Thanks for letting him know you told me about his engagements. I wasn't sure how I'd bring that up."

"Yeah, I thought it might be uncomfortable for you. Are you satisfied with his answers?"

"Sort of."

"That's why it's a good idea for you to take your time. Get to know him. Find out if your feelings are real or just infatuation." She chuckles. "I mean, he is awfully cute, and I can see how that would make you swoon."

I laugh. "Sounds like words of wisdom coming from experience."

"Oh, trust me. They are. I've kissed more than my share of frogs who looked like princes . . . until they didn't." She clears her throat. "I know you're super busy, but I have a huge favor."

"Sure, you know I'll do anything for you."

"You might change your mind when you hear what I'm about to propose."

"Just ask."

"Okay, here goes. Puddin' and I have decided to rent the space next door, and we're putting in several lines of children's apparel. We'd like to feature some of your hair bows and anything else you'd like to put in there."

Sara and I once discussed opening a shop with children's accessories, but we both decided we like not having to keep regular hours. This might be perfect. "Sounds like a good plan, but I will have to discuss it with Sara. When?"

"After the first of the year. The carpet company just moved out this week, so we have to get our design people in there to put in some walls and shelves."

"Perfect. I'll definitely tell my sister."

"Can y'all stop by sometime this afternoon?"

"We're at the rehab center, so maybe we can come by on the way home."

After I get off the phone, I pick up a magazine and wait for Sara to come out to the lobby. I'm excited to tell Sara what Shay said. But instead of being overjoyed, she frowns and shakes her head. "I don't think that's such a good idea."

37

MARYBETH

You'd think someone asked Bucky to dig ditches, the way he's been carrying on after Digger talked to him about building a boxcar. He hates the very thought of working with his hands, since he seems to think he's above all that now.

Well, I've got news for him. What attracted me to him in the first place was the fact that he's from a family of doers. I've always liked men who are self-sufficient and don't mind getting their hands calloused and dirty. Now his hands are softer than mine. It takes so much effort to get him to fix something around the house that I don't even ask him anymore. Instead, I call someone, and he doesn't even know it was ever broken.

I'd probably give up on the boxcar thing if it weren't for Julius being so excited about being in that race. For the first time since we came into money, our son is acting like an eager child who has family values and wants to spend time with one of us rather than a spoiled brat who can't be pleased no matter how much money we throw at him.

So I figure it's high time to talk some sense into Bucky. As soon as he lets out another gripe about having to build a boxcar, I turn and face him.

"Can't you see what you're doing?" I cough to try to clear some of the shrillness in my voice. "Our son is excited about spending time with his daddy and helping build something together."

"It's just a silly boxcar." Bucky downs the last of the water in his glass before putting it on the edge of the counter. "Maybe I can hire someone to build it for us."

I walk over and put the glass in the sink. "It's not just a silly boxcar, and you are *not* going to hire someone to do your work. Why aren't you listening to me? It's not about the boxcar. It's about your relationship with him. He wants to spend time with you."

He scowls. "We just went on vacation. We spent night and day with each other. What more does he want?"

"That vacation was last summer, and we were so busy with tours y'all didn't even have time for conversation."

"I don't get you, Marybeth. You nagged

and nagged until I agreed to go on a family vacation. Then when I booked our tickets to Europe, you griped about that."

"I was talking about some family time without distractions. We didn't really spend time bonding as a family on that so-called vacation." The truth of the matter is that I came back more exhausted than before we'd started, and now all I have are pictures to show for it. I know Bucky likes to show them to everyone so they'll think he's a world traveler, but I would have been just as happy booking a week at a fishing lodge in Tennessee.

Bucky just keeps saying the same thing. "But we were together. Isn't that what matters?"

He clearly doesn't get it. I just let out one of my grunts that irritate him and walk away.

I'm almost to the stairs leading to the bedroom area when I spot Julius coming out of the kitchen. His expression is softer and reminds me of how he looked as a little boy. He glances over at me. "Have you seen Daddy?"

"He's in the den." It's weird for Julius to ask for Bucky, since they hardly ever see each other at home, except at the dinner table — and that's only when I insist we all sit down for a meal together once or twice a week. "Why?"

"I want to go get the stuff to make the boxcar."

I can't help wincing at the sound of hopefulness in his voice.

"Good luck with that." I head on upstairs before he has a chance to say anything else. I'm tired of making excuses for Bucky.

This reunion we're about to have here has me nervous. I want Bucky to cook a pig in the backyard, since it's his family's tradition, but he says he doesn't want to mess up all the fancy landscaping he had put in.

Just when I think Bucky is getting better and realizing that the oil money shouldn't rule his life, he slides backward. One thing I realize now is that until he's ready to change, he won't. There's no amount of nagging I can do to make it happen. Unfortunately, it might take a major disaster — something even worse than what we've already experienced — and that makes my stomach hurt.

I glance around at the magazine-perfect room. Living life like this might look good in the movies, but in reality, I feel like I can't move anything, or I'll mess up the pretty picture. Bucky doesn't even want me to walk across the yard because he's afraid I'll crush the grass. I want to plant a vegetable garden in the sunniest spot, but Bucky says the tomato cages will take away from the beauty of the yard and the herbs look like weeds. Quite frankly, I'm at the point where I'd rather see a row of tomato cages and herbs than the expensive flowers and shrubs Bucky had put in. I finally found a spot he agreed to, but it's not ideal.

Every now and then, I think he gets what I'm saying. He even relents on occasion. But then he goes into town and hangs out with some of the people I don't even know, and that sets him back.

In my heart, I know I was born a redneck, and that's not something I can change. But I like the way I am at my core, which is probably why I come across so grouchy sometimes. Most of the people in Bucky's family roll their eyes when they think we're not looking. But I know. I can sense that they don't much care for our lifestyle, and I agree with them.

Shay once asked me if I needed help, and I totally came unglued. I let her have it, and when I was done with her, she apologized and backed away. I know she has no idea how emotional I was at the time, but Bucky had just gone out and bought himself another ridiculously expensive car. When I try to explain, she holds up her hands and says not to bother — that she doesn't want to interfere where it isn't any of her business. Ever since then, I've detected an invisible shield when I'm around her. That breaks my heart because I know how respected Shay is among the Bucklin family.

If I hadn't acted like such a nutcase, I might have had a good friend who is kind and willing to run interference for Bucky and me with his family. Shay has the reputation of being a good mediator because she has so much common sense like her granny and grandpa — something Bucky obviously didn't inherit.

Maybe I should call Shay now to grovel. I pick up my phone and pull up her number, but I chicken out. I put the phone down and walk over to my immense walk-in closet that's filled to the brim with expensive designer clothes, handbags, and shoes. If it were up to me, I'd wear jeans every day — and not the ones with the fancy stitching on the pockets to show we overpaid for them. I like good, old-fashioned Levis. They're comfortable, and I never mind having a few faded spots on the seat and knees. That just means they're worn in like I like 'em.

After looking through my things, I decide to get over my fear and call Shay and use the excuse that I need something casual for the reunion weekend. That'll make it a little easier to strike up a conversation.

She answers right away. "What can I help you with, Marybeth?" The formal tone in her voice lets me know she hasn't forgotten, but she's still not rude like some folks in her family.

"I'm trying to figure out what to wear to the reunion. Can you help me?"

"Um . . . we do have some things, but they might not be up to your —"

I cut her off before she has a chance to say something based on perception. "I'll be there in twenty minutes."

She sighs. "Okay, but you realize Puddin' is here, right?"

"Of course. Tell Puddin' I'm looking forward to seeing her."

"Will do."

After we get off the phone, I take a long, hard look in the mirror. I've taken on the appearance of the women I used to hate. My hair is perfect, my makeup is flawless, but inside, I'm the biggest mess ever.

That gets me to thinking. Maybe I can change things up a bit. I walk into the bathroom and open the bottom drawer beside my sink. I use a makeup-removing wipe to get rid of what I'm wearing, and I slap on what the cosmetics gurus call a five-minute face. Now as I see myself in the mirror, I look more like the real Marybeth.

Next, I change out of the pretentious jeans and shoes that cost more than the monthly mortgage payment on our last house and slip into an old pair of Levis that I have to lie down on the bed to zip. I yank off the cashmere sweater and pull on one that's a blend of cotton and rayon. A pair of sneakers I only wear around the house finishes off the outfit.

I'm running a little behind, but I don't think Shay will mind. She does a double take when I walk into the shop.

"Marybeth?" Her voice shakes as she tilts her head.

I nod and smile. "I need something cute and comfy for the reunion."

She looks me up and down before gesturing for me to follow her to the back corner of the shop. "We've been getting quite a few new lines in. Have you thought about style or color?"

"Not really."

She stops at one of the round racks and pulls something out. "How about this?"

I look at the things she's showing me and shake my head. "That stuff is rather pretentious, isn't it?"

"Not really." The look she's giving me now

lets me know she thinks I've completely gone off my rocker. "I was thinking you'd like it, since it matches your current style."

"To be honest, I'm tired of my current style. I want to go back to the kind of stuff I used to wear." I let out a low chuckle. "Well, not exactly the kind of stuff, since most of it came from the thrift store. Something a little more current but not quite so . . . well, not so—"

"Stuck up?" The sound of Puddin's voice catches my attention. "What's going on, Marybeth? Are you out slumming today?"

38

SALLY

As soon as I walk into La Chic, I know I've stepped into a minefield. Not only is Puddin' standing there glaring at Marybeth with a hand on her hip and flames shooting from her eyes, but Shay looks like she's afraid to say a word.

"Hey there." I offer a meek wave and forced smile.

All three of the women turn to face me, and I instantly wish I could melt into the floor and ooze on out of there. I swallow hard. All I wanted to do was leave some flyers about the next cooking class.

"Hi, Sally." Shay is the first one to recover. She walks toward me and takes the flyers. "We'll make sure everyone gets one of these. So, how are Sara and Justin?"

"He's doing quite a bit better, and she's feeling very pregnant."

Finally, Puddin' drops the scowl and manages a smile. "I know that feelin' all too well.

307

I can't imagine how she'll deal with an injured husband and a new baby."

Marybeth coughs, so we all turn toward her. "If there's anything I can do to help out, please don't hesitate to call me."

Puddin' belts out a sardonic laugh. "You? Who are you trying to kid? You're so busy getting your nails done and hanging out with all those hoity-toity women that you won't have time to —"

"I hate getting my nails done. I don't even like those women you call hoity-toity. I'm sick of my life. I want to be needed." Tears stream down Marybeth's cheeks as she melts down in front of everyone in the shop. I'm thankful we're all family, because if anyone else had been in there, we'd have some explaining to do.

Puddin' blinks as though she's never seen Marybeth before. "Are you serious?"

Marybeth nods. "Absolutely. And I feel terrible about how Julius has been acting."

"Well, I'll be a —"

Shay gives Puddin' a stern look before she steps up and gently places her arm around Marybeth. "Why don't you come on back to the fitting room area and have a seat?"

Marybeth wipes her nose with the back of her hand and shakes her head. "No, I came in here to get something new to wear, and I don't want anything too . . . too . . ." She looks at Puddin' and offers a shaky smile. "As you would say, nothing too hoity-toity. I don't like the way I've been since we struck oil. I don't even like myself anymore."

Shay and I both watch as Puddin's face softens, and the two of them close the distance between them and hug. And hug and hug. I hear one or both of them sniffling, until finally, Puddin' pulls away.

"I never thought I'd ever see this day," Puddin' says.

Marybeth's chin quivers as she nods. "I know. I wasn't sure I'd ever be able to do this, but I'm sick of pretending."

"Then stop doing it. Let's see what we can do to make you real again."

Shay pulls her head back and raises her eyebrows. "Looks like you've got this one, Puddin'."

Her sister-in-law nods. "I most certainly do." She takes hold of Marybeth's arm and pulls her toward a display of moderately priced weekend wear. "Let's start here and see what we can find."

Once Puddin' has Marybeth's full attention, Shay smiles at me. "So, how's the new condo deal coming along?"

I shrug. "The seller keeps acting all skittish, so I'm thinking about backing out of the deal."

"Can you do that?" Shay looks concerned. "Didn't you sign the papers?"

"Yes, but she hasn't. Nate says she's already past the date she's supposed to sign them, so I can get out of it if I want."

"Speaking of Nate . . ." Shay tilts her head. "How is everything between the two of you?"

"Good, I guess." I don't want to come right out and say that I'm holding my feelings back because I don't want to get hurt, even though I know she'll understand. But I really enjoy being around him. He's sweet and fun, and he always makes me laugh. Not only that, he gets along really well with Justin, but he doesn't forget about me like Tom did. But we've only been dating for a few weeks, so I figure it's best to let things play out for a while before I get too caught up in what I'm feeling.

Shay smiles. "Have you considered asking him to the family reunion?"

"I've thought about it, but I'm not sure he's ready for our family just yet." I remember when she brought her boyfriend Elliot to the last reunion. He didn't seem fazed, but he's been around the Bucklins for years.

Shay lets out one of her hearty laughs. "I know what you mean. Fortunately, Elliot already knew most of our family before he went, and he said he'd always wanted to go to one of the famous Bucklin family reunions."

"I'm sure he wasn't disappointed."

Shay leans toward me, cups a hand over her mouth, and whispers, "It shook him up when Brett and Julius blew up the barn. He said if it happens again, he'll have a talk with both boys."

"I'm sure that'll go over big with their mamas."

Speaking of the boys' mamas, Puddin' comes out of the fitting room area with a humongous grin on her face. "Hey, y'all, looks like Marybeth has come back to earth. Now all she has to do is work on Bucky."

I've known Bucky all my life, and I can't imagine that happening. I'm sure he has a sweet side, but I've never seen it. I was really young when they struck oil. After he got rich, he acted like he was better than everyone else, even though we all know he didn't do a single thing to earn that money.

This is one of the reasons Sara and I don't brag about how much we're making, even though I'm sure it's not as much as Bucky gets from the oil company. However, I suspect we're bringing in quite a bit more than he ever did before they struck oil.

People naturally assume we're barely squeaking by and enjoying our little hair bow business. If they only knew.

Marybeth comes walking out wearing leggings and a tunic-length sweater that's not only super cute on her but will make her fit in better with the rest of the family. I know she has spent a fortune on her other clothes, but they aren't the least bit stylish. They make her look like some of the old rich women who do lunch at the country club. In fact, I suspect that's where she's been getting her fashion advice, since she's been doing that for the past several years.

"Well, what do y'all think?" She gives a little spin while the rest of us stare at her. "Does it look cheap?"

I quickly glance over at Shay, who appears amused, and then at Puddin', who looks annoyed. Rather than risk having Puddin' be the first to speak up, I step closer. "I think you look absolutely darlin'."

She grins at me. "You do?"

I nod. "It takes a good ten years off you, and it's so in style now."

"It's super comfy." She walks over to the triple mirror and inspects herself from all angles. "The only thing I need now is a pair of boots." She faces Puddin'. "Do y'all have any of those fur-lined boots with the fuzzy dangling balls?"

"No, but I'm pretty sure they have them down at Sure as Shoe-Tin," Shay says.

Marybeth contorts her mouth. "Oh, Bucky doesn't want me buying footwear at a discount shoe store."

"And that's the very reason you need to go there." Puddin' snorts. "Their *footwear* is just as good as what they have at those overpriced stores with the dowdy shoes."

Everyone gasps, but Marybeth laughs. "Ya know, you're right. I used to buy all my shoes there before, and I never had a single solitary complaint. In fact, when I go by the window and see those cute shoes they have, I start droolin'."

"Then what are you waiting for, girl?" Puddin' looks over at Shay for support before turning back to Marybeth. "As soon as you leave here, go straight there and buy yourself some cute boots."

Marybeth nods. "That's exactly what I'll do. Now let me try on a few more things." She lets out a little squeal of delight as she scurries back into the fitting room.

Shay drops her voice to a low volume. "I hope we're not about to start a family feud."

"Don't be silly," Puddin' says. "We're doing something important." She lifts her chin and squares her shoulders. "We're helping to empower one of the women in the family. If Bucky makes noise, we'll all go to her rescue."

Shay gives her a sideways glance before looking at me. "If you say so."

I see the twinkle in her eyes. An image of a family female army rushes through my mind, and it makes me laugh.

39
SHEILA

I walk right up to my daughters' condo and bang on the door. As soon as Sally answers, I let her have it. "What have you girls done?"

"What are you talking about, Mama?" She gives me a confused look before stepping aside. "Come on in so I can close the door."

As soon as I walk inside, I turn back to my daughter. "I heard Bucky hit the roof when Marybeth went home with a bunch of stuff that she said you, Shay, and Puddin' told her to buy."

Sally chuckles. "I never told her to buy anything, but even if I did, she's a grown woman who can do whatever she darn well pleases."

"Don't take that tone with me, young lady. You might be all grown up and living on your own, but I'm still your mama."

"Sorry." A contrite look comes over her face. "But seriously, Mama, you know we can't make her do anything she doesn't want to do."

"What happened? Why were you even in the store with her?"

Sally explains what she was doing there and how Marybeth wanted to try on a few things that weren't dowdy. "So we helped her find a few cute things, and she loved them. What's wrong with that?"

"What's *wrong* with that?" I shake my head. "What's wrong with that is her husband doesn't want her dressing that way."

As soon as those words leave my mouth, I hear the lack of logic in my words. In fact, if George ever told me how to dress, I'd laugh my head off. After a few missteps early in our marriage, he's learned to tell me how great I look, no matter what he thinks.

"Hey, Sheila."

The sound of Justin's voice snags my attention. I quickly glance over toward the kitchen and see him slowly walking toward me, a huge grin on his face.

"Justin! What are you doing here?"

He laughs and cuts a glance over to Sara before looking back at me. "I live here."

"Oh, I know." I drop my handbag to the floor and rush over to him for a hug. "What I should have said is why didn't someone tell me you were coming home?"

Sara steps out from behind him. "We didn't know until this morning." She gives her husband a loving look. "He's been working so hard at getting better, so they said he could come home early as long as we don't overdo things." She lowers her voice. "I have to make him behave, which isn't so easy with someone as bullheaded —"

Justin interrupts her with a snicker. "This will be a vacation compared to what they put me through." He looks at Sara. "Speaking of which, what time is the therapist supposed to be here?"

"Not until after lunch."

"Oh, I thought —" He grimaces and leans against the wall. "I'm still having a little trouble processing things."

Sally looks at me with a playful expression. "Which is why he won't be working on cars for another couple of months, so we're putting him to work making bows."

"That's not —" I begin before Justin interrupts.

"I really don't mind. In fact, I think it's good therapy for me, and it helps them fill the crazy number of orders they've been getting."

"He's actually quite good," Sally adds.

"That's because I'm used to working with

my hands." He pulls away from the wall and goes over toward the sofa. "Why don't you come on over and have a seat?"

I have quite a bit on my to-do list, but I need to show support. As I lower myself into the chair next to the sofa where Justin is sitting, I spot a sheet of bubble wrap cluttering the table. My OCD kicks in, so I reach for it, but he grabs it before I do.

He pops a couple of bubbles before grinning up at me. "Therapy."

Sara groans. "You know that drives me insane."

Justin tilts his head and then pats the spot next to him. "Come sit down beside me and I'll stop."

"You know I have a ton of stuff to do," Sara says, her whiny voice reminding me of when she and Sally were little preschoolers.

He pops another bubble as he lifts his eyebrows and gives her a hangdog look. "Please?"

She lets out a low growl and plops down beside him, yanking the sheet of bubble wrap from his hands. "I'm gonna talk to your therapist and see if we can find something less annoying for you to do with your hands."

Clearly feigned shock washes over his face. "No! Don't talk to my therapist."

I can't help laughing. "So, what kind of therapist prescribed bubble wrap?"

"My UPS therapist?" He scrunches his face as he looks back and forth between Sara and me. "Am I busted?"

Sara stands up and throws a decorative pillow at him. "Afraid so, buster. And just for that, I'm going to tell your *real* therapist to crack the whip next time."

He holds his arms over his head in pretend fear. "No, not the whip."

"Yep." Sara folds her arms and snaps her head in a nod. "Afraid so. You're not gonna get away with anything around here." She looks back and forth between Justin and me. "Anyone want some tea?"

I stand. "No, thanks, sweetie. I need to run."

"Wait a minute," Justin says. "I heard you say something about Marybeth and Bucky. What's going on with them?"

Sara waves him off. "You're just nosy."

"No, I want to hear what's going on."

Sally rolls her eyes. "I can't stand any man telling his wife what to do."

"I know that's true." Justin laughs. "That's why I never boss my wife around."

Sally shakes a finger at him in a joking manner. "And you better not ever start either, or you'll have me to answer to."

Now that Sally has explained what happened at La Chic, I agree with her wholeheartedly. How dare Bucky micromanage his wife's wardrobe when he can't even manage anything about his own life. He was always somewhat belligerent with a few sweet moments thrown in, but ever since money found its way to his bank account, he's become a flat-out jerk.

What I feel bad about now is how I'd assumed Marybeth was just as bad. Sure, she took on a condescending tone around the family, but it's understandable, knowing what she's had to put up with to stay married to Bucky. Most of us have wondered what on earth she saw in him to begin with, but over time, we assumed it was something we never saw or ever would see, so we quit talking about it. He's the one who's blood related, but deep down, she's the one most of us prefer to claim — that is, until she started acting just as bratty as Bucky.

"Gotta run, y'all." I get up and walk toward the door. "Let me know if there's anything I can do for you."

All the way home, I think about our family and how insane we must look to other people. Fortunately, Justin has known George's family for most of his life, so he knew what he was getting into when he married Sara.

I pull into the driveway, hop out of my car, and make my way to the front door. As soon as I open it, I hear what sounds like George speaking on the phone. "No, she's not home, so I can talk now."

40

SALLY

I have to admit that I'm amazed by Justin's progress. If someone didn't know he'd had such a tragic accident, they might not see anything wrong with him. Right after it happened, the medical team wasn't sure he'd survive. Then a few days later, after he woke up, the doctor thought he'd be okay but said it would take a long time — maybe many months — before he'd be able to walk and talk like normal. Now, after only six weeks, they're discussing letting him go back to work soon.

It's hard to imagine why he'd even want to work on cars again, but he does. When Sara and I argue with him, he claims it's in his blood and says he might as well die if he can't do what he loves to do. Sara is worried, but she's taking his side, so I don't even bother trying to reason with him.

"Should I wear the red shirt or the orange one to the family reunion?"

I glance up and see Justin standing at the door of our workroom. "Why are you asking me?"

"Sara says you've become quite the fashion expert, so I thought you'd know."

Justin clearly doesn't get the fact that Sara is being sarcastic, so I shrug. "It really doesn't matter."

He walks into the room and holds the orange one up to his chest. "Just give me your opinion. This one?" He switches them out and holds up the red one. "Or this one?"

I keep my focus on the layers of ribbon in front of me as I point to the first one he held up. "That one."

"You're not even looking at me."

"Yes, I was. Wear the orange one." Now that the ribbon is the length I need, I pick it up and start wrapping it.

"Are you sure it doesn't make me look washed out?"

I glance up from the bow I'm constructing and narrow my eyes. "Who are you and what have you done with my brother-in-law?"

A hurt look comes over his face. "I'm just trying to impress your family."

I make a face. "Since when?"

He puts both shirts down on the table by the door and walks even closer. "Look,

Sally, you might not have noticed this, but some of the people in your family look down their noses at me."

"That's *their* problem." I'm sure he's right, but who cares what they think? I don't know anyone better than Justin to be married to my sister, and if they don't see it, they shouldn't matter.

He contorts his mouth. "I also don't want them to think the accident affected me."

"But it did."

He shrugs. "Maybe so, but they don't need to treat me like I've lost half my brain."

He clearly needs to have this conversation, so I put down the bow and turn to face him. "What makes you think they'll do that?"

"I don't know." He lowers himself into one of the chairs. "It's just that this whole thing has been so frustrating for me. I want to fit in with your family, and it seems like everything is stacked against me."

I ponder that for a moment. "Justin, this is probably the most important thing I'll ever say to you." I pause and smile. "You don't *want* to fit in with my family. You're unique and someone they should try to emulate. Not the other way around."

A slow grin spreads across his face. "You really think so?"

"Absolutely. I don't know anyone else who would have worked as hard as you to recover from what could have been tragic." I shrug. "A lot of folks in my family would have given up and expected to be waited on for the rest of their lives. You're one of the strongest people I've ever known."

"I did it because I love your sister and that baby she's carrying. I want to be a good daddy and show my son or daughter the world."

I have to fight back the tears that threaten to fall. "There is no doubt in my mind that you'll be the best daddy ever."

Sara appears at the door. "Hey, what's going on in here?"

"We were just talking." I stand up. "I've been sitting here long enough. Why don't you take over for a little while so I can go for a walk? I need to get some exercise."

"Where are you going?"

I shrug. "Just around the block. My back is starting to hurt."

Justin turns to Sara. "She wants to go walk past her new condo."

"Looks like I might not get it. Jeanine is acting so weird I'm not sure it's the right thing to do."

"You can stay here as long as you like," Sara says as she turns to Justin. "Right?"

He nods. "Yeah, it'll be fun. We'll have a built-in babysitter and not even have to worry about taking you home when we get in from our dates."

"Since you put it that way, I think I'll go put some pressure on her to let me have the place as soon as possible."

Justin laughs first, and a few seconds later, Sara lets out a shaky chuckle. He seems to get my humor even better than my own sister does — at least now that she's super hormonal.

I leave them in the workroom and head on out. It's an unseasonably warm day, so I push my sleeves up as I start my walk.

I've walked about twenty feet when my phone rings. It's Mama, so I answer it.

I don't have a chance to say a word when she blurts, "Your daddy wanted to go on a cruise instead of the reunion."

"Well? Are you going?" I stop walking.

"No, I told him we can't do that, since I've already committed. Besides, I'm trying to help plan this, and I don't want to drop the ball."

"Mama, they can manage without you."

"The timing still isn't good for me." She pauses. "I'm still happy that's what he's been up to."

"What do you mean by that?"

"I overheard him talking to someone on the phone, and it sounded mighty suspicious. I thought —"

"Please don't." This is something I don't want to hear.

She sighs. "At any rate, I think it's sweet that he wanted to surprise me, but I'm glad I caught him before it was too late. He was trying to reschedule the nonrefundable trip. You know how I am about wasting money."

"Yes, I certainly do."

After we get off the phone, I resume my walk. I'm about twenty feet from the edge of Jeanine's condo when I hear my name. I turn around, and there she is. I'm not sure what to say or how to act, so I just lift my hand and wave.

Jeanine shades her eyes from the sun. "Can we talk?"

I glance around and then look at her again. "Now?"

"Yeah, before I chicken out."

I'm not sure this is such a good idea, but I nod. "Okay, what do you want to talk about?"

"First, I want to apologize for acting the way I have been. It's just that I never thought . . . well, I always thought everything was fine and would continue to be that way forever."

A strange sensation prickles the back of my neck. I'm tempted to turn and run, but she clearly needs to talk, so I stand there staring at her, hoping the feeling passes.

"If I don't do something soon, I risk losing everything, including my job." She glances down at the pavement and sheepishly raises her gaze to mine as she gestures toward an older-model Chevy. "I lost the Jag, and this is all I can afford."

"I'm sorry." Deep down, I don't think the Jaguar is all that big a deal or even what's truly upsetting her, but she's clearly distressed over it.

"Thank you. That was the car of my dreams, so Dean bought it for me."

"Dean?"

She nods. "Yeah, that's the guy who gave me the other house — the one I'm still living in."

"Oh." I still don't know who she's talking about or what house she lives in, but I don't want to pry.

She holds up a key. "I still have this. Want to go inside where we can have some privacy?"

Now I'm nervous. What if she does something when we're alone? I remember that the last time I was around her, she acted really strange.

"Please?"

Well, I am curious. "Okay, but just for a few minutes. I need to get back and finish some work. My sister and her husband are expecting me." At least now she's aware that someone is expecting me. "I'd hate for them to have to go looking for me." *Okay,* I tell myself. *I've already driven that point home.*

"It won't take long. I just need someone to talk to."

As soon as we walk into the condo, she bursts into tears. "I thought we had everything going for us. I loved him, and I assumed he loved me . . . at least he told me he did. But then when I started pressing to find out when he was planning to make our relationship more permanent, he . . ." Her chin quivers as she looks at me with red-rimmed eyes and tears streaming down her face. "He told me his wife won't give him a divorce."

I gulp. "His wife?"

She nods. "Yeah, I met him after they were separated. He said he'd filed for divorce, but now I know that was all a lie. I've been a . . ." She sniffles again. "I've been the other woman for more than a year. I can't believe how stupid I was to believe him."

This is so far out of my realm of understanding that I don't even know what to say.

"I'm really sorry."

"Why would you be sorry?" She gives me an incredulous look.

"I hate when people have problems."

She belts out a sardonic laugh that completely catches me off guard. "Have you always been this naive?"

41
CORALEE

I still can't believe how stupid I've been. After Puddin' has advised me to have a heart-to-heart talk with Kyle about my feelings, I go and do just that. I thought it would be a back-and-forth conversation and we'd wind up coming to some sort of agreement. I expect disappointment and hurt, but no, that's not what I get from him.

"We don't have to date, but will you at least sit next to me during the final exam?" he asks without missing a beat.

"What? Why?"

He rolls his eyes. "I can't fail sociology, and you're my only hope."

"But sit next to you — ?" Then it dawns on me. He wants to cheat. "I've helped you study. Why on earth would you want to cheat?" Then I go off on a tangent, letting him know how important it is to me to do the honorable thing and actually study for the test.

I've barely told him my feelings when he starts laughing at me. "Coralee, you're not as bright as you think you are. Yeah, you're good in sociology and English, but in real-life matters, you're pretty clueless."

"I'm not only not into being a cheater, I don't want to date one either." I want to make it very clear where I stand. And I have a deep need to be the one to blow him off. "You're not the man I thought you were."

"Maybe not." The smirk on his face makes me sick to my stomach.

"Do you understand what I'm saying, Kyle?"

He shakes his head. "You still don't get it, do you? If I could have afforded to hire you, I would have, but I had to figure out some other way to get your help." He gives me a pitiful look. "That's the only reason we were dating."

It's not that I'm all that heartbroken about losing a boyfriend. I'm just furious and hurt that I allowed myself to be used like that. "That's all the more reason I don't want anything to do with you."

I start to walk away, until he places his hand on my shoulder. "I didn't really mean that, Coralee. I'm sorry. It's just that I say things when I'm hurt, and I don't have a lot of experience in the romance department."

I look at him and shake my head. "Sorry, Kyle, but it's over." Then I leave him standing there.

So now here I am, on my way home from finding out I've been played for a fool, knowing someone will ask why I'm so upset. Now that I look back, I realize I should have seen some signs, like the fact that he ignored me until I walked in with what he said was confidence. In actuality, that look I gave him was all he needed to make his first move. There's no way I'll be able to talk to Mama about it, and I certainly don't want Daddy to know, or he might do something to hurt Kyle.

A blue light in my rearview mirror gets my attention. Oh man, it's a police officer, and I think he wants me to pull over. A quick glance at my speedometer lets me know my hunch is correct. I'm going sixty in a forty-mile-per-hour zone.

I pull over onto the shoulder, lower my window, close my eyes, and lean my head back. Can things get any worse?

I open my eyes in time to see the police officer leaning over and looking at me with concern. "Are you okay, ma'am?"

"Yes, I'm fine."

"May I see your driver's license and proof of insurance?"

I rummage through my wallet, pull out the cards, and hand them to him. "Am I in trouble?"

He gives me a half smile. "Do you know how fast you were going?"

As tempting as it is to lie, I can't bring myself to do it. "Yes, sir. As soon as I saw your blue light, I looked."

His smile widens as he jots some things down and hands the cards back to me. "Are you running late for something?"

I slowly shake my head and fight back the tears as I think about why I was driving so recklessly. I'm not a lawbreaker. I follow all the traffic rules, so being a speed demon is new for me.

His smile fades into a frown. "Is there a reason you're in such a hurry?"

Now I can't control my emotions. My chin starts to quiver as the tears spurt. I wipe my face with the heel of my hand, smearing makeup all over my sleeve.

"Ma'am, would you like for me to call someone?"

"No, I'm fine." I sniffle. "Just a few personal problems, but nothing all that major."

He glances over his shoulder and then looks back at me. "Tell you what, Ms. Bucklin. I'll follow you to wherever you're going to make sure you arrive safely if you promise to pay attention to your speed in the future."

"I'm not getting a ticket?" I glance at his name tag and make a mental note.

He shakes his head. "Not this time, but consider it a warning."

"Thank you, Officer Murdoch. I'll be fine."

"Um . . ." He straightens up, rubs the back of his neck, and then looks back at me with a smile that makes me think there's something else he wants to say but won't. Or can't.

I look into his gorgeous brown eyes and find myself speechless. I clear my throat and manage to squeak, "May I go now?"

He nods and gives me the handsomest smile I've ever seen in my life. His teeth aren't perfectly straight, but they have character. He has a strong chin that evokes confidence and strength. There's something about him that makes me feel warm all over — and safe — something that never happened when I was with Kyle.

As I drive away, I glance in my rearview mirror and see him standing there on the side of the road, watching me. I'm almost home when I realize something. I'm totally attracted to him, but I don't know how to finagle a way to see him again. My lack of experience has caught up to me once again.

Okay, breathe, I tell myself. This isn't the end of the world. And Pinewood isn't a big city, so if he wants to find me, he will. But what if he doesn't? What if he didn't feel the magnetic pull between us? I have no idea what to do.

The one person who will know is Shay. She's the smartest person I know, and I can trust her.

I pull off to the side of the road to call her, but before I click the Send button, I decide this would be better in person. So I make a detour and head to downtown Pinewood, find a parking spot in front of La Chic, and say a short prayer that she's working today.

She is. As soon as I walk in, there she is, smiling. "Hey, Coralee. Back for more cute things?"

I shake my head as I glance around. "Are we alone?"

A frown quickly replaces her smile. "Yes. Is everything okay?"

"Sort of . . . but not really." I give her a pleading look. "I need help."

A soft laugh escapes her lips. "Why don't you tell me what's going on, and maybe we can figure it out?"

I start out by letting her know how much I love my new clothes, hoping I'll get the

nerve to tell her how attracted I am to Officer Murdoch. I'm about ready to transition
when I see her gaze darting to something
outside. I glance over my shoulder to see
what has her attention, and then I have to
do a double take.

It's Officer Murdoch. Suddenly, I start
stuttering, and she looks back at me with
concern.

She looks out the window before turning
back to face me. "Are you okay, Coralee?"

I nod, but I can feel my face heating up.
"I . . . uh —" I'm silenced by the jingling
bell as the door opens.

Shay's face lights up. "Hey, Trace. What's
going on?"

I can't bring myself to look directly at
Officer Murdoch — or Trace — so I stare
down at the floor. He apparently doesn't realize or remember I'm the one he stopped
less than a half hour ago.

"Since you're part of the Bucklin family, I
figured you might be able to help me out.
I'm looking for Coralee Bucklin. I wanted
to get her phone number, but I couldn't
while I was on duty."

My heart hammers as I look up and meet
his gaze. His face instantly turns as red as
mine feels.

Shay whispers, "Okay, I think I know why

you're here." Then she laughs and backs toward the hallway. "Why don't the two of you talk while I finish up something in the office?"

I feel like I'm back in middle school as we look at each other, both of us at a loss for words. The situation is extremely awkward, but it's not terrible.

He finally smiles and licks his lips. "Sorry. I had no idea it was you."

"That's okay." I glance down at the floor and clear my throat. "Shay's my cousin."

He nods. "I figured that. I suppose you heard what I said when I first came in here."

My face gets even hotter. "I did."

"Then can I have your phone number? I'd like to call you sometime." He clears his throat. "That is, if you'd like to talk to me again."

"Sure." I put my handbag on the counter and dig around for a slip of paper. After I jot down my information, I hand it to him.

"I wanted to ask when I stopped you, but it's against our policy."

I'm so excited I feel like jumping out of my own skin. "I understand."

"Would you like to go out with me sometime?"

My lips are dry and my tongue sticks to the roof of my mouth, so all I can do is nod.

I see movement in the hallway, and it's Shay giving me a thumbs-up.

He shifts his weight from one foot to the other before taking a step toward the door. "I guess I'd better leave so you can talk to your cousin." Then he leaves.

Shay walks back into the shop area, still grinning. "So, one problem settled. Now, do you need help with anything else?"

I tell her about the traffic stop, and she listens. After I'm finished, she chuckles. "The Lord has a way of working things out, doesn't he?"

"He obviously does."

"There's something else you probably don't know about Trace."

I brace myself for some bad news. "What's that?"

"Grandpa Jay has hired him to work at the family reunion."

"Doing what?"

"Security." Shay smiles. "Grandpa Jay figures having an officer of the law present will keep everyone on their toes and hopefully out of trouble."

I think about that before grinning right back at her. "That's probably wishful thinking."

Her grin widens. "I know."

42

SALLY

I have to admit, after talking to Jeanine, I'm having some reservations about buying her condo. There's something about her that makes me unsure if I want any connection with her at all.

As soon as I walk back into the condo I'm already living in, Sara confronts me. "Is your new place still standing?"

I tell her all about my conversation with Jeanine, and she nods her understanding. "So, what do you think?" I ask.

"I totally get why you're worried." She places a hand on my shoulder. "I would be too."

"Do you think I should go through with trying to buy it?"

"I'm not sure. There are more issues you need to consider." Before I ask what they are, she starts naming them. "First of all, she has proved she can't be trusted by being involved with a married man, which

340

means she doesn't mind hiding information. That leads me to think there might be something she's not telling you about the condo."

I nod. "I have thought about that."

"Another thing is that if she has people mad at her — like the man's wife — what if they come looking for her, and they find you instead?"

That's something I hadn't thought about. "That could be dangerous."

"I know. And then there's the issue of her being so strange. What if she has seller's remorse and decides she wants her place back?"

"I'll change the locks, first thing."

"I don't know, Sally. Maybe you should reconsider this whole thing and wait for something else to come on the market."

"But the baby —" I point to her belly. "You'll need to get your nursery set up."

"Justin and I have been talking, and we've decided to keep the baby in the room with us for a couple of months."

"Are you sure?"

Sara nods with enthusiasm. "Positive. Even if you move out, I don't want to be separated from the baby at first."

I let out a sigh of relief. "That settles it. I'm going to call Nate and let him know that I don't want the place."

He answers on the first ring, and I tell him what happened as well as my thoughts and reservations. "I agree with you," he says. "We've always known there's something not right about that woman, and I'm beginning to think it's worse than we thought."

"So, what will the bank do with the place?"

"What we always do. We'll finalize the foreclosure, make sure everything is in order, and put it on the market." He pauses. "To be honest, I'm relieved you're not still on for buying that place. In this business, we've seen a lot of weird things happen. I'd worry about you because I like you too much."

"You do?" My heart pounds so hard I'm afraid it might jump right out of my mouth. I consider myself very independent, but I still love the fact that he's trying to be protective.

He lets out what sounds like a nervous laugh. "This isn't something I wanted to tell you on the phone, but I'm sort of falling . . . well, I'm pretty crazy about you."

My heart hammers hard. "I like you a lot too."

"Now that we have that out of the way, what do you want to do this weekend?"

We talk about several options and settle on ordering pizza and watching a movie on Netflix. Then I decide I might as well bring up something I've been thinking about. "Would you like to go to my family reunion?"

"I thought you'd never ask."

"Really?"

He lets out a soft chuckle. "Yes, really. First of all, I'm honored that you'd want me to meet your family. And second, the Bucklin family reunions are known as the event of the year around here."

"Even in Hattiesburg?"

He laughs again. "Even in Hattiesburg. When people find out I'm dating you, one of the first questions I usually get asked is whether or not I'm going to your next reunion."

"Maybe we should charge admission."

"You'd probably make a few bucks if you did."

"Then it wouldn't be as much fun because we'd have to perform to make sure everyone got their money's worth. As it is, every single act of misbehavior comes natural — and that's something the Bucklins do so well." I glance at the clock. "I need to go. See you tonight."

I head on back to the workroom and give

Sara a report. "He sounded excited when I asked him to the reunion."

"Are you sure you want him to go?" Sara gives me a long look. "What if he finds out how crazy our family really is and decides he doesn't want any part of it?"

"Well, first of all, we haven't discussed anything long-term — at least not yet — so that's not an issue . . . yet. And second of all, I think it'll be good to see the family's reaction to him and how he deals with the craziness."

She bobs her head. "Yeah, there is that." She points to some ribbon she's laid out. "We have a huge order for some gold-lined green-and-red-plaid bows, so I figured it would be best to knock those out before we start on the smaller orders."

I get right to work on the new order. By the time I finish the last one, I know that if I never see another green-and-red-plaid print, I'll be happy. This happens when we get huge orders, but I'm not complaining. This business might be monotonous, but it keeps us from having to go to work for someone else, doing something we dislike even more.

As soon as we're finished, Sara leans back and turns to me. "Do you ever think about what you'd really like to do with your life?"

I shrug. "Not really. Why?"

"I know we're making a boatload of money, but it seems that there's something else. Something more rewarding."

I lift an eyebrow and point to her belly. "You already have something more rewarding, but if we're talking about a career, what are you thinking about?"

"I'll tell you when I figure it out." She grins. "But in the meantime, I suppose we'll just keep on making hair bows as long as mamas are willing to buy them."

"Which will be forever." I clean up my workspace and stand. "I don't think there's ever been a time when mamas didn't want to put some crazy stuff in their daughters' hair."

"I know. Remember when our mama used to pull our hair back and stick those insane ribbons in our hair?"

I nod. "The only thing that was worse was when she bought some comic strip bows from a craft fair."

Her eyes widen as she remembers. "Yeah, those were the ones someone made by covering real comic strips from the newspaper with contact paper."

"I was embarrassed to leave the house when she stuck those in our hair."

Sara shakes her head. "Which was why we

conveniently lost them in the bushes right outside the church." She drums her fingers on the table and gets one of those familiar looks on her face. "Do you remember what they looked like so we can replicate them?"

"Don't go getting any ideas." A familiar feeling of dread washes over me at the very thought of putting a child of today through that kind of torture.

"Why not? If they sell, we'll make a fortune. All we have to do is buy a bunch of Sunday newspapers, and we can ask people to save them for us."

She has a point. "Well, the cost will be lower than all the ribbon we're buying."

"Let's see if we can find instructions on YouTube." Without waiting for me to respond, she pulls her laptop toward her and starts searching. "Look. There's a bunch of 'em. All we have to do is pick one, make a prototype, and add it to our Etsy page."

As we study the different types of comic strip hair bows, we chuckle about the fact that we're actually doing this. "It's like we're in cahoots with the mamas to torture their little girls."

Sara crinkles her nose as she gives me one of her looks. "They're not as bad as I remembered."

"You're kidding, right?"

"No." She scrolls down to the next tutorial and smiles. "In fact, I actually like this one."

"I pity your baby if it winds up being a girl."

She rubs her belly. "I have a feeling it just might be."

43
BRETT

If someone had told me Julius would be excited about building a boxcar, I would have said they were crazy. But here he is, asking questions about what'll make the thing run faster.

"How would I know?" I stand back and stare at the pile of junk he and his daddy have put together. "All I know is we get in it, someone gives us a shove, and it's over when we reach the bottom of the hill."

"How did you build it if you don't know what makes it work?" Julius continues staring at his boxcar.

I shrug. "I just did what Daddy told me to do. He knows how to build those things."

"I wish my dad was as cool as yours," Julius says. "He keeps griping about all the money he spends on my cars, and he says all I want to do is put together a homemade mess that I'll never be able to use again."

I stare at Julius. He thinks my daddy's

cool, yet his dad makes sure he has the best wheels at Pinewood High School. I don't know of a single girl who wouldn't jump at the chance to go for a ride in his car . . . or a guy, for that matter. And he wants to be in some silly boxcar race? He's messed up even more than I realized.

"So, what can I do to fix this thing?" Julius stands back and shoves his hands into his pockets as he gives me a questioning look.

I walk around it, bend over to check how the wood is screwed together, and finally stand up straight. "Ya got any tools?"

"Yeah, my dad has a toolbox in the garage."

"How about screws and brackets?"

He looks confused. "What do you need screws for?"

"You'll need screws and brackets to keep the sides from falling off."

"Oh."

I vaguely remember the steps we went through to put mine together. "Maybe we should go to the hardware store and pick up a few things."

"Let me go tell my mother where we're going. I'll be right back."

As Julius runs into his family's ridiculously big mansion, I rock back on my heels and ponder what to do. Mama dropped me off,

349

hoping Julius and I would hang out here and find some common ground. Maybe this will be just what we need. I'm actually surprised she wanted me to come here because of what she found in my room. But Daddy has convinced her that I'm a good kid, and I need to figure out how to stay out of trouble without her constantly hovering.

He comes back with a grin on his face. "She said go on ahead." Then he holds up a credit card. "And we can buy whatever we want."

"You have your own credit card?"

"Get real." He makes what Mama calls an *Elvis* mouth. "I got this off my dad's dresser. He won't even know as long as I put it back when we come home."

If I did something like that, my daddy would tan my hide and ground me for a solid month. But this is Julius, and I doubt his dad would even flinch, since they have more money than they got sense, according to Mama.

While we're in the hardware store, we pick up a bunch of things, including the screws, brackets, and some spray paint. I'm surprised he picks the bright orange.

"That way they'll know it's me," he says. "I like to make a statement." He picks up a can of black spray paint. "This is for the stripe down the side."

"Why don't you just get some black tape? That'll be easier."

He shakes his head. "Nope. I want it painted on."

"Okay. I think that's about all we need."

When we get back to his house, his dad's in the front yard waiting for us. Julius groans. "Uh-oh."

"What's-a-matter?"

"I know that look on my dad. He's mad as all get out." He pounds the steering wheel, and I jump.

"Why?" I glance back and forth between Julius and his dad.

"Who knows?"

As soon as he puts his car in Park, I hop out. Julius's daddy storms over to me. "Where have you boys been?"

I glance over my shoulder and see that Julius is still sitting in his car, and then I turn back to Bucky. "Just to the hardware store."

"You expect me to believe you?" His tone of voice scares me, and his shoulders are up around his ears, making him look not only fierce but crazy.

"Yes, sir. That's where we've been."

His shoulders drop a few inches. "Okay,

since it's you tellin' me, I believe you. What I don't get is why on earth two teenage boys would steal my credit card just to go to a hardware store."

"We didn't . . . I mean, I didn't . . ." It's hard for me to get the words out with him staring at me like a bull getting ready to charge.

He steps even closer to me and gets right up in my face. "What didn't you do, Brett?"

"I didn't steal anything." I turn my head and cough before looking back. "I promise."

"My credit card is missing, and my son took off without telling anyone, so all I have to do is put two and two together." He glances over at Julius, who still hasn't gotten out of his car. "What did y'all get at the hardware store?"

"Just some stuff for his boxcar."

"We've already finished building it."

"But —" I stop myself before telling him that they did a horrible job. My mind races as I try to think of something to say. Finally, all I can come up with is a lame "He wanted to paint it."

His face gets all scrunchy before it relaxes, and he nods. "Okay, that makes sense. What'd y'all get?"

"Mostly paint."

"I didn't think about making it pretty."

He starts to turn back toward the house and stops to smile at me. "Tell Julius to put my credit card back on the dresser along with the receipt."

"Yes, sir."

After he goes into the mansion, Julius gets out of the car and walks toward me. "That was a close call."

I put my hands on my hips, just like Mama does when she fusses at me. "What are you talking about? You didn't even talk to him."

He grins at me. "I know. You're so good at it I thought I'd let you explain."

Some of the stuff Mama has said about Julius pops into my mind, but I certainly can't tell him what it is. Instead, I point toward the shed behind the garage. "Let's go fix up your boxcar."

It takes me a couple of hours to reinforce the sides of the boxcar and to secure the wheels that would have fallen off within seconds of the start of the race if I hadn't done that. Julius keeps asking when we can start painting it, and I keep having to tell him when we're done.

"All the paint in the world won't hold this thing together when you're flying down that hill in Hattiesburg."

"I just want it to look cool."

I open my mouth but quickly close it. Julius is being true to form when all he cares about is how he'll look. Daddy's words about building the foundation before adding the prettiness play in my head. Mama always says when I grow up I'll look back and see how smart she and Daddy are. Maybe that's what's happening with me now.

Finally, I take a step back and point to the bag with the paint. "Now you can paint it."

He pulls out one of the cans of orange paint and pries off the lid. Before he points it toward the car, I hold up my hand.

"What?"

"You have to shake it first, but we need to take it outside so we don't have to breathe the fumes." I reach into the bag and pull out the face masks I talked him into buying. "And put this on first."

"Nah, I don't need one of those."

"But you'll —"

Before I finish, he starts spraying the paint, and next thing I know, he's having a coughing attack. "That stuff's horrible." He sputters again. "I can't breathe."

"That's why you need the mask."

He grabs it from me, puts it on, and starts spraying again. The thing is a real mess because he didn't give me a chance to show him how to tape off the car to protect what shouldn't have paint on it.

After he's finished, he steps back, squints, and stares at it. "Looks like I'm gonna have to paint the wheels black. They look stupid in orange." He pulls out the can of black paint.

"You need to wait for it to dry."

"That's ridiculous." He starts spraying down the side of the car.

I sigh. I don't think he'll listen to anything I say, so I stand back and watch as the black paint drips into the orange. Now it looks even worse than it did before.

When he's done, he straightens up and grins. "Well? What do you think?"

44
SALLY

Tomorrow we'll be piling everything into our cars to take to Bucky and Marybeth's house for the reunion. We heard Grandpa Jay is cooking the pig, since Bucky doesn't want to mess up his expensive lawn, so Justin has volunteered to help him out.

"I don't like this one bit," Sara says as we wait for Justin to change shirts.

I glance up at my sister. "What don't you like? I think it's sweet that Justin is helping Grandpa Jay."

"It's not that. It's just that every stinkin' time Bucky gets too involved, something bad happens."

"Nothing bad has happened."

"Not yet, but you know it will." Her frown deepens. "I don't know why they want to have the reunion at his place."

"Maybe because they want him to show off the house."

"Oh, I doubt that. I don't think anyone in

the family is impressed enough by what Bucky buys with money he never earned."

"Yeah, you're right."

"Based on how he and Marybeth act, you'd think they did something important to get all that money, when all they did was sign the papers to put those hideous oil rigs on their property." Sara makes a face. "I know we keep talking about that, but it still doesn't make sense to reward Bucky for being the family snob."

"Or maybe it's a way to bring him down a notch or two. I'm sure there's a learning opportunity in there somewhere."

"Maybe you're right." Sara gives me a goofy look. "Again."

Justin walks out of the bedroom and smiles at Sara. "This should be fun. Your grandpa is one of the coolest guys I've ever met."

"I know, I know." Sara rolls her eyes as she casts a smirk in my direction. "You can't believe how lucky you are to get to hang out with him all night while the pig roasts."

"That's right." Justin grins as he holds up a duffel bag. "I'm bringing my reunion outfit and taking a shower at your granny and grandpa's place." He hesitates before pulling the keys to his truck out of his pocket. "I thought I'd drive."

"Oh no, ya don't." Sara's no-nonsense tone startles me, but when I glance at Justin, I see a look of amusement. "We're not taking any chances."

He lifts his hands in mock surrender. "Yes, ma'am. Whatever you say."

As they walk out the door to Sara's car, I hear her lecturing him about getting some sleep. "You're still not completely healed, and I don't want you going back to the hospital."

I smile at the sound of my sister showing her maternal side to her husband. There's no doubt in my mind that she'll be an awesome mama.

After I pour a cup of coffee, I head into the workroom to get as much done as possible, since I'm taking off some time for the long weekend. By the time Sara gets back home from taking Justin to Grandpa Jay's farm, I've completed a couple of rush orders.

"Grandpa Jay is as excited to have Justin there as Justin is to be there." Sara takes in a deep breath and loudly exhales. "He says I married a good man who reminds him of himself when he was younger."

"Justin has done a good job of making himself part of the family."

"I know, right?" She holds out her hands.

"On the one hand, I'm happy about that, but on the other hand, I can't help being jealous of his time."

I put down the ribbon and clip I've been preparing. "You need to remember that the time he spends developing relationships with the family is sort of like time spent with you."

"How do you figure that?"

"It's easy. He's doing it for you. And based on my experience, I'm sure the more they get to know him, the more they'll love him."

"Oh, okay." She turns to the ribbon and pulls off a length to work on a bow before lifting an eyebrow and glancing back at me. "When did you get so smart?"

I laugh. "I've always been smart. You're just now getting around to realizing that."

"You sound like Mama." She lets out a grunt. "She said the exact same thing to me last week."

We work until midafternoon, when I stand up and announce that it's time to start working on the food I'm bringing to the reunion. "Shay said I can do the meatballs again, and I'm going to add a noodle dish from the cooking class."

"The doctor says I need to add more fruit to my diet, so I'm bringing an apple pie."

I laugh. "I don't think that's what your

doctor meant."

"I figured you'd say that, which is why I'm also bringing a fruit platter with yogurt dip."

"The dip we made in the 'Cooking for Toddlers' class?"

She nods. "Yep. That's the one."

"Yum. At least I have one thing to look forward to. There's no telling what'll happen this year."

"What makes you think something will happen?"

I shrug. "Something always happens. Sometimes I wonder why we keep going." I pause. "Maybe it's like a car wreck. We don't want it to happen, but we can't stop looking."

"C'mon, Sally. You know it's not that bad. Don't let a few bad apples ruin your time with the rest of the family."

"I know. It's just that . . ." I let my thoughts take over in my head to keep from saying them out loud.

"Look. You'll have me and Justin, and I'm sure Shay will be more than happy to spend time with you."

"Is she bringing someone?"

Sara shrugs as she opens the fridge door and bends over to pull out the yogurt. "How should I know? I hardly see her anymore. I reckon we'll find out soon." Then she scrunches her face. "Now that you brought that up, I thought you were bringing Nate."

"I am." My face heats up merely at the sound of his name.

She giggles. "You don't sound all that excited, but you look flustered."

"I'm not flustered." I clear my throat. "But I'd be excited if I didn't have such a bad history with men."

"And if *he* didn't have such a bad history with women." She bobs her head. "Maybe that's why y'all are such a good match."

"So you're saying two bads make a good?"

"Yeah," she says with a chuckle. "Pretty much."

If anyone but my sister had said that, I'd be offended. I roll my eyes. "That's just messed up."

She levels me with a look. "Seriously, Sally, you don't have a bad history with *men*. Just one man."

"You have to admit I had bad judgment when I thought he was so wonderful."

"Well, yeah." She laughs. "But hopefully, you learned what to look for."

We continue this pointless conversation as we prepare the dishes we're bringing to the reunion. One thing I can count on with my sister is being able to hold a meaningless conversation with her for hours, and she doesn't judge . . . or at least she didn't in the past. I'm discovering so many new things about her that I'm not sure anymore.

"How much do you like Nate?" She stops stirring and looks directly at me.

"A lot."

"Does he know?"

I shrug. "I don't know. Why?"

"At some point, you need to show it. Most guys need some words or at least signs that you have feelings."

I force a smile. "We'll have to see about that. Let's concentrate on what we're doing."

She gives me a closemouthed smile. "Okay, but think about what I said."

After we're done, I turn to Sara, lift my hand, and give her a high five. "What now?"

Her eyes widen. "Now we call Shay and invite her over for a preview of our cooking."

"Great idea." I pull my phone out of my back pocket and punch in her number.

She answers right away. "Sure, I'd love to come over. Puddin' is staying a little bit later, since I haven't even started cooking yet."

"Isn't she cooking something?"

"Are you kidding?" Shay laughs. "She had

362

her stuff finished and in the freezer days ago. All she has to do is pull it out and reheat it."

We make plans for her to arrive at five. After I hang up, I look at my sister. "We need to do something special for her."

"I could make her a bow."

We both crack up. Ever since we started our business, when it's time to give someone a gift, one of us says we can make a bow. Once I said that to Mama, and she just gave me a look like she thought I'd lost my mind. So now Sara and I keep it as our personal inside joke.

She contorts her mouth as she often does when she's coming up with an idea. Finally, her eyes light up. "Tell you what. We can go to Walmart and get her a potted poinsettia, and then we can come back and make her a platter of samples."

"Great idea."

She tilts her head. "Do you think we should get her something else?"

"Like what?" I think for a moment. "It's not her birthday, is it?"

"I don't think so, but after all she's done for us, we didn't even bother getting her a housewarming gift. Let's see if they have something good at Walmart. She can probably use some new pot holders or something." She crinkles her forehead. "Or one of those squishy mats you can put in front of the sink to keep your feet from hurting while you're doing dishes."

I lean back and laugh. "You crack me up. You've never been the least bit interested in house stuff. Now that you're married and pregnant, you've gone and gotten all domestic on me." I'm still laughing as I shake my head. "Pot holders? Floor mat? Really, Sara? What's up with this?"

"I know. It's weird. Justin said his mama told him women start nesting while they're pregnant."

"Maybe that's what you're doing. It just seems strange that you've changed so much in a matter of months."

"I haven't really changed. I'm just starting to say the things I'm thinking."

I narrow my eyes and give her a long look. Apparently, I don't know my sister as well as I thought I did.

We find everything we need at Walmart, including the poinsettias by the entrance and some serving platters on clearance. "What's wrong with them?" Sara asks as she turns them over and inspects the bottoms. "You'd think they'd go on sale after Thanksgiving, not before."

"Most people have probably already

bought that kind of thing."

She grins at me. "Looks like procrastinating isn't always a bad thing."

We find some cute matching dish towels and pot holders for Shay, take them to the cash registers, and then wait in one of the long lines. "I hope this line moves fast. We spent way too much time looking at serving platters."

Sara smiles at one of the employees who motions her over to a lane she's about to open. Some guy makes a rude comment about us cutting in line when it was his turn.

As soon as we get in the car, I groan. "I can't believe how rude some people are."

"But not everyone. Justin's mama says as soon as I start showing, people will start being super nice."

I lean back and close my eyes while she backs the car out of the parking space. Sounds like Justin's mama has a lot of wisdom that can help Sara — more than I'll be able to, since I've never been married or pregnant.

As soon as we turn onto our street, I see Shay standing in front of the next building, chatting with Jeanine. After what she said about Jeanine, I'm concerned that something bad might be happening. My heart thuds as I turn to Sara, whose eyebrows have shot up almost to her hairline.

45
MARYBETH

I'm down on my hands and knees in the master bathroom, scrubbing behind the toilet, when I hear footsteps. I pause for a moment before I continue cleaning. The footsteps stop. "Just what do you think you're doing, Marybeth?"

I drop the brush and scramble to my feet. "What does it look like I'm doing?"

Bucky closes his eyes and lets out a throaty sound of frustration. "How many times do I have to tell you not to do that kind of stuff? You're supposed to supervise the household help, not do it yourself."

"But —" I stop myself because I know that no matter how many times I explain that no one else can clean my bathroom like I do, Bucky will argue.

My husband curls his lip in disgust. "Get up and change into something nicer. I don't want my wife looking like a cleaning lady."

But I am a cleaning lady. Before we came

into money, having a clean house was one of the things that gave me satisfaction. Some people might not understand this, but knowing I did it myself made it all the sweeter. And something Bucky doesn't know is that when I needed extra money, I called one of my old high school friends who owned a cleaning service, and I did an occasional job or two. To this day, I look back on those times with fond memories.

I wait until Bucky has left the bathroom before finishing the job and standing up to admire the sparkling tile floor. It still makes me smile. I understand why Bucky is the way he is. He thinks that rich people don't do manual labor and that they hire folks to do the dirty work. If that's the case, maybe I'm not cut out to be rich.

It takes me an hour to take a shower, get dressed, and put on my makeup. When I go downstairs, I see Bucky pacing in the foyer.

I pause at the bottom step. "What's wrong?"

"The cleaning people forgot to dust the chandelier."

I glance up and squint to see the few particles of dust on one of the prisms. "It's not that bad. I can —"

"No, you can't." He glares at me before looking back up at the light. "I'm going to call them and have them send someone out to finish what they started."

"But it's a holiday," I argue.

He lifts his hands and lets them fall to his sides. "It's not a holiday until tomorrow."

"They probably have a ton of places to clean."

"I don't care. I paid them good money to clean our house, and now I expect them to do it right."

This is an exhausting conversation, and my blood pressure is rising by the second. So I take off for the kitchen to make myself a sandwich. It's clear that Bucky has forgotten his promise to take me to Mack's for some catfish. He's not a fan of what he calls the *common* dining area, but it's always been one of my favorite places to eat. You get to sit at a long picnic table with a bunch of people you probably don't know. They bring out baskets of fried catfish, french fries, coleslaw, and hush puppies. It's an all-you-can-eat place, and when Bucky and I first got married, it was the best place for us to eat because we never left hungry. Now I have to beg him to take me there.

Bucky is getting increasingly difficult to live with. In fact, I've actually considered demanding we get counseling and moving out until we get things straight. I think that deep down, he knows he's acting like a snob, and his internal demons are fighting so hard they're showing their horns. Just when I think he's making progress, he slides back even more.

People who think money takes away all their cares haven't seen what it can do to people like my husband. And I have to admit, people like me. I don't think it's changed me all that much deep down, but I do see how people react to my frustration. They probably think it's snobbery, but it's not. I just don't know what else to do or say when my husband acts like he's too good for his own family, and our son is becoming a spoiled brat.

I've expressed my concern to Bucky about Julius, but he says, "Boys will be boys." When I look around and see sweet boys like Brett and some of the other kids close to our son's age, I don't see the same attitude. Sure, they get in trouble, but they always seem contrite when they do. Not Julius. He acts like he's entitled.

"Mama, I'm bored."

I glance up to see my surly son dragging his feet as he walks into the kitchen. He flops into a chair.

"Sit up straight, Julius."

He tips his head forward and gives me one

of his why-should-I-listen-to-you looks. "I'm hungry."

"I was too." I can't stand his expression, so I look away. "So I fixed myself something to eat, just like you can."

He cranes his neck. "What are you eating?"

"A sandwich." I take another bite and resist the urge to hop up and fix him one.

"I want one." His head bobs, making me want to knock it off his shoulders.

I turn slightly away from him so he can't see my face. "Then get your fanny out of that chair and fix yourself one."

"But —"

I turn and give him one of my sternest looks and force myself not to crack. Finally, he gets up and saunters over to the refrigerator. I have to remind myself to breathe as he opens the fridge door and just stands there, looking inside without pulling anything out.

After a couple of minutes, I clear my throat. "Get what you need and close the door. You're letting all the coldness out."

He glances over his shoulder, his lips turned downward in a cross between a frown and a scowl. Finally, he yanks open the meat and cheese drawer, pulls out a couple of packages, and closes the door. I

remain seated as he fixes himself a sandwich, but it's hard because he's making a
humongous mess.

It takes him what seems like forever, but
he eventually joins me at the table. He casts
a long look at my sandwich before looking
at his. I half expect him to ask me to trade
with him, but he doesn't. He lifts it to his
mouth and chomps down.

"So, what are you doing today?" I ask.

He shrugs as he chews with his mouth
open. "There's nothin' to do."

"Close your mouth while you eat, son. I
don't want to see your chewed food."

He stares down at his sandwich and
pushes it away. "It's too dry."

"Then get up and put some mayonnaise
on it."

He rolls his eyes and lets out a sound of
exasperation.

"Why don't you hang out with some of
your friends?"

"They're all busy doing lame stuff."

"Lame stuff?" I narrow my eyes and meet
his gaze. "Like what?"

He shrugs and looks down. "I don't know,
like cleaning and cooking and raking and
washing cars and stuff."

Deep down, I'd love for Julius to hang out
with Brett more than the few times they've

been around each other, but Bucky says Digger and Puddin's young'uns are all a bunch of wimps who'll never amount to anything. I have to bite my tongue to keep from reminding him that we barely scraped by before the oil company came along. In fact, we were both ecstatic about the five thousand dollars they were paying us annually to lease the rights on our property.

I glance out the back picture window and see the rigs all lined up about fifty yards away. They're ugly as all get out, but Bucky likes to remind me of the beautiful life they've enabled us to have. I reckon there's a lot of truth to the old saying that beauty is in the eye of the beholder. However, I can't help seeing the ugliness of what's become of us.

46
SALLY

I have no idea how Shay does it, but she has managed to calm Jeanine down and gotten her to actually listen to reason. Somehow the condo deal is back on — with Nate's approval. Shay managed to get Jeanine to part with her furniture for a fraction of what I'd offered, and she has a signed paper to prove it.

Now Shay, Sara, and I are inside the condo I still share with my sister and her husband, looking at the paper. I tap the edge of the paper and look directly at Shay. "I can't believe you even thought to do this."

"I've been in the business world for a long time." Shay pauses and smiles back and forth between Sara and me. "People do a lot of talking, but until they sign their names, it can be hard to hold them to what they say they'll do."

I glance at Sara and see an unfamiliar expression. "Are you okay?"

She starts to nod but stops. "I can't lie. I'm sad you'll be moving."

"You know it'll have to happen sooner or later. You and Justin were already talking about moving out . . . or having me move out anyway." I pause and give her a few seconds to think about that. "Besides, based on how Jeanine has been acting, that can still change."

Shay holds up a finger to get our attention. "One thing you need to do is be firm. Offering her more money than she originally wanted for her furniture made her perceive you as a pushover."

I ponder that. "I want to be fair."

"Oh, trust me, you're being very fair. If someone doesn't come along and purchase that place, her credit will be messed up for a very long time. And I'm sure she'll probably have quite a few sleepless nights." She gives me a comforting smile. "In a way, you're saving her from a much worse situation."

"True." I smile at Shay before focusing my attention on my sister. "And remember that I won't be far. This is actually the best of both worlds for you. You'll have your family home, and I'll be less than five minutes away."

Sara's lips form into a pout. "It still won't

be the same."

"It never is after we become adults." Shay nods toward the kitchen. "I can't wait to taste what y'all have been working on for the reunion."

I pull the cold items out of the refrigerator while Sara takes the other plate to put in the microwave. As soon as Shay sees the array of food, her eyes widen. "Y'all did all this?"

Sara and I both nod with pride, and I hold up my hands. "With our own four little hands."

Shay's expression lets us know she's surprised but impressed. "Y'all's food will be the hit of the reunion. I have to admit I didn't see this one coming."

I laugh. "Quite honestly, neither did we. I never saw myself as domestic, but now that I've had a little experience in the kitchen, I actually enjoy it."

Sara sighs. "And I'll need to be a good cook so I won't have to take my kids through a fast-food drive-through for every meal."

I look at Shay, and she makes a funny face. "Glad I could save your kids from that."

"I know, right?" Sara laughs. "I remember when we were growing up, I felt neglected because everyone else ate fast food most of

376

the time, and our mama cooked all our meals."

I nod. "And then we moved out on our own and fell into the fast-food trap until you came along."

Shay takes a bite of one of my fruit and prosciutto appetizers and lets out a deep sigh. "This thing is heavenly. Whatever made you think of doing this?"

Before I have a chance to say a word, Sara gives away my secret. "She's been watching the food channel. The chefs on there do stuff like this all the time."

Shay gives a thumbs-up. "Whatever you're doing, keep it up. This will definitely be a huge hit at the reunion."

"Yeah, it might even make the favorites table, alongside Aunt Willa Dean's Coca-Cola ham."

Shay laughs. "Willa Dean's ham has lost some of its standing. In case you haven't noticed, it's edging its way toward the second-tier table." She glances down at her plate before picking up one of the celery spears. "What did you stuff this with?"

"Hummus." Sara offers a shaky smile. "I made it myself."

"Homemade hummus, huh?" Shay's eyes light up as she takes a bite and chews. "I feel like I've died and gone to heaven. Seriously, ladies, y'all have become quite the culinary twins."

Sara nudges me. "Maybe if we get tired of making hair bows, we can apply for our own show on the food channel."

I start to tell her we're not good enough for that, but Shay speaks up. "Y'all have an interesting angle that they just might like. You can play up the fact that you're twins, but you're very different in your approach." She takes a bite of one of my stuffed mushrooms and sighs again. "And both of them work."

"Before we start having dreams of being famous chefs, let's see how the family likes our cooking first." Someone has to be the voice of reason, and for some reason, it's not Shay. Unless our food is better than I think it is. "At least let's give it another year or two."

Shay laughs and tries one of my meatballs next. "This is even better than mine. Seriously, Sally, you might want to consider trying out for the food channel. I think they'll actually consider you." She takes another bite, chews, and swallows it. "Or you can continue perfecting it and try in a year or so. Y'all can be the 'Appetizer Twins.'"

Suddenly, it feels as though everything in my life has gone totally haywire. Shay has always had her feet firmly planted, but now she's talking just like Sara.

After Shay finishes trying all the samples on the plates in front of her, Sara stands up and walks over to the counter. "Now for dessert. I made a mini apple pie so you can try it out."

"Wait a minute." I tilt my head and narrow my eyes. "You made the apple pie? You didn't buy it from the bakery?"

She holds up both hands and wiggles her fingers. "I did it with these two hands, and I think it turned out really good."

Shay has already taken a bite, and she's nodding with enthusiasm. As soon as she swallows, she gestures toward the pie that's left on her plate. "This is your pièce de résistance. It is absolutely fabulous." She takes another bite and closes her eyes in what appears to be ecstasy. "I cannot believe you've gone from never cooking to something like this." She glances at Sara and then me and smiles. "Good job, ladies."

We chat for a few more minutes about the reunion that starts tomorrow. Shay gets up and takes a step toward the door. "I need to get my food ready, but it's going to pale in comparison to what y'all have made."

She walks toward the door, but I stop her.

"What do I do next with the condo situation?"

"Talk to Nate and let him know you want this thing over with as quickly as possible. She's a very skittish woman, and we don't want to give her a chance to change her mind again."

I nod. "Okay, I'll talk to him tomorrow."

"Oh, and before you move in, you'll want to get the locks changed." She offers a closemouthed grin. "And you might want to consider getting a motion-activated camera for the front door."

47
SHEILA

"What's wrong with you, Sheila?" George points to the handful of olives I dropped on the floor. "You've been like this for a couple of days."

"Like what?"

"Unsteady. You've been dropping things, running into furniture . . ." He gives me a worried look. "You don't think you might have had a stroke, do you?"

"No, of course not." I force a smile. "I'm fine."

"Then what's gotten into you?"

I don't want to admit it, but I figure I might as well, since George knows the girls as well as I do. "Sara says they made a bunch of food for the reunion without Shay's help."

He gives me an odd look. "I don't see how that can be a problem."

"They've never been very domestic. Remember the time I told them to heat something up while we were out, and when we got home, the house was filled with smoke?"

"Is that what you're worried about?"

I nod. "I don't remember them doing any cooking . . . or any successful cooking without Shay or me watching over them."

He laughs. "Then it should be interesting."

"What if people get sick?"

"I doubt they'll get sick, but they might not eat it after the first bite."

"True." I point to the pantry. "Would you mind getting me another jar of olives?"

He does as I ask and then leans against the counter to watch me prepare the food I'm bringing. "At least you'll wow 'em with your cookin'. I just happen to think you're the best cook in the family."

"Thanks, Georgie." I blow him an air kiss and continue putting the olives on top of my potato salad. I used to bring it without garnishment, but I saw an ad in a magazine that showed how much nicer food looks with something colorful to decorate it. After experimenting a bit, I discovered that sliced green olives with pimentos provide a nice touch to top off almost any kind of salad.

We chat a little about what we expect to happen. "At least we have nice enough weather to have it outdoors," he says. "I know their mansion is big enough for the entire town of Pinewood, but I like not being all closed up."

"You just want it to be easy to escape," I remind him.

He laughs. "Yeah, there is that."

After I finish everything I'm bringing, I head to the bedroom to start getting ready for the big day. Bucky and Marybeth have said we're supposed to spend the whole weekend at their place, but I doubt if we will. In fact, I've been working on an excuse to leave tonight after everything is put away and we've had some time to chat with everyone.

There are only a few out-of-town folks, so they'll definitely spend the weekend there. However, I've heard several people say they're doing the same thing I plan to do.

The only problem is George. He wants to stay with them because he doesn't want to hurt their feelings. He joins me in the bedroom and starts putting on the clothes I have laid out for him.

I remind him of how Bucky and Marybeth have acted since they came into all that oil money. "They used to be more normal."

"Bucky isn't a horrible guy." George steps into his shoes before looking back at me. "Maybe a little misguided, that's all."

383

"Too much money can do that to you."

He shakes his head. "I don't think it would change you all that much." He pauses and grins. "Me? I'm another story. I'd go out and buy the biggest, most expensive car on the lot."

"Oh, you would, would you?" I toss a playful grin in his direction.

He pulls the shirt over his head and nods. "Yeah, and while I'm out shopping, I'd find you the most luxurious mink coat I can find in Hattiesburg."

I scrunch up my nose. "I don't want a mink coat. They make me sneeze."

"Then I'd find you something else that lets everyone know we've made it."

"As far as I'm concerned, we have made it." I tilt my head forward and level him with one of my loving wifely gazes. "And I don't have to do a thing to show off, because I'm confident without having to prove anything to everyone else."

In spite of his hearing impairment, George clearly hears me just fine. I know this because he puts his arms around me and gives me one of those kisses that make my leg kick up — just like in the old movies.

He gives me a gentle pat on the rear and tells me he loves me before walking away. When he gets to the door, he stops, turns around, and says, "Do you need me? Because if you don't, I need to clean the car out before we go."

"I'm fine." I grin at him. "I just need to put on some makeup so your kinfolk don't think you married a hag."

"Trust me, Sheila, they won't think that at all." He gives me one of his smoldering glances. "If anything, they'll wonder how I managed to get such a gorgeous wife . . . and keep her."

I think my husband really believes what he just said because he sees me through the lens of love. But I know the truth. I've given up coloring my hair, and it's now more salt than pepper. My midsection has spread out quite a bit, and no amount of diet or exercise is doing me any good. The one thing I have a little bit of control over is my face, so I spend a lot of time working on making it the best it can be, although I know the wrinkles and fine lines remind me I'm not getting any younger.

After I finish putting on my makeup, I go back down to the kitchen, where George has put some boxes on the counter to carry the food. I used to have to remind him to save boxes for me, but now he does it without my having to ask.

I fill one box with cold food and the other

with hot stuff. He comes back inside just in time to carry them to the car.

"Ready to face my family?" He puts his hand on my shoulder and gazes lovingly into my eyes.

"Ready as I'll ever be. Let's go."

All the way to Bucky and Marybeth's house, we chat about what we expect to happen. "Do you think the boys will try to blow something up again?" George asks.

"I doubt it. I heard that your grandpa has hired a police officer to just hang around. The boys aren't stupid."

He rolls his eyes as he turns toward the family property. "Even though they act like they are."

"Maybe so, but I doubt they'll pull any pranks with a police officer there."

"You never know how teenage boys think."

I ponder his comment for a moment. "You're right, which is probably why it's good we never had boys."

He chuckles. "In case you've forgotten, teenage girls can be quite a challenge too."

"Oh, trust me, I haven't forgotten. And they can still frustrate you after they're adults."

George knows better than to add a comment now, since I've gone on and on about how worried I am about them. With one daughter pregnant and her husband seriously injured, I'm concerned about their future. And with the other daughter looking to live completely on her own, I'm a basket case. Having both of them moving out at the same time made me sick to my stomach, but it was somewhat tempered by the fact that they had each other.

"They'll be just fine, Sheila. They're smart women." He grins at me. "Just like their mama."

I reach over and pat him on the arm. I appreciate George's compliments, but I still can't help worrying. And my immediate concern is having our daughters' feelings hurt when people don't eat their food.

"Make sure you load your plate up with whatever the girls bring," I say. "And try to eat it if possible."

George shakes his head. "Why don't we let things happen in a more natural way?"

"I don't want their feelings to get hurt."

"They can handle it. I'm sure their feelings have been hurt before, and it'll happen again. That's the kind of thing that adults have to deal with."

"I know, but —" I stop myself to keep from bringing up the times they both came crying to me when they were little and how it hurt me as much as it did them.

He pulls into a spot on the massive circular driveway in front of the mansion, puts the car in Park, and turns to me. "Let it go, Sheila. They're grown women. Stop trying to baby them." He glances over toward the crowd in front of the house. "Speaking of the girls, they're already here."

I open my door. "C'mon, let's go."

We're about twenty feet from the front porch when George stops and gives me a look of concern. "Looks like there might be trouble."

"What?"

He nods toward the group. That's when I notice that boy Sally brought to the last reunion making the rounds, chatting up some of the family. Sally and her new guy are standing off to the side, watching him.

"This could get awkward."

"Uh-oh." I cringe. "I invited him, but then I heard Sally uninvited him. I wonder why he decided to come anyway."

"There's no telling." George closes his eyes momentarily and shakes his head. "With my family, if there isn't enough natural drama, someone will create it."

48
SALLY

When we first walked up and spotted Tom, my first thought was that there was some confusion. I remember how he'd gotten the invitation, but I thought he was clear about being uninvited. Maybe he'll see that I have a date and take the hint that he needs to leave.

That thought is quickly squelched as he approaches with his hand extended to Nate. "Hi there. Welcome to the Bucklin family reunion."

Nate smiles and shakes Tom's hand. "Were you born into this family, or did you marry into it?"

Tom leans back and belts out a strange sound that only remotely resembles a laugh. "Obviously, Sally hasn't told you about me yet."

Nate gives me a look of concern. "Is there something I need to know about?"

I don't want to lie, but I don't want to say

something mean about Tom either. So I just shrug and try to act nonchalant. "Tom and I have been friends for a while. We met at a children's fashion trade show."

I cut my gaze over to Tom with the sternest look I can manage. I hold my breath until he nods. "Yeah, we're old friends," he says.

I'm pretty sure Nate has picked up on the lack of sincerity, bordering on sarcasm, in Tom's tone. "It's nice to meet you, Tom."

Is that icicles in Nate's voice, or is it just my paranoia kicking in?

Tom gives a clipped nod. "Nice to meet you too. I'll say good-bye to a few folks and head back to Jackson." He gives me one last look, shakes his head, and walks away.

"Sally!" The sound of Mama's voice causes me to turn around. "I'm so happy to see you." She cuts a warning look in Tom's direction and then faces Nate with a smile. "And who have we here?"

I see Mama all the time, but if someone were to hear her now, they'd think we're never around each other. And her voice sounds tight and tinny.

"Hey, Mama. This is Nate."

Mama looks up at Nate, shifts the box she's holding to the side, studies his face for an uncomfortable several seconds, and then gives him a warm smile. "Nice to meet you, Nate."

I think most guys would be nervous in this situation, but Nate seems perfectly at ease as he flashes a smile back at her. "So nice to meet you too, Mrs. Wright. Would you like for me to take that?"

"Um . . ." Her lips twitch as she glances at me before looking back up at him. "Sure, that would be nice. Why don't we head on around back so we can put this stuff with the rest of the food?"

Since Nate and I arrived with the food I brought, he knows where to go, so he leads the way. Mama and I follow close behind.

She whispers, "I brought enough to cover for you and Sara . . . that is, if y'all aren't sure about what you made."

"Are you saying you don't think we did a good enough job?"

"No, of course I'm not saying any such thing. It's just that . . . I don't know. Y'all weren't exactly little Suzie Homemakers."

"We're grown women now. We know how to cook."

Mama pulls her chin back. "I'm just sayin'." She holds her hands out. "I'm sure your daddy and I will enjoy whatever you brought."

Nate stops at a table. "How's this, Mrs.

Wright? Is it okay if I put it here?"

"Just place the box on the corner of the table. I'll put everything out where it belongs."

Again, she whispers, "Where's the stuff you brought? We can move it to the back and put mine in front of it."

If this weren't Mama, I would be offended. But I know her well enough to understand that she's trying to save Sara and me from public humiliation.

"Okay, before you say another word, I want you to try a few things." I lead her over to the hummus-stuffed celery Sara made, pick one up, and hand it to her. "Here, try this."

She takes it, looks it over, and then nibbles at the edge. When she tastes the hummus, her eyes widen. "Did you make this?"

"No, Sara did. What do you think?"

"This stuff is delicious. Did Shay help y'all out again?"

"No, we did it without any help. Now I want you to try one of the things I made."

She sees the meatballs that are exactly like the ones I brought to the last gathering. "I'd love to try a meatball. Did you do something different?"

"No, I used the exact same recipe Shay showed me before. I want you to taste

392

something else I made." I pick up one of the prosciutto-wrapped melon slices, place it on a napkin, and hand it to her. "I think you'll like it."

She eats all of it before giving me a thumbs-up. "Good job, Sally. Y'all are good at making appetizers. How are you with actual cooking?"

"Gettin' pretty good, if I must say so myself." I blow on my fingertips and rub them on my shirt in an exaggerated manner.

"Amazing. Y'all are all grown up now."

I hold my hands out to my sides. "It happens."

Nate points to something he brought. "I would ask you to try my brownies, but I'm sure they're good because I bought them from the bakery."

"Hey, what's going on over here?"

Mama and I glance up in time to see Marybeth coming toward us.

"We're not supposed to touch the food yet."

"I was just tasting my daughter's food." Mama places her hands on her hips, looking just like she used to when she was getting ready to lay into Sara and me when we misbehaved. "You can't —"

A contrite look comes over Marybeth. "I

didn't mean to sound like I was fussin'." She makes a big deal of scurryin' over, exaggerating her arm motions as she sidles up to us. She tilts her head sideways as she looks up at me with a conspiratorial grin. "Mind if I try one of those?"

"You're not supposed to —" Mama stops when I give her a glare and hold up one of my hands. I can tell she didn't get the hint that Marybeth was trying to bond with us, but now I think she does. She gestures toward the melon and prosciutto wraps. "Help yourself."

Marybeth leans over, picks one up, says, "Shh, don't tell anyone," and then pops it into her mouth. Her eyes roll in appreciation. "That is off-the-charts delicious."

She reaches for another one, but Mama playfully swats at her. "Not until it's time to eat. We don't want to eat up the whole buffet."

Marybeth giggles — something I've never seen her do. "Spoilsport. Hey, do y'all want to see what I'm doing out back?"

I look up at Nate, and he nods. "Y'all go on ahead. I think I'll grab something from the drink table and go talk to Shay for a few minutes."

"Are you sure?" I tilt my head to see if he's really okay being left.

"Positive." He grins. "I'm a big boy."

Mama glances at me, I nod, and then we both look at Marybeth. "Are you getting back into gardening?" Mama asks.

"I am, but Bucky doesn't want me to mess up the lawn after he had the whole thing redone." She makes a face. "I'm having to work around his precious landscaping."

"Let's go see what you've been up to." Mama takes me by the arm and pulls me toward Marybeth. "C'mon, Sally. Stop lollygagging."

49

CORALEE

I'm so annoyed I could spit. After all that excitement over Officer Murdoch asking for my phone number and giving me hope that he'd call, I haven't heard squat. But I know he's here at the reunion. Not only did I spot his patrol car in the front yard, Grandpa Jay told me he'd been asking about me.

If he'd called, I'd be happy to know he's been talking about me, but as it is, it's like he's being a tease. I'm totally done with guys who play games after what Kyle did to me. Granted, I wasn't all that into him after a while, but couldn't he at least have let me think I broke his heart?

Speaking of Kyle, what's he doing here? I blink, hoping my eyes are playing tricks on me, but there he is, walking toward me with a half grin on his face.

"Hey, Coralee."

I squint and bob my head as I place a fist on my hip. "Just what do you think you're

396

doing here, Kyle?"

"You invited me, remember?"

I think back and can't recall being specific and actually telling him where this place is. "How'd you find the place?"

He laughs. "You've told me so much about your cousins I know where all of them live."

That's just creepy. "I still don't know why you're here."

"Now, that hurts my feelings, Coralee."

The fake pain in his voice makes me want to smack him, but I'm not into violence, especially in front of my family, so I refrain.

"I'm your guest. You're supposed to be nice to me."

"But we're not an item anymore, remember?"

"Doesn't matter. You still invited me, and you didn't tell me you changed your mind about having me here." He glances around before looking back at me. "And I didn't tell you I wasn't coming, so it would have been rude not to show up."

"Says no etiquette expert, ever." I roll my eyes as I back away from him.

"I said some things I didn't mean, and I really want to talk to you. Maybe we can —" He shrugs. "You did invite me, you know."

"It doesn't matter if I invited you because now I'm uninviting you."

"You can't do that. I'm here, and I even brought food."

"You did?" I glance around and see that some of my cousins have stopped talking and are now watching us.

He nods. "I brought a variety of chips and dips as well as a plate of cookies from a recipe my mother gave me."

"You baked?"

"Yeah. Want to try one? They're delicious." He places his arm around my back, but I yank myself away from him. I'm totally not in the mood to play whatever game he's into.

"Is this guy bothering you, Coralee?"

The sound of a familiar deep voice coming up from behind me snags my attention, so I turn around and find myself face-to-face with Officer Murdoch. My heart starts pounding, and my palms instantly go damp.

"Um . . ." I look over at Kyle, whose eyebrows are practically in his hairline. "We were just —" I stop because I can't think of anything to say that wouldn't be a lie.

Kyle quickly recovers. "Coralee and I haven't seen each other in a while."

"Oh?" Officer Murdoch gives me a questioning look. "So everything's okay?"

I shrug. "I guess."

He takes a step back and gives Kyle a menacing look that makes me want to smile. But I don't.

"I reckon I'll let the two of you finish up your conversation while I make the rounds." He smiles at me, and that melty feeling in my abdomen returns. "I'll check with you later, okay?"

I nod. Maybe there's still hope.

As soon as he's out of hearing distance, Kyle folds his arms and glares down at me. "Who is that guy?"

I bob my head and meet his gaze. "The police officer my grandpa hired to make sure nothing goes wrong at this reunion."

Kyle puckers his lips and whistles. "Your family reunions must be doozies to have to hire cops."

"They can be." I think back and can only remember one major incident that happened at the last one. "Folks in my family like to blow things up." Maybe that'll scare him away.

"Sounds exciting!" He wiggles his eyebrows. "I can't wait to see what happens at this one."

I let out a groan. Kyle is clearly determined to make my life miserable.

"Look, Kyle, I don't want to make a scene, but we broke up, remember?"

399

He bobs his head a few times and then shrugs. "I might have made a mistake."

"No, you didn't make a mistake." I give him the biggest frown I can manage. "*We* didn't make a mistake. We're clearly not meant for each other, and I don't like being used."

"Are you saying I used you?"

Is he stupid or what? "You needed tutoring, remember? And you used me to get what you needed."

"I just said that, Coralee, but I didn't mean it."

"This conversation is going nowhere, and I really think it's time for you to pick up your chips and cookies and go home." My voice cracks.

He widens his stance. "I'm not going anywhere, and I don't think there's anything you can do that won't cause a scene."

Once again, he has my number. I've always made an issue of the fact that I hate drama, so he's confident that I'm not going to say or do anything that would create it. The problem with that line of thinking is that he's forgotten about having the police officer here. I can let Officer Murdoch know that Kyle isn't an invited guest at this private party.

I look around until I finally spot the police

officer. "Excuse me. I need to go speak to my friend."

Kyle doesn't say a word as I walk away. I'm hoping he sees me chatting with Trace and takes a hint. However, after I've tapped him on the shoulder, I glance around and see Kyle still watching me.

"Hey, Coralee. Did you need something?"

"Yeah. Um . . . would you mind telling that guy . . . um —" I can't bring myself to come right out and let him know what's going on because it would cause drama, and the very thought of my being responsible for it makes my stomach churn.

"Tell what guy what?" He glances over in Kyle's direction. "Are you talking about your boyfriend?"

"See, that's just it. He's not my boyfriend. He's —"

"He's not?" The look of joy on Officer Murdoch's face catches me off guard. "Then what's he doing here?"

I take a deep breath and blow it out. "We were sort of dating, until I found out he was just using me to help him study and I got upset even though I wasn't really all that into him and . . ." My voice trails off as I realize I'm rambling. "It wasn't working out, so we broke up."

"A n d he didn't take the hint that once

y'all broke up, he was uninvited?"

"Yeah, pretty much."

"That's a tough one." He smiles down at me in a warm way that kicks my pulse into an even higher gear. "Let me think of something, but it might be a few minutes. Your grandfather has asked me to chat with the teenagers, just to remind them that I'm here."

"Thanks, Officer Murdoch."

"Please call me Trace."

"Is that okay? I mean, with you being in uniform and all?"

"Yes, it's fine. A lot of people call me Trace when I'm in uniform."

As I walk away from Trace, I feel a sense of relief that everything will be fine. That is, until Mama comes up to me with a big ol' honkin' grin on her face. "Why, Coralee, don't you have the cutest boyfriend ever? Kyle is such a sweetie pie, I can't believe you've been hiding him from us all this time."

50

SALLY

As Marybeth goes on and on about the flower beds she talked Bucky into letting her have in the backyard, I start to get a clearer picture of what's going on with her. Most of us clearly misread her, but now we're seeing something different. She's frustrated as all get out.

Mama has told me that Bucky was always the cousin most likely to show off — whether it's a new stunt on his BMX bike or something new he bought or got as a gift. I can tell Mama is getting annoyed — not so much with Marybeth but with Bucky.

Marybeth continues talking about what Bucky will and won't like, so I decide it's time to speak up. I know I have to choose my words carefully, or they'll come out making Bucky sound bad.

"What flowers do *you* want to plant?"

She taps her index finger on her chin for a moment. "I'm thinking marigolds would be nice to start with. According to what I'm reading, they don't have to be watered all that often, and they bloom all season."

Mama nods. "Yes, that's true, and I think marigolds are lovely."

I glance over at Mama, who is clearly looking for someone in the crowd that has started to overflow into the backyard. I can tell when she spots her target because she excuses herself and storms over there.

Next thing I know, she's facing off with Bucky, who appears stunned. I try my best to keep Marybeth from seeing, but that's impossible with the way Mama took off so abruptly.

Marybeth's hand flies to her mouth. "Oh no. Bucky is gonna be furious with me."

"That's okay, Marybeth. He'll get over it."

Tears well in her eyes. "You clearly don't know Bucky."

"What are you talking about?" Then it dawns on me. "Are you afraid of your husband?" When she doesn't answer, I lean closer and place my hand on her shoulder. "Does he hit you?"

She shakes her head and sniffles. "No, but he's very hardheaded." Her chin quivers. "He keeps harping on me to stop acting poor."

That actually doesn't sound all that bad

to me, but she's clearly not in the mood to hear that. "Why don't you just tell him he's lucky to have a wife who's as supportive as you are?"

Her chin quivers again. "He wouldn't like that."

My opinion of Bucky was never great, but now it's even lower. "Sometimes, Marybeth, you have to stick up for yourself, even if he doesn't like what you say."

She blinks and sniffles. "But what if he leaves me?"

"Is that what you're afraid of?" I take her hands in mine so she won't try to cover her face.

"Yes."

"I don't think he'll leave you." I leave out the fact that no other self-respecting woman would have him if he did.

"Maybe not, but if he does, I don't have anywhere to go." She lowers her head. "I came into the marriage with nothing, and I don't have decent job skills, so I'm pretty much stuck."

"You do realize that you're half of this marriage, so he can't turn you away without providing for you."

"He can't?"

"He absolutely can't." It bugs me to say something like this because I'm afraid it sounds like I'm advocating divorce. But I'm not. I just want to see Marybeth stand up for herself and find some way to make her marriage work without basing it on fear of not being able to support herself. "From what I can tell, you've been a good, supportive wife, and he should be delighted you'd even want to be by his side. I'm sure he hasn't forgotten the fact that you were there before y'all acquired all this."

She ponders this before nodding. "Yeah, I'm pretty old-school like that, and I always stand by my man. Too bad he doesn't realize that."

"Oh, I'm sure he knows, but maybe he needs to be reminded."

"Every time I try to tell him how devoted I am, he reminds me of where I came from."

I gesture around toward the crowd. "Look around, Marybeth. In case you haven't noticed, he didn't exactly come from royalty."

As if I need someone to help make my point, Uncle Bubba lets out a booming burp. I hear nervous laughter from a couple of the guests, but the family members are so used to it that they just keep on doing whatever it is they were doing before.

I give her what I hope is a comforting smile. "See what I mean?"

Marybeth nods and grins back at me. "Thank you so much, Sally. You sure are wise for being so young."

"I'm not sure about being wise, and there are days when I don't feel so young."

"You have your whole life ahead of you." Marybeth pauses and glances over toward the field with the oil rigs. "Have you and your sister decided what to do with y'all's land yet?"

"What do you mean?"

"The land you're getting from your great-grandparents."

I tilt my head and try to remember if I've heard anything about getting land. "I don't think I'm getting land. I'm sure Mama and Daddy will get some from my grand-parents."

"Nope. Your great-grandfather has already started working on passing down the rest of the acreage that he hasn't already handed out."

"Marybeth! You're not supposed to tell her yet. That's the big surprise."

I look over my shoulder and see Nana coming toward us, shaking her head and making one of her tongue-clicking sounds.

"Oops." Marybeth lifts a hand to her lips. "Sorry. I thought y'all already knew. We've told Julius about his land, but he can't have it until he's twenty-one."

"I don't think —"

Nana puts her arm around me and gives me a huge hug. "Yeah, sometimes it's best not to think."

Marybeth gives Nana an apologetic look. "Sorry, Fay."

"That's quite all right. The grands and great-grands were going to find out this weekend anyway. Daddy wanted to make a big announcement." She lets go of me and gives me a conspiratorial smile. "Do me a favor and keep it to yourself."

"Can I tell Sara?"

Nana hesitates before shaking her head. "No, you can't tell a soul. Daddy has a big old speech he's been working on to let everyone in the family know that he's sharing the remainder of the land." She purses her lips and then lets out a sigh. "He also said there won't be any strings attached. Y'all can farm it, bring in the oil companies, live on it, put a cabin on it, or sell it to another family member if you don't want to be burdened."

"How much land does Grandpa Jay have?" I ask. I thought he'd given it all away.

"Several thousand acres. His daddy bought it when it was real cheap, and since his brothers and sisters didn't want it, they sold him their shares for a dollar an acre."

"I bet they're kicking themselves now." Marybeth shakes her head. "This land is worth a fortune."

"Daddy's the only one of his siblings still living, but his nieces and nephews are okay, since he gave each of them a hundred acres."

This is all news to me, but I realize that's partly my fault, since I've never been interested in some of the family business. Now I'm speechless.

And now I'm worried. Sara and I have never kept secrets from each other before, and I'd hate for this to be the first time. It's such a doozy. A strange feeling washes over me at the realization that I'm about to have to make some life-altering decisions soon, and my life is about to change.

My concern must be obvious because Nana brushes my hair from my face. "I can see how difficult this will be. Let me go talk to Daddy and see if he can go ahead and let y'all know so you don't have to be so secretive."

"No, that's okay. If he has something planned . . ."

51
BRETT

"Get outta here." I can't believe a word Julius says. He's lied before, and I'm sure he's doing that now. "You are not a millionaire. Maybe your daddy is, but you're not."

"I am too a millionaire." Julius's voice drops. "Can you keep a secret?"

"What kind of secret?" I don't trust my cousin any farther than I can throw him. "What kind of lie are you gonna tell me now?"

Julius holds up his hand, like that proves he's telling the truth. "This is the honest truth, I swear."

Mama and Daddy don't allow us to say *I swear,* which used to bug me, but now I get it. "Okay, so what's your secret?"

"Promise you won't tell?" He narrows his eyes and gives me a half-threatening look.

"Okay, I'll play. I promise I won't tell."

His expression changes, and he grins real

big. "You're gonna be a millionaire too."

"Now I know you're full of it. Stop saying things like that."

"No, really. Grandpa Jay is giving all us young'uns some land."

"That doesn't make us millionaires." I look past the fields and toward the forests lining the land where Julius's mama and daddy built their mansion.

"It does if you put some oil rigs on it, and that's what I fully intend to do."

Then something dawns on me. "Wait a minute. How come I'm getting land if my own mama and daddy haven't gotten any?"

"Maybe Grandpa Jay doesn't like your mama and daddy. They are kinda different, if you know what I mean." Julius pretends to flick something off his shoulder. "Just sayin'."

I know he's spoilin' for a fight, so I tighten my jaw to keep from saying what's on my mind — first of all, my parents might not be perfect, but I like them a whole lot more than his. And Grandpa Jay isn't like that. He's true-blue loyal to his family and the fairest person I know, which is one of the reasons everyone loves him, even though a lot of them can't stand each other. And I'm sure he and Granny Marge are the reason we're still getting together like this. It makes them happy to see the family all hanging out.

Julius gets in my face. "Did you hear me?"

"I heard you, but I'm trying to ignore you."

He laughs. "Your dad is out driving packages to people, while my dad gets to have fun and do what he wants to all day because he's smart. And your mom . . . ." He shakes his head and snorts. "My dad says he can't believe she owns a fashion store, 'cause she doesn't know one end of an outfit from another."

"Hold it a second." I can't take it anymore now that Julius has crossed the line. "My parents work hard for a living."

"That's just it. They have to work hard because they're losers."

I make a fist and take a step toward him when I hear someone from behind. "Whoa there, boys. What's going on?"

I turn around and see the police officer who has obviously snuck up on me and Julius. I relax my fist and take a deep breath.

"Is there something I can help y'all settle?" The officer looks at me with a half smile, and then he turns to Julius with a warning look in his eyes. I can tell he knows who started this whole thing, but I'm still on guard.

412

"Nah, we were just having a little fun." Julius gives me an I-dare-you-to-say-anything look. "Weren't we, Brett?"

I tighten my jaw and don't say a word. Julius doesn't deserve to be defended.

The officer puts his hands on his hips, glances over his shoulder, and then turns back to face me. "I think your mama could use some help at the food table." He pauses, tilts his head forward, and gives me a look like we have a secret. "She could use some *muscle.*"

"Okay." I take a couple of steps back before I turn around and run. When I get to where Mama is standing with some of our cousins, I look back at Julius, who appears to be getting an earful from the officer. And he doesn't look the least bit happy.

"Hey, Brett. What are you doing over here?" Julius's mom leans over to check out her son. "Why aren't you over there with Julius?"

I shrug. "I figured I could help Mama with some of this stuff."

Mama gives me a curious glance, but I can tell something has dawned on her when she smiles and steps closer. "Yeah, you're right. I want to move the dessert table."

"No," Julius's mom says. "Bucky wants it there."

"But it'll get all clogged up here with folks from the main course table and those who want dessert."

"You'd better ask Bucky before you start moving tables around." Julius's mom has dropped her niceness, and she sounds like she did at the last reunion. "He says it'll make for better photo ops where it is now."

Mama clears her throat. "Brett, why don't you stand right here while I go talk to Bucky? I'll be right back."

Now I'm stuck standing a couple of feet away from the woman who has always made Mama feel bad about herself. My parents said she's been a lot nicer lately, and I sort of saw that, until now. She has that pinched-face expression that reminds me of the mean lady in the lunchroom back when I was in elementary school — kind of like she's been eating lemons. I can't stand the thought of her judging me, which I'm sure she's probably doing now, so I look down at the ground.

"Did you see Julius's car?"

I look up at his mom and see that her expression has gone back to being nice. I nod. "He took me to the hardware store in it."

"No, not that car. I'm talking about the boxcar."

An image of the orange crate pops into my head, and I nod. "I saw it last time I was here."

"What do you think of it?"

I hate being put on the spot like this, but I have to say something. "I think the orange color will stand out."

She lets out a crazy laugh before catching herself. Then she places her hand on my shoulder. "Now, that's an understatement if I've ever heard one."

I sigh with relief. It sounds like she's come back to her senses, but I don't want to take any chances and get caught off guard again, so I look around for Daddy. He's over by some of the guys he calls his *nice* cousins, clearly talking about what he calls *man talk*. That's where I want to be, but I can't because Mama told me to stay right where I am.

"Uh-oh." Julius's mom nods to something behind me, so I turn around. "Looks like Bucky didn't tell her what she wanted to hear."

52
SALLY

You'd think someone told Bucky his house is on fire based on his crazy reaction to someone coming up with a better idea on how to arrange the serving tables. He's ranting and raving, flailing his arms around, while Puddin' stands there staring at him like he's lost his mind. And that's pretty much what everyone is thinking from the looks on their faces.

"This is my house and my yard, so who on earth do you think you are?" If Bucky's face gets any redder than it is, it'll catch on fire. "Don't even bother answering that because I know you're nothing but a loser."

My heart stops for a second as I wait for Puddin's reaction and pray that she doesn't make things worse by spouting off. But she doesn't. Instead, her chest expands with a deep breath, and a smile gradually spreads across her lips.

A strange expression comes over Bucky.

416

"What are you grinnin' at me like that for?"

"If people start trippin' over each other and someone gets hurt, it's all on you. Don't say I didn't try to help." She folds her arms and smirks at him without saying another word.

Bucky's expression changes as he processes what she said. Finally, he lifts his arms in surrender. "Fine. Do whatever you want. Ruin my yard while you're at it. I'll send you the bill when this thing is over."

"Seriously?" Puddin' tips her head forward and gives him one of the looks she's known for giving her kids. Then her nostrils flare as she takes a breath and lets it out, never once losing eye contact.

"Whatever. There's no reasoning with you, Puddin', but what can I expect from anyone who's foolish enough to marry Digger?"

She shakes her head, turns around, brushes her hands together as though she has just finished an important but dirty job, and walks away, leaving Bucky staring after her. It takes me a minute to realize she has just taken Bucky down.

Five minutes later, some of the stronger men are rearranging the tables while Bucky stands there with his hands on his hips, nostrils flaring, and not saying anything. I'm so proud of Puddin' I almost can't stand it.

In the past, she always acted like she had something to prove, but now she has the confidence that being a successful business-woman has given her.

Everyone at the reunion knows that the only reason Bucky has all this expensive stuff is that he inherited the land with oil, so they don't pay much attention to any-thing he says. And we also remember where he and Marybeth lived before they had the means to build this pretentious mansion.

When people start praising Puddin' for coming up with a new serving table arrange-ment, she grins for a while but eventually holds up her hand and tells them it's time to talk about something else. I can tell she's practicing humility, but she really loves the compliments.

Each reunion we have someone different — most often a guest pastor — give the blessing, but we don't have clergy present at this one. So Grandpa Jay stands on the top step of the mansion's back porch and lifts his hands. Everyone instantly grows quiet, with the exception of those who don't or can't see him. But someone gives them a nudge, so within seconds, the only thing we can hear is a few birds that dare make noise.

As he praises the Lord for bringing our loving family together and asks for forgiveness for our sins, I hear a few people chuckle. But when he moves on to giving thanks for the food we're about to eat, I hear the squirming from more than a hundred hungry people. They know it's almost time to eat.

After the blessing, a resounding shout of "Amen!" comes from my hungry family members before they converge on the tables filled with everyone's best casseroles, salads, and desserts. It's a good thing the tables have been moved, or there would be a logjam, something that could be a disaster with this hungry family.

"They act like a pack of starving animals." I glance over my shoulder and see Sara smiling and shaking her head. "You'd think they never saw food before, the way they're pouncing on the food."

"I think it's all in how they've been conditioned." I point to the table holding most of the meat. "In case you haven't noticed, it's mostly men."

"Yeah, I have noticed." She nods toward her husband, who is right up there with Uncle Bubba, Uncle Irby, George, Digger, and a large group of our other male cousins and guests. "And I know for a fact that Justin has eaten today. He told me he fixed Grandpa Jay and himself each a six-egg omelet with ham, potatoes, and tons of cheese."

"I sure wish I knew where he put it. If I ate like that, I'd have to buy a whole new wardrobe."

"Where's Nate?"

"With all this craziness, he's had to fend for himself." I look around and spot him approaching the meat table on the other side. "There he is."

"Why don't you stop worrying about everyone else and give him more attention?" Sara shakes her head. "He's such a good guy, and I think there might be something there if you allow it to happen."

"Yeah, I know. I really do like him." He makes me feel safe.

"So you've said. Speaking of Nate, has he given you any indication of when you'll be able to close on the condo?"

"He thinks it should happen before Christmas." I try to remember all the details he said I'd have to take care of first. "We need an inspection, and we have to make sure everything that's broken is fixed."

"Can't it wait until after the holidays?"

"No, if I don't act quickly, she might back down, and then I'll have to start over. I really need to move forward with this."

"That's just sad." Sara's bottom lip protrudes in the same way mine does when I'm not happy about something. "I was hoping we'd all be able to sit by the tree and sip hot chocolate on Christmas Eve."

"We can still do that," I remind her. "It's not like I'll be all that far away."

"I know, but —"

"Hey, Sally, you'd better get some meat while there's still any left."

I turn and see Nate walking toward us with a plate filled with chicken, pork, and fish.

"I don't see any vegetables." I clamp my mouth shut as soon as I realize I'm sounding just like Mama.

A sheepish look comes over him. "Yeah, I reckon I'd better go get some salad or carrots or something."

"Puddin' makes an awesome broccoli casserole," Sara says. "Or if you like cold veggies, you can try some of the stuffed celery."

"Okay." Nate turns back toward the table filled with sides, leaving Sara and me alone again.

Sara raises her eyebrows. "He's so much like Justin when it comes to food I can't stand it."

"And they're both like Daddy."

She crinkles her nose. "Are you saying we're attracted to our daddy?"

"That doesn't sound right, but I've heard that happens."

"You girls better go on up and get yourself something." Daddy has a plate in each hand as he stops beside us. "I don't want y'all missing out on the good stuff."

Sara looks at me, and we both laugh. "We were just about to hit the salad table."

"Okay, but don't wait all day."

As soon as he leaves, we both snort, until Sara pipes up. "I guess that just proves what we were saying."

"But I'm not married to Nate," I remind her.

We approach the table where Nate is standing. He smiles at me, warming me from the inside out. I feel my cheeks flame, so I tilt my head forward so my hair will cover it.

"This is unfamiliar territory to me," he says.

"Me too."

He gives me a tender look. "I'm talking about the vegetable table."

Again, my face heats up. "Oh. Why don't you try a little of each and dip it in some of the dressing? Everything's good with ranch dressing."

"Great idea." He looks at me again. "By the way, the way I'm feelin' about you is unfamiliar to me too."

"I'm sorry I haven't been as attentive as I should be."

"Don't worry about it, Sally. I totally understand. Besides, it's giving me a chance to chat with some of your relatives. I'm actually having a great time."

I love the fact that he doesn't need hand-holding, but I also feel like I need to give him more attention. I make a vow to myself to do better.

Sara approaches and gestures toward Nate, who is loading up his plate with broccoli, carrots, and celery. "Look at that. How did you manage that?"

Nate glances toward her with a goofy grin. "She told me it'll be good with ranch dressing."

She opens her mouth to say something, but the sound of folks hollering echoes through the air. My heart pounds as I look at her widened eyes.

Seconds later, I hear Grandpa Jay's thunderous voice coming from the top step on the back porch. "Everyone stay put. We don't need everyone getting involved. Officer Murdoch will take care of whatever's going on." Without another word, he comes down off the porch and heads in the direction of the hollering.

I hear someone say, "I bet it's those boys again. Didn't they learn their lesson last time?"

53

MARYBETH

"Wait right here, Marybeth. I'll deal with this." As soon as Bucky takes off to see what on earth the boys are up to, I close my eyes and send up a prayer for our son. And I add an extra plea for Grandpa Jay to have mercy on him for not obeying.

There's no doubt in my mind that the screaming and screeching sound is the result of one of Julius's shenanigans. My husband clearly doesn't see that he's spoilin' Julius to the point where there may be no return, and I'm afraid that might be happening at this very moment.

"What on earth?" Puddin' steps up beside me.

"Brace yourself," I whisper so only she can hear. "I have a feeling we might be dealing with our sons getting into trouble again."

No sooner have I said that than I see Julius and Brett running around the corner of the opposite side of the house from the noise. "Did y'all just hear something?" My son looks sincerely concerned.

"It wasn't y'all?"

"Wait, what?" Julius narrows his eyes and gives me a look of disbelief. "Are you kidding? We've been working on the boxcar and planning our strategy."

Puddin' lets out a sigh of relief. "These boys must have learned their lesson."

"Then who — and what — was it?" I move a few feet away and shield my eyes from the sun as I glance in the direction of the sound.

Bucky comes out from around the house shaking his head, and Grandpa Jay is right behind him looking equally bewildered. They both stop about twenty feet from the crowd that's holding its collective breath. Grandpa Jay glances over at Bucky, who is shuffling his feet and clearly not in the mood to convey the message we're all waiting to hear.

Finally, after what seems like forever, Grandpa Jay speaks up. "Resume whatever you were doing before this incident. It's nothing any of you need to worry about."

Since folks in this family rarely defy him, several of them go about their business. But this isn't going to work for Granny Marge, who marches right up to her husband, stops a couple of feet from him, and plants her fists on her hips. And then I think she does a little head bob, sort of like what I see the young women in the family doing. I have to stifle a giggle.

Then she pulls out the dreaded index finger and wags it at Grandpa Jay. "If you think you can get away with not telling us what just happened to cause all that commotion, you've got another think coming."

The helpless look on Grandpa Jay's face is priceless and makes him seem more human to me. His very presence has always been so huge I forget he's a mere man.

"Okay." He holds up his hands to let everyone know he's about to say something profound. "We had a bit of a romantic brawl."

"Ooh, sounds interesting." Granny Marge widens her eyes. "I hope you don't think you can stop there."

"What more do you want?" he asks.

"Whose romantic brawl, for one, and what happened?"

He looks down at his wife and speaks so softly I can barely hear him. "Can we discuss this privately?"

"Sure." Without another word, she takes him by the hand and leads him to the back of the house. Bucky is right behind them, and after he says something I can't hear, they go inside.

Once they're away from the crowd, Puddin' joins me again. "It was Coralee."

I pull back and look at her with caution. "How would you know this?"

She gestures over toward the side yard, where Coralee is talking to a young man who appears pretty miserable. "Apparently, there's a love triangle with her, that boy she's talking to, and Officer Murdoch."

"You've got to be kidding." I shield my eyes as I scan the crowd. "Speaking of Officer Murdoch, where is he?"

"According to Digger, Grandpa Jay sent him home."

"Oh wow. It just goes to show that anything can happen, even when you bring in a cop to make sure nothing happens."

Puddin' nods. "Words of wisdom if I ever heard 'em."

I see someone walking toward the back door and turn to see that it's Coralee. A warning bell goes off in my head. It's one thing to have craziness outside where everyone is hanging out but another thing to go into my private space. This is one of the reasons I didn't want to go along with Bucky's plan to have everyone here for the weekend. "I think I'll go check on things and make sure —"

Puddin' interrupts me. "Make sure nothing gets broken?"

I force a laugh. "Yeah, something like that."

"Then I'm coming with you." She grins when I turn around and look at her. "You know. For support."

I can't even begin to describe the feeling that surges through me, merely from Puddin's promise of support. If being close to my husband's family does this for me, I want more of it, and I'll do whatever it takes to have it.

54
SALLY

Sara nudges me in the side. "Even after hiring a cop, this family has more drama in a day than most see their whole lives."

"We don't know that." I pause. "I suspect others are just as bad, but they keep it to themselves."

"It's these reunions that are making us famous in Pinewood and parts of Hattiesburg."

I nod. "But as long as it doesn't go beyond Pinewood and the 'Burg, we'll be fine."

"Yeah, we don't need someone taking our dirty laundry to the tabloids." She holds her hand up as if pointing to a headline. "I can just see it now. *Rabble-rousing with Rich Rednecks.*"

"Rednecks?" I give my sister a pretend glare. "Speak for yourself. I like to think of this family as eclectic — with a smattering of redneck blood but just as much southern charm and grace."

She tilts her head back and laughs out loud. "Right."

"Do you really think we're all rednecks?"

Sara smiles and then shakes her head. "Not really. But you have to admit that anyone who sees us at a family reunion would jump to conclusions."

"I suppose you're right." I look around to make sure no one else can hear. "There are some pretty rough edges on a few of our family members."

"Ya think?"

"Hey, what're you girls so talky-talky about?" Justin comes up from behind and puts his arms around Sara. "Looks like you might be tellin' secrets."

"Of course we are," I say. "That's what we do best."

I notice someone else approaching in my peripheral vision, so I look up and see that it's Nate. He smiles and gives me a look that nearly turns me inside out. "Hey. Did y'all get everything worked out?"

A wave of guilt washes over me. "As much as possible."

"And that's not saying a lot," Justin retorts. "There's always something to work out in this family." He chuckles. "That's not always a bad thing though, and there's never a dull moment."

I'm amazed by how chatty Justin is right now. He's been keeping Nate company, and knowing Justin, he wouldn't bother if he didn't like him. That makes me smile because I really like him too, in spite of the fact that I haven't been as attentive as I should be. It's just that sometimes I'm not sure what to do with someone other than my sister. And after our conversation at the salad table, I don't feel quite as bad.

If given half a chance, I think I might even be able to fall in love with Nate. I just have to be careful to guard my heart so I don't wind up being failed fiancée number four. But now that everything has calmed down, I decide to try to make amends.

"I'm so sorry I've been a bad date," I say. "I hope you don't hate me."

"I don't hate you." He gently turns my face toward his.

I look him in the eye, and he smiles. "I promise I won't leave you alone with my family again."

He holds up his hands before taking one of mine. "I've already told you not to worry about it. I've had a good time seeing first-hand what so many folks have been saying. You really do have a lot of excitement at these things."

Justin nods. "That's putting it mildly."

Sara and I exchange a glance, and she speaks up. "Let's try to have a good time while we're here, okay? Put all this stuff behind us."

I nod. "Sounds good to me."

The four of us stand around and discuss the food, and since Sara and I haven't had a chance to eat, the guys walk with us over to the tables, where it looks like a bunch of buzzards have hit. Sara gives me a sideways glance before picking up a plate and trying to figure out what to do next.

Justin points to a very unattractive casserole. "That tastes a lot better than it looks."

Sara makes a face, baring her teeth. "What is it?"

"Um . . ." Justin looks at Nate, who shrugs. "I think it's chicken."

"All righty, then." Sara picks up the serving spoon and scoops a little bit onto her plate. "I think I'll go see if any of Missy's chili is left."

"I saved you some." Missy's voice catches Sara's and my attention. "I have a whole 'nother Crock-Pot of it in the garage, but don't tell anyone." She smiles. "I figured something might happen, so I decided to have backup this time."

I let out a deep sigh. "I think you just

saved us."

"What's a cousin for if she can't be there for ya?" She takes a couple of steps toward the garage, stops, and gestures for us to follow. "I don't want to bring it out, or folks'll converge like the monkeys from *Wizard of Oz*."

That cracks Sara and me up, and we laugh all the way to the edge of the garage. Missy holds up her hands to stop us. "Somethin's going on in there. Listen."

Sara and I both lean forward. Missy makes a zipping motion across her lips to tell us to be quiet.

"I don't give a hoot what you want, I'm done." It's clearly a young woman's voice, but I can't quite make out whose. "So why don't you just leave me alone?"

"I can't, Coralee. Not after what I did to you. I feel awful."

"Stop worrying, because I'm over it."

"But I'm not." The man's voice has turned all gravelly, almost like he's on the verge of tears. "When I told you I was only using you to help me study, that wasn't exactly true. How many times do I have to tell you that?"

"Then what's the truth?"

"I was covering up how I really felt. And

now I'm ready to admit that I'm in love with you."

Sara's eyes grow huge as saucers as she looks back and forth between Justin and me. "We can't go in there."

Missy makes a face and whispers, "Why don't y'all stay right here? I can go in there and pretend I didn't hear a word of it."

"Nah, that's okay." I take a step back. "We can find something else."

Sara shakes her head vehemently. "Speak for yourself, Sally. I'm starving, and I'm determined to have some of Missy's chili, no matter what I have to do to get it."

The pleased expression on Missy's face makes Sara's comment all the more comical to me. I let out a nervous laugh, and Nate stifles a grin as he winks at me.

Before I have a chance to say another word, Missy goes straight into the garage. I hear her greeting Coralee, rattling the Crock-Pot, and making an issue of apologizing for interrupting. When she appears in front of us holding the Crock-Pot, she has a humongous smile on her face — almost as if to say *ta-da!*

55

CORALEE

It takes me forever to get rid of Kyle. His profession of love is way too late, but even if he'd said it when we were still seeing each other, I wouldn't have been all that happy. Red flags kept popping up, and then there was the matter of the chemistry that fizzled out for me pretty quickly. But I stuck around a little longer than I should have because it was convenient. Now I understand why folks stay together even when they don't seem to care a lick about the other person.

I'm surprised that Marybeth took me to one of the guest rooms, insisting I stay for the weekend. It's gorgeous in here with the forest-green furniture and deep coral accents. But I'm not in the mood to enjoy my surroundings. I plop down on the loveseat, lean forward, and bury my face in my hands.

Now I have to figure out what's going on with Officer Murdoch. Trace. He acted awful strange when he realized Kyle was the one who made me cry. And I'm talking strange in a good way. Like he was happy that he could be there for me.

If I weren't so confused about my attraction to him, I'd be laughing about what happened when he walked up to Kyle and me. He gave me an odd look and asked again if Kyle and I were an item. I said no at the same time Kyle said yes. Officer Murdoch then asked if Kyle was being a nuisance. I started to say no, but Kyle decided to make it his business to talk for me. That's when things got out of hand. Kyle shoved Trace, who told him to keep his hands to himself. Then Kyle acted in a way that shocked me. He started to shove him again, but Trace warned him that it was against the law and that he'd be in a lot of trouble. Instead of making physical contact, Kyle tried a little bit of taunting, until Grandpa Jay came in and took over. This is as close to having anyone fight *over me* as I've ever experienced and probably ever will. Go figure.

I'm the girl who has never had a long-term relationship. I'm the girl who never had a date until college. And now I'm the girl who is confused between two guys — one who has come right out and said he wants me but I don't trust him and the other who hasn't made the first move but he makes my heart feel like it has wings. I know I'm not into Kyle, but my feelings for Trace could be based on any number of things, like he's so cute in uniform, like he was there to save me, or it's a real feeling that can blossom into something really special. I don't want to make a colossal mistake like I've seen so many people do, so I decide to let things happen naturally and not force them.

After I take a few minutes to regroup, I reluctantly go back out to join the family. A few people give me a double take, but no one pounces on me, demanding to know what happened. I'm shocked. I fully expected everyone to crowd around me, asking questions, making a big deal of what happened.

It appears that a bunch of hungry hogs hit the table, but I go over there to see if I can find anything decent. I put a few things on my plate and start for one of the picnic tables when Missy approaches carrying a disposable bowl. I glance down at it and see the steaming chili.

"I thought this might make you feel better." She holds it out to me. "It's from my secret stash that I hid for times like this."

I feel a smile coming on as I take it. Missy

has always been very sweet, but she tends to fade into the background for me. That'll never happen again. She's my hero now.

"Want me to join you, or are you in the mood to be alone?" she asks.

"You can join me if you want." I look around and see that there's already at least one person sitting at each table.

She nods and points off to the distance where a portable table sits beneath one of the big pecan trees. "Why don't we go over there?"

As we walk toward the table, I take a deep breath. It's unseasonably warm for November, but a gentle breeze keeps it from getting too hot.

I sit with my back to the house, and Missy sits across from me. "This is my award-winning chili." She pauses as I scoop the first bite into my mouth.

"I can see why. It's delicious." After I swallow, I take another bite.

Missy smiles. "It makes me happy to hear nice things about my cooking. Foster has never been one to heap praise on me."

There's something in her tone that catches my attention. I stop eating and look her in the eye to see a deep sadness that breaks my heart.

"How long have you and Foster been married?" I ask.

She chuckles. "More than twenty years."

"That's a long time." I leave out the rest of what I'm thinking — that it's way too long to be as miserable as she appears.

She sighs. "Yes, it certainly is."

"I hope I can find someone to spend my life with." I put down my spoon and clear my throat. "I mean, I want to finish college and get a good job, but sometimes I get lonely."

"Looks to me like you don't have to stay lonely." Missy's smile returns. "Both of those boys are totally smitten."

I ponder how much to tell her and quickly decide to let her know all about what happened. She listens attentively and gives me an occasional nod. When I finish with the scene that occurred earlier, she widens her eyes and shakes her head.

"So I don't know what to believe." I shrug. "Maybe I just need to go meet more people and start over."

"If only it were that easy." She pulls her lips between her teeth, and I can tell she's itching to say something.

I narrow my gaze as I stare at her. "What?"

"I hate giving advice when I'm not asked, but I have some if you're interested."

I shrug. "Sure. I'm open to advice, since

I'm clearly clueless."

"Well . . ." She fiddles with a paper napkin she's been holding. "I can't attest to that boy Kyle's feelings, but I think you and Officer Murdoch should get to know each other."

"He seems nice."

Missy laughs. "He's more than nice, and it's obvious he likes you enough to stick up for you." She pauses. "I think it's clear how much he likes you."

It's not that I want anyone fighting over me, or getting hurt in my honor. But it sure does feel good to hear this coming from someone who isn't directly involved. "You really think so?"

"I do, and that's not all."

I lean forward. "Don't keep me in suspense."

She giggles. "I might shouldn't say this, but according to Granny Marge, he asked Grandpa Jay if it was okay to take you out to dinner next week."

"He did?" I ponder that for a moment. "It takes guts to approach Grandpa Jay."

Missy nods. "I know, right? He's clearly super interested, or he would never have done that." She glances over her shoulder. "Why don't we go inside where there's a little privacy?"

I nod and follow her into the house. Now I'm so excited I start blabbering my head off. At first, I let her know how my life has changed over the past couple of months, and that leads to the fact that if I'd known before what I know now, I would have had a social life much sooner. Being a mousy wallflower in ill-fitting clothes and not putting myself out there because I was too afraid of rejection only perpetuated my lack of socialization.

Mama used to tell me that there was no in-between with me. When I'm out and about, I don't utter a peep, but when I get home, I'm a motor mouth. But I can't help myself. And Missy remains sitting there listening, although she does have a strange look on her face.

56

SALLY

"Have you seen Nate?"

"Yes, sweetie. I was chatting with him a few minutes ago." Mama gives me what appears to be a pitying look. "I know you're all wrapped up in your own thing, but you really should give him more attention. He's such a sweet young man."

"He's fine." This time he's the one who wandered off. "Where is he now?"

Mama shrugs. "Justin came and got him. Apparently, Bucky wanted them to come look at a boxcar he built for Julius."

"Where is it?"

"In the garage, I think."

I leave Mama with one of our cousins and head on over to the garage, where Nate and Justin are deep in conversation with Bucky and Digger. They're clearly talking guy talk, so I wander toward the house, where the back door is standing open. I push it a little farther and go inside.

As I walk into the house, I hear Coralee going on a rant about how tired she is of being the last to know anything, while Missy just stands there with her mouth hanging open, looking like she wishes she could be anywhere but here. Before I have a chance to sneak back out, Coralee spots me.

"Hi." I give her a shaky grin. "Sorry. I didn't mean to walk in on —"

"No, you're fine." Coralee motions for me to step closer. "I want your opinion on something."

"Um . . ." I glance over at Missy, who gives me an apologetic look and a shrug. "Okay, what do you want my opinion about?"

She doesn't waste a second before telling me about how she was pulled over when she was crying about Kyle and that she was instantly attracted to the police officer. "I mean, with a cute face like that, how could I not be?"

Once again, I look at Missy, whose face is expressionless — sort of like she's afraid to commit to a smile or frown. Then I glance back at Coralee. "I get it."

"Okay, so then he doesn't call me, and I've lost hope, but then here he is at the family reunion." She goes on to tell about how Kyle crashed the reunion and then he

444

got into it with Officer Murdoch. "Who gets in a fight with a cop?"

I'm not sure, but I don't think she wants an answer, so I shrug. "Not someone I'd care to be with."

She scrunches her face into the frowniest look I've ever seen. "I thought maybe Trace would ask me out, but he didn't, and then Missy here tells me he asked Grandpa Jay if it was okay to take me to dinner." She pauses. "What guy does that these days?"

Now I'm pretty sure she wants an answer. "A guy who wants to do the right thing?"

"I don't know." She tilts her head and gives me an odd look. "Do you really think so?"

I nod. "Absolutely."

Missy steps forward and touches Coralee's arm. "I agree with Sally. I think he's an honorable guy who wants to get off on the right foot."

"Guys might have done that back when you were my age, but that's not how it's done now."

"How would you know?" Missy pauses and tips her head to the side as she looks at Coralee. "You've already told me you don't have much experience with guys."

Coralee lets out a nervous giggle. "I probably shouldn't admit this, but I'm sort of addicted to reality TV. I've seen how people are on those shows."

Missy lifts an eyebrow. "If you're trying to do what those rude reality TV stars do, you'll never find true love." She gives Coralee an I-feel-for-you grin. "And to be honest, I don't think those shows are all that real. They're staged. There are truly some honorable folks out there who know how to stay out of trouble."

I swallow hard, hoping Coralee doesn't come back with Missy's past. Most people over the age of twenty-one know that her daughter arrived six months after they got married.

To my relief — and I'm sure Missy's — Coralee taps her finger on her chin. "So you're saying that Trace is doing things the old-fashioned way because he likes me?"

This is the first time I've heard her call the officer by his first name, and I'm thinking that's a good sign.

Missy cuts a glance over at me and gives me a forced smile before turning her attention on Coralee again. "Yes, that's pretty much what I'm saying." She takes a sideways step toward me.

Coralee folds her arms and stares down at the floor for a few seconds before lifting her gaze back to Missy and then to me. "Okay, so what do I do now?"

"When he asks you out, you say you'd love to go." As I state the obvious, I look at Missy, hoping for backup.

Her reaction catches me off guard. "Or you tell him you're not interested."

I want to ask her what on earth she's talking about, but Coralee speaks up. "But I am interested."

Missy grins as she holds out her arms. "Then it's settled. You accept the date."

"And then what?"

Now that I see what Missy has done — get Coralee to commit — I chime in. "You go out and have a good time getting to know him."

Something behind me catches Coralee's attention. "Like *you're* not doing with *your* boyfriend?" I glance over my shoulder and see Nate standing there with Bucky, whose voice I heard.

"Oh, hi." Now I feel silly offering advice I'm not heeding in my own life.

Missy gestures toward the door. "Why don't you go have some fun, Sally? I can take over from here."

As I join Nate, Bucky runs his hands through his hair. "Is everything okay in here? Do y'all need me?"

Coralee makes a face as she and Missy

both speak at the same time. "No."

"All righty then, I'll just head on back out and make sure everything is running smoothly." He walks toward the door with Nate and me, mumbling something about folks wandering off, acting like they own the place.

As soon as Nate and I are alone, he puts his arm around my shoulder. "Can we go somewhere and talk? Privately?"

"Sure." I shield my eyes from the sun and look around. "Why don't we go over to the other side of the house?"

I'm pleasantly surprised to see a two-seater swing beneath a large oak tree. Nate points to it. "How's that?"

As we sit down and start swaying, he pulls me closer. I have to admit it feels good to be in the protective arms of a guy I really like.

"So, have you managed to solve all your family's problems?"

I look up at him and see the teasing grin on his face. "Pretty much."

"I could tell it was important for you to handle some things, so I tried to leave you alone as much as possible."

"I'm sorry."

He shakes his head and waves his hand around. "Don't worry about it. I've had a good time getting to know some of the guys. Justin and I get along great."

I've noticed that Justin gets along with almost everyone, but I don't say that. "I'm glad."

"Me too." He lifts a hand and brushes the hair from my face as he gazes at me with adoration. "I really like you, Sally."

"Even though I've invited you here and left you to fend for yourself?"

He chuckles. "I like the fact that you are your own woman and not someone who clings."

"You don't think I've been rude?"

"Not rude, but I would like to spend more time with you."

I take his hand in mine and look him in the eye. "I promise I'll be more attentive. I'll spend the rest of the day with you."

"And I'd like nothing better."

Before I have a chance to say another word, he lowers his face to mine and kisses me. I'm sure he can feel my pulse through my lips, but I don't care. This is how I'd always imagined a kiss making me feel but never really knew if that would ever happen.

57

SHEILA

Whoa. I should have known better than to leave the group I was chatting with, but I've already done it, and now I've seen something I can't unsee. Sure, Sally is a grown woman, and her twin is already married and pregnant. But she's still one of my babies.

I duck back around the house, hoping Sally doesn't notice me and praying that she doesn't think I'm spying on her. I let my head fall back as I suck in some air, since every ounce of it left my lungs the instant I saw her in a lip-lock with Nate.

Nate. The boy who's smack-dab in the middle of stealing my baby. The boy I want to hate but can't for more than one reason. First, he's very sweet. Second, he's cute as all get out, and I can see why my daughter was attracted to him to begin with. And third, she clearly likes him, and I've always told my girls that anyone who's a friend of theirs is a friend of mine. But still.

"Sheila?"

I spin around and see my husband standing about ten feet away, looking apprehensive. "Hey, Georgie."

"Are you okay?" He takes a step closer but stops before he's within reach. I can tell he's not sure what to do with his hands or his feet, since he's shuffling around and kicking his toe on the ground. I must have a crazy expression for him to be acting like that.

I take a deep breath and try to relax my facial muscles. "I'm fine."

"So, what's going on?" He tips his head to one side.

I swallow hard because I'm not sure what to say. I don't want to lie to my husband, but I'm not sure I should tell him I've been snooping. Actually, it isn't exactly snooping, but there's no doubt in my mind it'll sound like that's what it is.

He shuffles his feet and studies the ground before meeting my gaze with an odd look. "Did you see what I just saw?"

I tilt my head to the side and give him a questioning look. "All depends. What did you just see?"

"Sally and . . . uh, her fella were sort of . . ."

"Kissing?" I can't help laughing at his reaction that seems even more overblown than mine.

"Yeah." Now he looks so pained that an overwhelming urge to comfort him washes over me.

I close the distance between us and put my hands behind his neck and clasp them. "You mean like this?"

Before he has a chance to answer, I put my lips on his and give him a big ol' honkin' smackaroo. It takes a few seconds, but his tense body eventually relaxes. I have to admit it's good to know I still have that effect on him after all these years. It's been quite a while since I've kissed him spontaneously like that.

"Hey, you two."

We break our kiss and look off to the side. There stands my father-in-law chuckling and shaking his head.

I keep my hands clasped behind Georgie's neck as I continue looking at Dennis. "Are you spying on us?"

"Not any more than you're spying on my granddaughter." He laughs again. "There's definitely a lot of romance in the air around here."

"Then you'd better go find Fay. There's a lot of good-looking men around here too."

"Don't forget," Dennis says as he holds

up an index finger. "She's related to most of them, and as far as I know, this family tree has branched out quite nicely."

"But you still might want to know where she is," Georgie says. "After what happened at the last reunion, it's not a bad idea to keep track of folks."

"Oh, trust me, I know where Fay is. She's busy chasing after Digger's little one. That little guy sure is a handful, but he's definitely lovable. We need us some great-grandchildren."

"Which you're getting soon enough."

Dennis rubs the back of his neck. "Yeah, I have to admit I'm surprised by that. Me and Fay always figured Sally would be the first one to get hitched. I never imagined Sara making a decision that big on her own."

"This family is full of surprises," I remind him.

As he turns around to leave, I hear him mutter, "You can say that again."

Georgie drops another kiss on my lips before letting go of me. "I think it's time to get back to the party. I don't want folks to worry about us."

I take his hand and walk with him. When we get to the group, I see Sally and Nate standing off by the barbecue pit talking with Sara and Justin, and it brings a plethora of feelings. On the one hand, I'm happy to see my grown daughters acting all . . . well, all grown up. But on the other hand, I'm not so sure I'm ready for this.

"Why don't we —"

As I'm about to suggest joining our daughters and their guys, the sound of something rumbling toward us catches my attention. A bunch of people hop out of the way, and that's when I see a bright orange hunk of wood with a helmet-clad head sticking out of the top coming toward us. I don't have a chance to hop out of the way before the boxcar is right upon me.

"Mama!"

That's the last sound I hear before I fall to the ground.

58
SALLY

I can't get to Mama fast enough, and Sara is right behind me — the only thing slowing her down is exhaustion from her pregnancy. She says she could take a nap any time of day or night now that she's pregnant. Before I reach Mama, Julius has hopped out of the orange hunk of junk and removed his helmet. But the instant he gets out, he just stands there and stares down at her with an odd expression I can't read.

Mama is lying on the ground, clearly unconscious. I kneel down beside her, lift her hand, and check her pulse. Relief floods me as I feel that she still has one, and it seems normal.

Grandpa Jay is right there, holding out his phone. "I've already called an ambulance. Everyone needs to back off." He looks at Daddy, Sara, and me. "Except her husband and daughters."

I look up at Daddy, whose eyes have filled

with tears. He gingerly kneels down, something that I know is difficult since his knee surgery last year. Justin comes up behind Sara and puts his arms around her, while Nate stands off to the side looking like he's not sure what to do next.

I meet his gaze. Within seconds, he's by my side. "I couldn't get to her fast enough." He gives me an apologetic look. "But I said a prayer for her as soon as I saw her get hit."

"Thank you." I turn back to Mama, who is making moaning sounds as she starts to move. "Be still. I don't want to take any chances on making this worse than it already is."

Her eyes pop open. "Am I in heaven?" She blinks and then focuses on me. "I guess not yet." Then she tries to push herself up on her elbow but falls back. "Ouch."

"Where does it hurt?" I ask.

"My shoulder. I think I got the wind knocked out of me."

As soon as those words leave her mouth, I hear the sound of a siren approaching. "Sounds like the ambulance is here."

"I don't want —" She squirms and grimaces, clearly in pain.

"Shh, just try to relax and let them take care of you." I gently stroke the back of her other arm as I glance around and look for Julius. He's nowhere in sight, but I figure Grandpa Jay will deal with him.

Once the ambulance arrives, I get up and take a step back to get out of the way of the paramedics. Nate doesn't hesitate to pull me into his arms. Now I understand what people mean when they talk about finding comfort in someone else holding them. If it weren't for his being there for me, I'd be pacing and fretting, probably making things worse.

"Looks like she might have a broken bone or two," the ambulance driver says as the others take her to the ambulance. "But we won't know for sure until she's checked out and x-rayed at the hospital."

"Is there anything life-threatening?" Those words catch in my throat, and I feel tears welling in my eyes.

"We can't tell yet." He looks at me and offers a comforting glance. "But I don't think so."

He turns around and runs to the ambulance. As it pulls away, Nate gestures toward the cars. "I'll take y'all to the hospital."

Without another word, Sara, Justin, Nate, and I pile into his truck, and he manages to maneuver it through the rows of dozens of parked cars and out onto the road leading to the hospital in Hattiesburg. I'm thankful that he's here because I'm shaking too hard to drive.

Sara and Justin whisper in the backseat, but Nate and I don't say a word until he pulls up in front of the emergency room entrance. "I'll let y'all out here and go find a parking spot."

The receptionist calls for someone to come and get us. By the time she arrives, Nate joins us.

"Are you all family?" the woman asks.

Nate clears his throat, but I don't give him a chance to speak. "Yes, we're all family."

She casts a doubtful look at each of us before leading us down the hall, through the double doors, and into a small holding room, where Mama is propped up in a hospital bed looking around in a daze. My heart breaks from seeing her in such a fragile state.

"They're taking me for X-rays in a few minutes." Mama tries to move, but she's been immobilized, so she gives up. "I reckon I don't have to tell y'all I hurt like the dickens."

Daddy's voice at the door catches our attention. "What took y'all so long getting here?"

"I'm sorry, sir." Nate gives Daddy a

contrite look. "I had to get around a lot of cars."

"I was just kidding. I'm surprised you got here as quickly as you did." His levity brings me a sense of relief because I know he wouldn't be kidding about anything if he thought Mama's injuries were life-threatening. "It doesn't appear to be serious."

"Thank the Lord. Sounds like our prayers have been answered."

All of us turn to face Nate. The fact that he's thanking the Lord and praying brings even more comfort.

"You're so right, son." Daddy walks up to Nate and pats him on the shoulder before doing the same to Justin. "I appreciate you boys being here for our girls."

Nate gently places his arm around me, and I continue to find comfort in his embrace. I can tell Daddy likes him because he doesn't even flinch when he notices. He originally had a different reaction to Justin back when he and Sara eloped, but over time they have developed a good relationship.

Sara and I take turns whispering our thoughts and prayers in Mama's ear. When the guy comes to take Mama to the X-ray lab, the rest of us remain standing in her room, looking at each other but not saying anything.

After she leaves, Nate nudges Justin. "Want some coffee? My treat."

Justin looks like he wants to turn Nate down, but after only a brief hesitation, he nods. "Sure."

As he gets to the door, Nate looks over his shoulder. "Want us to bring y'all anything back?"

Sara asks for hot cocoa, but Daddy and I don't want anything. As soon as they're gone, Daddy takes Sara and me by the hand.

"Your mama and I love both of you girls more than you'll ever know, and even though these aren't the best circumstances, your actions today have shown us what you're made of. It's nice to know we raised some loving daughters who don't hesitate to be there when we need you."

Sara hugs Daddy. "I love both of you more than you know too."

He nods and smiles as he looks me in the eye. "I can tell. By the way, I appreciate how Nate gave us a few minutes alone. That is one smart boy, and I hope you don't let him get away."

If Daddy had said that about anyone in the past, it would have annoyed me to no end. But now it makes me smile. Yes, there definitely is something special about Nate.

Nate and Justin return about forty-five minutes later, and some guy in scrubs wheels Mama in right behind them. He gives us a thumbs-up.

"Good news?" Daddy asks.

"Yep. Doesn't look like there are any broken bones or internal punctures. Just a dislocated shoulder that a little physical therapy can take care of."

"Can she go home today?" Daddy asks.

"No, I want her to hang out here overnight, but when she goes home, she'll need someone to help her with some of her daily activities."

"Do you have any idea when the doctor will come in to talk to me?"

The guy in the scrubs chuckles. "I'm talking to you now."

Daddy's eyes widen as Sara and I stifle giggles — partly from relief about Mama but mostly from Daddy's reaction. "But you look like —" He cuts himself off.

"A teenager?" The doctor laughs again. "I get that all the time." He straightens up and gives us a full-frontal view of his face. Now that I see the day-old stubble on his chin and crinkles around his mouth, I can tell he's not the kid we thought he was. "I've been an emergency room doctor for almost five years now, so I know what I'm doing . . ." He smiles at all of us. "At least most of the time."

"Do we need to start having our family reunions at the hospital?" The sound of Grandpa Jay's voice grabs all of our attention.

Daddy reaches out to shake his hand. "Not a bad idea."

"How's she doing?"

Everyone turns to face the doctor, who gives his attention to Grandpa Jay. His eyes suddenly widen, and he moves toward the older man for a man hug. I look at Sara, and she shrugs.

Grandpa Jay pulls back and looks the doctor in the eye. "Why didn't you tell me you were back in town, Paul? I thought you were working at Emory Hospital in Atlanta."

"I just got back. Mom said she wanted me closer to home."

Grandpa Jay takes a deep breath and gives the doctor a questioning look. "I reckon it's about time to tell them about you."

The doctor makes a face as he takes a step back. "I don't know if this is the best place."

Grandpa Jay pats him on the shoulder. "I think it is."

59
MARYBETH

You could've knocked Bucky over with a feather when Sally and Sara came back to the reunion and told him his grandfather had paid the college tuition for all of his childhood friend's grandchildren. I mean, it's not like he did anything wrong, unless you consider not telling the family about another good deed a bad thing.

Tears streamed down Sara's cheeks as Sally explained how Grandpa Jay's friend was killed in a factory accident, so he did what he could to help out, since he had the means from some of the oil money. My heart melted at the very thought of Grandpa Jay helping someone become an emergency room doctor.

"That money should have been ours." Bucky shakes his head in disgust. "All this time I thought he put his family first." Bucky's all hunched over on the couch, acting like his world just ended. But it didn't.

Everything will remain the same, except his grandfather is even more awesome than I realized.

I glare down at him. "I think you're over-reacting."

Bucky lifts his face from his hands, and I see the anguish on his face. "How can you say that, Marybeth? He's giving away our inheritance."

"Wait a minute." There's clearly something he hasn't considered. "It's not like it was your land or money. It's his, and he can do whatever he wants with it."

He scrunches his face and squints. "What are you talking about? Make some sense, will ya?"

"Okay, think about it for a minute. If he had a friend who couldn't afford to send his children to college, and he was willing to cover the expenses, most people would consider him a hero."

He leans back and folds his arms as he thinks about it. "What do you think? Is he a hero in your eyes?"

I nod. "Yes, I've always thought your grandfather was awesome, and now he's even better than awesome." I force a smile. "He is a real-live superhero."

He pulls his lips between his teeth and squeezes his eyes shut before looking directly at me. "It's still not rightfully their money. It should have come to us. You don't get it because you're not blood related."

I let out a low growl of frustration. "Maybe not, but there's still nothing you can do about it."

"There might be. I know a lawyer —"

"Don't you dare cause trouble for your grandfather, Bucky. Not only will it hurt him, it'll show our son that you're greedy and self-centered."

Bucky contorts his mouth. "Yeah, you're probably right — not about the greedy and self-centered part. Just the part about causing trouble for my grandfather."

"Then why don't you look at it in a positive light? You can even bring those people he helped into the family. Call them your honorary cousins or something. It wouldn't hurt to have a *doctor* in the family."

"Yeah, that's true." A grin spreads over his face. "And I like the fact that one of 'em's a doctor."

"Yeah, you can introduce him as your cousin Paul the doctor." Apparently, having a doctor in the family appeals to him more than missing out on this relatively small amount of inheritance, so I give myself a mental high five.

Bucky sighs. "Great idea, Marybeth. It's

not like I'm losin' a thing. I'm gaining family, and the Lord knows, you can't have too many kinfolk."

It's obvious the whole doctor-cousin thing is what has brought him to this way of thinking, but whatever. "Now, why don't you go splash some cold water on your face and get back out there to make sure our guests are having a good time?"

"We need to figure out who's gonna sleep where," he says as he stands up. "Since a lot of 'em have decided to go home, everyone who wants to stick around for the weekend will have their own room."

I see movement in the doorway, so I look up to see who it is. He doesn't look even remotely familiar. "Who are you?"

He smiles as he walks toward Bucky and me. "My name is Paul Mason. Your grandfather asked me to come here when I got off my shift at the hospital."

Bucky shakes his hand. "So you're the doctor everyone's making such a fuss about." He stands back and looks Paul up and down. "You sure don't look like a doctor to me. I'm not even sure I'd trust you to look in my ears."

"Bucky!" I give him the elbow in the side — something I rarely do but have discovered it works to temporarily shush him. There's so much going on that I'm not sure it'll faze him. "It's nice to meet you, Paul. Or should I call you Dr. Mason?"

"Paul is fine." He takes a step back and glances back and forth between Bucky and me. "If you'd rather I —"

I interrupt him. "We are so happy to meet you, Paul." I glare over at my husband. "Aren't we, Bucky?"

"Yeah, sure."

"I wish we had more food left, but the vultures have already swooped." I take him by the arm and lead him toward the backyard. "Why don't we see if there's anything left on the dessert table?"

As we walk out the door, I glance over my shoulder and make a face at Bucky, who looks like he has no idea what to do next. I'm getting tired of trying to act a certain way just because we have money now. It's exhausting, and it makes me feel bad for everyone I'm around. Bucky claims we're supposed to behave like rich people, but I don't agree with him. Besides, I'm not even sure how rich people are supposed to act. I want to go back to being myself.

"I hope my coming here isn't causing a problem," Paul says. "I just thought —"

"Don't worry about it. I'm delighted to have you join our family. Sally and Sara didn't have enough good things to say about you, and if they like you, so will everyone else."

We stop at various clusters of people, and I introduce them to Paul. He's very gracious, but I can tell he's overwhelmed.

His eyes light up when he spots Sally coming toward us with Nate right behind her. I can tell he's comfortable around them.

I don't know what Julius was thinking about when he plowed into the crowd like he did. The area where Sheila was standing was at the bottom of a sloping section of our yard — a spot I've been after Bucky to do something about. He claims it's a rolling hill and adds character and interest to the yard. I bet he won't be saying that now.

"Hey, Dr. Mason." Nate comes out from behind Sally with his hand extended. "I'm so glad you took Mr. Bucklin up on his invitation."

Paul gives Nate a big ol' honkin' grin that near 'bout splits his face in two. "It's good to see your familiar faces."

Sally stands there watching the two men chat, appearing more interested than I suspect she really is. I can tell she really likes this boy Nate, which makes me happy. That guy she brought to the last reunion seemed too clingy, and I think that would be a problem for her relationship with Sara, since the two of them have such a special bond.

"Hey, Marybeth."

I turn around and see Bucky walking toward us. "Did you need me?"

"Yeah." He shifts his weight from one foot to the other. "Well, actually, it's Julius."

I roll my eyes. "What about Julius?"

"He's in the garage bawling his eyeballs out, and I don't know what to do." Bucky's helpless look grows more intense. "I should have let you talk to him first."

And I shouldn't have let Bucky push me away, but I don't tell him that. "Did he say anything?"

"He says he doesn't want to live here anymore because he's sick and tired of being rich." Bucky shudders. "He even said he doesn't want to drive his car anymore. He wants an old heap like all his friends have."

I have to hold back a smile. My son . . . our son is asking for a heap; maybe he is finally realizing that a person's value doesn't come from money. "I'll go see what I can do."

60
SALLY

I am so glad I brought Nate to the family reunion. He's not only kind and smart, he's there when I need him but gives me space when I don't. It's amazing, really. I've never met a man like him.

"Whatcha thinkin'?" Sara asks.

"I bet you can guess right on the first try."

She grins. "I bet I can too. You really like Nate, like a lot, don't you?"

I smile back at her. "I've already told you I do."

"Then why did you let him go home after he brought us back? He could have come in."

I shrug. "I don't know. I sort of figured he could use a break after all that crazy family drama."

"I hear ya."

Justin laughs as he puts his arm around Sara's neck and playfully ruffles her hair. "You never worried about giving me a break from the family drama."

"I'm not as nice as my sister."

I look at both of them. "Plus, y'all were married before the last reunion, so a break wasn't an option."

Justin bobs his head. "Good point."

"So, what's for supper?" Sara looks at me.

"Who am I, your mother?"

"No, but you're not exhausted from being pregnant, so I figured you could fix us something."

Justin points toward the sofa. "Both of you, sit down. I'll fix supper, and y'all can talk about the craziness of the day." He starts toward the kitchen but stops. "And after I finish cleaning the supper dishes, I'll take y'all to the hospital to see your mama."

Why did I ever not think Justin was good enough for my sister? He's been nothing but a dream guy to both Sara and me, with very few exceptions that are probably more our fault than his. And I have no doubt he'll be an awesome daddy. Maybe a little over-protective, but that's okay.

We've barely gotten into a conversation about the day when someone knocks on the door. I hop up and open it to see Daddy standing there looking uncomfortable.

"Mind if I come in?"

I take a step back. "Of course not."

Justin sticks his head around the kitchen wall, waves to Daddy, and says, "Hey, George. There's plenty of food if you want to have supper with us."

"I don't want to intrude."

"You won't be intruding at all." Justin laughs. "In fact, I'd love to have you stay."

Sara looks at me, and we both start laughing. Daddy gives us a confused look. "What's so funny?"

"Justin sounds like you and Mama when people would stop by at dinnertime." Sara turns to me for backup, so I nod.

Daddy rolls his eyes. "If y'all really want me to stick around for supper, I suppose I can do that, since your mama's still in the hospital." He rubs the back of his neck. "That house feels so empty without her in it."

Justin carries a serving platter out from the kitchen and places it on the dining room table. "I figured we could eat in the dining room, since we have company."

Sara whispers, "Justin is loving this."

"I can tell."

"Ya know, I think there's something to what people say about girls marrying their daddies."

I make a face. "Don't say that."

"I just did." She grins before we both turn

our attention to our daddy and Justin having a conversation.

As soon as Justin puts supper on the table, we all sit down to eat. Before anyone lifts their fork, Justin holds up his hands. "Our blessing."

Those two words have us bowing our heads. He thanks the Lord for our time with family, the blessing of Mama not being more seriously injured, and the food we're about to eat. After we all say, "Amen," I glance at Daddy and see the blatant admiration on his face as he looks at his son-in-law.

Then a knock comes at the door. I give Sara a curious glance, and she shrugs, letting me know she has no idea who that could be.

Justin hops up from the table, crosses the room, and flings open the door. "What took you so long?"

Nate steps into the dining area, grins at me, and turns back to Justin. "When you called, I'd just pulled something out to fix for supper, so I had to put it away." He glances at me. "You look surprised. Didn't Justin tell you I was coming?"

Justin shrugs and makes an *oops* face. "I reckon I forgot."

A look of concern washes over Nate. "I

hope y'all don't mind."

Before I can say a word, Daddy points to the chair next to me. "Of course we don't mind. Have a seat."

As we pass around the dishes Justin has prepared, a feeling of comfort and love washes over me. Sara grins at me, her eyes glistening, letting me know she feels it too. I can't think of anywhere I'd rather be than right here with these people, although it would be nice to have Mama here too. But at least we know she'll be back home tomorrow, and all will be right in our world.

Julius sure is in a heap of trouble, only this time without me. After he cried, I thought he might get off without punishment, but Grandpa Jay put his foot down. All his bribing was only slightly tempting, but even a weekend of ridin' around in his car wasn't enough to get me to go with him.

I'm home in my room now. Mama and Daddy are in the kitchen with Jeremy, whispering so softly I can't hear what they're saying. I reckon they're probably trying to figure out where they went right with me.

Right after Julius crashed into the crowd, I heard Mama's voice. "Where's Brett?" still rings in my ears. At first, my feelings were hurt, but then I remembered the last reunion. Now I can't say I blame her for expecting me to be involved.

I lean my head back and replay what happened. Julius wanted me to take the first ride in his boxcar, but since I don't even have the desire to ride in my own boxcar, I told him no. Mama would be so proud of me.

Next thing I knew, he was hopping into that boxcar and telling me to give him a push. Once again, I said no. He called me a few names Mama and Daddy don't allow me to say.

So he got out of the car, turned it to face the folks at the bottom of the hill, gave it a push, and hopped into it. Next thing I knew, there was a woman on the ground. At the time I had no idea who it was, but that didn't matter. All I could think about was how glad I was that I didn't participate.

I think back to when he first showed me his boxcar. It wasn't put together well, so I tightened things up a bit and made it so it wouldn't fall apart. Then it dawns on me. If it weren't for me, he wouldn't have made it to the bottom of the hill.

As a flood of guilt washes over me, I wonder what to do next. Should I tell Mama and Daddy or just let it be? If I tell them, what will they do? Knowing Mama, I'll be grounded for the rest of the school year. Daddy might back her up at first, but he'll eventually talk her into letting me off for good behavior.

The more I think about it, the worse I feel. Finally, I can't take it anymore, so I hop up, run out of my room and into the kitchen, and holler, "It's all my fault."

Mama turns around and gives me one of her looks. "What on earth are you talkin' about, Brett?"

"The boxcar. If I hadn't fixed it, Julius wouldn't have been able to knock anyone down."

Daddy chimes in. "What do you mean, son?"

I explain how I secured the boxcar with brackets and screws. Mama and Daddy listen, occasionally glancing at each other with expressions I can't read. Finally, Mama nods, and Daddy comes toward me with his arms outstretched. I take a hesitant step toward him, and then he gives me a big ol' hug.

"You did the right thing, son."

"I did?" Now this is getting weird.

"Yes, you sure did. You were trying to protect your cousin. What he did with that car after you fixed it has nothing to do with you. It's all on him."

I look over at Mama and see her nodding. "That's right, Brett. You are not the least bit guilty."

Now I let out a shaky sigh of relief as my

stomach emits a loud groan.

Mama grins. "Hungry?"

I'm pretty much always hungry, so I nod. "Yes, ma'am."

"Want me to heat you up a bowl of Missy's chili?" She gives Daddy another one of her looks, and he nods before she turns back to me. "She brought extra and sent some home with me."

"That sounds good."

"Want corn bread with it?" Before I have a chance to respond, Mama opens a plastic zipper bag and pulls out a wedge of corn bread.

Jeremy lets out a squeal, so I turn around. He's sitting in his high chair with a bowl of something upside down on his head. I can't help laughing at the little guy, but I quickly stop because Mama says I encourage him by doing that.

Next thing I know, Mama and Daddy are laughing too, so I relax. Something has changed in my family, and even though I'm not sure what it is, I reckon I'll find out soon enough.

"Do me a favor, Brett, and get Jeremy cleaned up while I heat up the dinner." Mama tosses me one of the dish towels.

I've done this so many times I can do it in my sleep. Jeremy keeps laughing when I wipe his face, and I laugh back. There's no doubt in my mind that he'll be the class clown when he goes to school.

After the chili is hot, Mama scoops it into bowls, and the three of us sit down to eat. My sister and other brother are out, so it's just the four of us.

"Is Julius in a heap of trouble?" I ask.

Daddy holds his spoon in front of his lips and turns to me with a goofy grin. "What do you think?"

Yeah, I suppose it was a stupid question. I take a bite of corn bread while the chili cools off a little.

Mama picks up her napkin and makes a big deal of putting it in her lap, something I know she does to remind me to do the same. "I think Julius might finally see the error of his ways."

I tilt my head and look at her. "What do you mean?"

"He cried like a baby after he hit Sheila. His daddy came running up to make sure he was okay, and Julius said he hated his life and wanted to be poor like the rest of the family." Mama grins as she breaks her corn bread in half and butters a piece of it. "I talked to Marybeth a little while ago, and she says they're all going to counseling. Apparently, she's been trying to get Bucky to go, but until now, he didn't think it was such a good idea. Now he doesn't have much of a choice."

Daddy nods. "Grandpa Jay and Granny Marge have Julius now, so he gets to start his counseling early."

"If anyone can whip that boy into shape, it's your grandparents." Mama takes a sip of her tea.

After we finish eating, I point to the table. "I'll do the dishes. Y'all can go relax."

Mama gives me a hug and gets Jeremy out of his high chair. "C'mon, let's get out of Brett's way."

I know I'm not as good at cleaning as Mama, but I don't mind doing it. There's something relaxing about going back and forth between the table and sink and then loading the dishwasher.

As I clean, I think about Julius and some of the things Mama and Daddy said. Maybe there is hope for Julius to be a decent guy, but in the meantime, I plan to stay as far away from him as possible.

62

SALLY

I'm sitting in Mama and Daddy's sunroom, enjoying the warmth of the rays making their way through the nearly naked branches of the trees in the backyard. Mama's sipping her tea while Daddy studies the sports pages of the newspaper.

It's been several days since Julius nearly killed Mama, but everything is calm now. Mama says she still hurts like the dickens, but her therapist declares her on the road to recovery. I'm relieved everything turned out like it did.

Daddy finally glances up at me. "When's your date with Nate?"

Mama laughs. "That rhymes."

"So it does." Daddy grins at Mama and then looks at me, waiting for an answer.

"He's picking me up at six."

Daddy glances at his watch. "Don't you think you'd best get going, then, so you can do whatever it is girls do to get ready for a date?"

Mama grins and shakes her head. "She's fine, Georgie. Our girls don't have to do much to look beautiful."

He grins right back at her. "Just like their mother."

I can't sit here and listen to all this mushiness, so I stand. "It's time to go. Call me if you need anything."

Daddy stands and gestures toward the door. "I'll walk you out."

We chitchat until we get to the front door, where he stops me. "Sally, I want you to know how much your mama and I appreciate you and Sara. We raised some mighty fine girls who turned out to be some of the best women we know."

"You've already said that."

"I just want to make sure you know how we feel."

"Thank you, Daddy." It feels strange to hear this coming from the man who rarely says anything personal like this. "Sara and I appreciate you and Mama too."

He clears his throat and shifts from one foot to the other, letting me know there's more. So I turn to face him directly and wait.

"I also want to tell you that I think your

482

sister married a good man. I wasn't so sure at first, but the more I get to know him, the more I understand why she picked him."

"Same here. Justin is turning out to be a pretty cool brother-in-law."

Daddy nods. "And that guy you're seeing. Nate. He seems like a good guy."

I grin back at Daddy. "I really like him."

"Just do me a favor, Sally. Keep your mama and me posted on how things are going with the two of you. As much as we like Justin, well . . . your mama would still like to be involved in the wedding plans."

I can't help laughing. "There's nothing to plan, so don't worry about it."

"There's nothing to plan *yet,* but you never know about these things." He pauses. "Oh, by the way, you missed the inheritance speech."

"Inheritance speech?"

Daddy nods. "Everyone in the family who hasn't already gotten land will get some soon, and the only string attached is that it has to stay in the family. You can farm it if you want to." He tips his head toward me and lets out one of his hearty chuckles. "Or you can let an oil company drill."

I scrunch my nose. "I think I'll just let it sit there for a while."

Daddy opens the door and holds it for me.

"You'd better go now so you're not late."

All the way home, I laugh about that conversation. Farm the land? I can't even imagine. My thoughts slide all over the place, and by the time I pull into the driveway, I'm reflecting on my own feelings about Nate. There is something special — something different — about him, and it appears Mama and Daddy can see it too.

Sally and Justin are having dinner at his parents' house, so I have the place to myself. It's quiet, so I tell my Amazon Alexa to play some music.

Then I take a quick shower and put on one of the outfits I picked up at La Chic. Shay says it's effortlessly stylish, whatever that means.

A few minutes after I make the last swipe of gloss across my lips, I hear a knock at the door. My heart hammers nearly out of my chest as I cross the condo to answer it. When I open the door and see Nate standing there grinning at me, a fluttery feeling washes over me and renders my knees wobbly. So I take a deep breath and smile back at him.

"You look beautiful, Sally."

"Thank you." I'm so glad Shay taught me how to accept a compliment. Before her tutoring, I would have argued. "Do you want to come inside, or should we go now?"

He hesitates for a split second before gesturing toward the living room. "Can we talk for a minute before we go?"

I nod and lead the way to the sofa, where we both sit. "What's on your mind?"

He takes my hand and kisses the back of it. "Sally, I know this is early in our relationship, but I can tell that there is something special between us."

My mouth goes dry as I continue looking at him. I want to say something, but I have no idea how to put my slippery, swirling thoughts into words.

"Since I don't want to make the mistake of rushing things, I'm not going to express all my feelings." He kisses the back of my hand again. "But I wanted to put some of my thoughts out there so you can be . . ." He chuckles. "So you can be warned. I love being with you, and I —" He gives me a helpless look that lets me know there's something he feels but doesn't want to say.

"I like you too." I smile back at him. "A lot."

He hops up and helps me to my feet. "Well, now that that's settled, how about going for a seafood platter?"

With all the butterflies still fluttering in my tummy and chest, I'm not sure how much seafood I can eat. But I nod anyway. "Sounds good."

Throughout the evening, Nate and I talk about anything that pops into our minds. This is how a relationship should be, I think. He and I have a connection that can't be put into words. Now I better understand those looks Sara and Justin keep giving each other. They're speaking without having to say anything, something that Nate and I are starting to do.

Nothing exciting happens during the date, but I'm beyond thrilled to be with him. And then when he walks me to the door, he tips my face up to his. "I've been praying for someone like you to come along."

As he kisses me, I know that the Lord has blessed both of us with a special kind of relationship that transcends anything else in my life. Now all we have to do is give our budding romance some time to go into full bloom.

ABOUT THE AUTHOR

Debby Mayne writes family and faith-based romances, cozy mysteries, and women's fiction and is the author of more than 60 novels and novellas — plus more than 1,000 short stories, articles, and devotions for busy women. Debby is currently an etiquette writer for *The Spruce.*

Debby grew up in a military family, which meant moving every few years throughout her childhood. She was born in Alaska, and she has lived in Mississippi, Tennessee, Oregon, Florida, South Carolina, Hawaii, and Japan. Her parents were both from the Deep South, so Debby enjoys featuring characters with Southern drawls, plenty of down-home cooking, and folks with quirky mannerisms. *High Cotton* is the first book in the Bucklin Family Reunion series.

Connect with Debby!
Website: www.debbymayne.net

Facebook: www.facebook.com/DebbyMayne
Author
Twitter: www.twitter.com/debbymayne